xx!

Mia Sheridan

TRAVIS

A PELION LAKE NOVEL

Mia Sheridan

To all the readers worldwide who first loved
a silent boy, and helped give him a voice.

PROLOGUE

Travis – Seven Years Old

"Mommy? What's wrong?" I approached slowly, my heart drumming as I watched my mommy's back shake. Her head was in her arms on the kitchen table in front of her, her soft sobs muffled.

But at the sound of my voice, she sat up. Her cheeks were wet with tears, her mouth twisted in what looked more like anger than sadness. My mommy's face did that a lot. Her eyes said one thing, but the rest of her expression, and even her words, said another. Sometimes my mommy confused me. I didn't know if I should try to help, or run away from her.

My daddy didn't confuse me like that. My daddy smiled with his whole face, and when he was sad, I could tell that too.

My daddy seemed sad a lot. But he loved me and I loved him. He was my hero and someday I was going to be a policeman just like him. Then he wouldn't be sad anymore, because I would make him proud and happy.

My mommy's shoulders rose and fell as she took a big breath. "Your daddy's left us," she said.

I blinked at her, my heart giving one strong knock in my chest. "Left where?" I whispered. On a trip? To the town on the other side of the lake to do policeman business?

"Who knows where!" she said loudly, suddenly, her eyes sparking with the same anger on her mouth. "He's snuck off like a thief with your aunt Alyssa and cousin Archer. He wants *them* to be his family now. He doesn't want us anymore."

I stepped back. Away from my mommy and the words she was telling me. "No," I whispered. "My daddy wouldn't leave me behind." *With you. He loves me.* "He wouldn't."

"Oh, he would and he did," she said, her tears stopping as she tapped her fingers on the table, her long fingernails making sharp clicking sounds. *Tap, tap, tap.* I wanted to clap my hands over my ears and make that sound *stop*. I wanted Mommy to stop. The crying. The yelling. The tapping. It felt like someone was pressing on my chest.

I felt scared and sad.

He wouldn't leave me.

He loves me.

2

But I didn't cry. I was tough, like my daddy, and I wouldn't cry.

My mommy glanced at her phone on the table next to her, her fingers tap, tap, tapping, harder and faster. "But maybe there's something I can *do*," she murmured, her lips tipping upward but her eyes still narrowed.

She grabbed the phone and began pressing the buttons, calling someone.

"Why, Mommy?" I whispered, my voice breaking, begging for a different answer than the one she'd given. Desperately needing something that made *sense*. "Why did he leave?"

My mommy stopped dialing, raising her head to stare at me. She watched me for several moments before saying, "Because I'm second best, Travis. We both are. We always have been."

It felt like something withered and fell inside me, like the shriveled apples that dropped to the ground in our backyard. *Thud.* They were the ones nobody wanted.

Second best. Second best. You're nothing but second best.

And second best didn't even deserve a goodbye.

CHAPTER ONE

Travis

The lake sparkled beyond the trees as I pushed open my brother's gate, the squeak from the rusty hinges breaking the silence of the still summer evening. Noise that was quickly and boisterously joined by the front door banging open and my nephews—and several mongrels—rushing from inside, racing up the sloping yard to greet me.

"Uncle Travis! Uncle Travis!" the boys yelled in unison, their short legs carrying them swiftly uphill, the dogs barking and dancing around, tails wagging in a way that would have let any knife-wielding burglar or serial killer entering the property know they were more than welcome to join the family.

I laughed as Connor and Charlie reached me, bending, and scooping them up, one in each arm. "I have two stomachs!" Connor declared. "My daddy says."

"It's a Hale trait," I explained. "It's how we grow big and—"

"I prolly have *three* stomachs!" Charlie stated, not to be outdone by his twin.

I peered down curiously at his stomach, using my fingers to tickle his side. Charlie shrieked with laughter. The dogs wove in and out of my legs and I sidestepped the brown one who seemed to always be grinning. I didn't trust it. Anything that grinned that constantly was obviously insane.

"Did you ever see an elephant, Uncle Trav?" Charlie asked.

"Not in person—"

"What about a bear?" Connor inquired.

"Too many to—"

"Elephants weigh more than cars!"

"Bears sleep all winter! It's called hide your nation."

"Hide your *nation?* What's a nation?" I asked.

Connor leaned in, cupping his hand over his mouth as he "whispered" loudly, "It's prolly his hairy butt!"

Then both boys howled with laughter, their little bodies shaking with hilarity. I laughed too, because if you were a guy, the phrase *hairy butt* was funny, whether you were five or over thirty. Or a hundred fifty, I was going to assume.

"Boys," Bree called, stepping outside, six-month-old Averie in her arms. "Let your uncle catch his breath." She smiled. "Hi, Travis."

5

"Bree." I set the boys down, just catching the slight nod Charlie gave Connor before Charlie stumbled. I reached forward, catching him before he hit the wood floor of the porch.

"Aha!" Connor yelled triumphantly from just next to me, holding up the pack of gum he'd slipped from my pocket while I was rescuing his brother from his fake fall.

"My God, you boys are Ninjas," I said, proud of their stealth, high-fiving them both.

They laughed and Bree eyed them disapprovingly, putting her one available hand on her hip. "Don't pick pockets, you two." She turned her gaze on me. "I thought you were supposed to be the law."

"Who said?"

"The citizens of Pelion, apparently."

"Ah, that's right. Now I remember. Your mother's right. Pickpocketing will eventually lead to the slammer."

Connor looked mildly intrigued, an expression that melted into innocence as he turned to his mother. "Can we have some gum?" he asked very seriously, holding up the evidence of his crime.

The corner of Bree's mouth twitched. "May we," she corrected. "One each," she said and the boys lit up with matching grins, Connor quickly doling out the gum and then with a nod of their mother's head, they scampered inside, yelling, "Thanks, Uncle Travis," behind them, chatting exuberantly about what sounded like a Lego castle. Those two definitely made up for my half-brother's silence.

The baby eyed me warily, laying her head on Bree's shoulder, her chubby hand gripping her mother's shirt as though she saw in my eyes that I intended to kidnap her at any moment. I felt mildly offended. It was *me* who had led the rescue charge when the kid had made the poor choice to be born during one of the worst snowstorms in years, only six months before, causing her parents to have to deliver her themselves. It was like she'd already forgotten.

"Looking for Archer?" Bree asked.

"Yeah. I brought the police department's data he asked for," I said, pulling the folded printouts from my back pocket. Archer had asked that I pull together crime statistics for the town's annual meeting coming up in July.

Bree nodded. "Lie down," she said to the dogs who were still milling around my legs.

"That's not a good idea, Bree. You're married to my brother and I'm attached to someone. You really have to get over me once and for all."

She rolled her eyes. "Funny."

She focused her attention on the dogs—her serious *mom* look—and I grinned as they lay down on the porch, the larger black dog and the small, curly-haired white one flopping onto their sides, the brown one still grinning up at me like some furry demented clown. I glared at it, letting it know that it should save its furry deranged clown business for someone who couldn't fight it off. Its grin stretched, widened. *Jesus.* I gave it an extensive berth as Bree stepped inside the house and motioned me to follow her. "Archer texted a few minutes ago. He's running a little late but he should be home shortly."

The house was small but homey. It smelled like vanilla and something savory cooking in the kitchen. The boys argued genially, their animated voices rising and falling as they played in their room at the back of the house. The windows were open wide and the curtains fluttered in the breeze coming off the lake. The hardwood floor creaked under Bree's bare feet as she walked to the kitchen, chubby baby perched on her hip. *Would this be so bad? A home like this? A life like this?*

"You're welcome to stay for dinner," Bree said. There was only the barest hint of hesitation in her tone, as though she wasn't a hundred percent sure she meant what she said. *I guess that's going to take a while—maybe forever.*

I set the papers down and leaned against the counter as I watched her juggle Averie, while checking something in the oven and then stirring what looked like pasta on the range. "I can't. I got tonight off so I can surprise Phoebe and take her to dinner."

Bree let out a small laugh but it died a quick death. "Sorry. I just wish your girlfriend didn't have the same name as my dog. It's . . . unsettling."

"So change its name."

She turned to me quickly, looking more than a little outraged. "You can't just—" She shook her head as though what she was about to say wasn't worth her time. "Anyway, I'm sure she'll be thrilled that you're off." She looked at me sideways. "How are things going with her? You've been seeing her for what? About a year now?"

I nodded, warmth infusing my chest as Phoebe's smile filled my mind's eye, the way she still sighed and looked nearly star-struck when I winked at her. "Ten months. She's good. She's great." *She worships me.*

Bree had gone back to her stirring, but now stopped, placing the spoon on the counter. She shifted Averie so she was holding her with two arms and leaned against the counter, resting her chin on the baby's head and watching me thoughtfully. "Travis Hale. I never thought I'd see the day. You're actually *serious* about someone, aren't you?"

"Jealous?" I grinned but she remained serious. My smile slipped.

"No. Glad. It's good to see you finding happiness."

There was a full, weighted silence that made me feel itchy. I didn't know what to say. In all honesty, Bree had every right to wish me *un*happiness for the rest of my days even though Archer and I had mended fences, and I tried my damnedest to be a good uncle to my nephews—which wasn't hard because, frankly, I enjoyed the hell out of them—and someday, if I was able to win her over, the niece still watching me cautiously. The way I'd acted when Bree first came to Pelion . . . the things I'd done to my brother all our lives, would forever be between us. Years had passed, holidays had gone by, I liked to think I'd matured, but even so, there was nothing I could do to change the way I'd hurt them in the past. The things my actions *might* have caused.

"She's the one, huh?" Bree asked, and I detected the barest hint of . . . uneasiness? Concern? I wasn't sure, and whatever had passed over her expression was there and gone in the blink of an eye. She bent her head and inhaled Averie's wispy brown hair, sighing softly.

Bree had met Phoebe on many occasions. She'd never said anything unkind about her, but I'd also gotten the sense they might never be best friends. Which was okay by me. Bree was into baking, and reading, and mucking around in the rocks with her kids and dogs. All worthy pastimes when you were a mom. But Phoebe wasn't a mom. Yet. She was into . . . well besides *me*, she was into . . . what *was* Phoebe into?

She liked to shop, I knew that. And tan. She was very good at both.

"Well, when you know, you know," Bree said, smiling softly, meeting my gaze and holding it for several beats.

When you know, you know.

I pushed off the counter just as the soft sound of the front door opening met my ears. The door clicked shut quietly and then Archer turned into the kitchen, looking unsurprised to see me. He'd obviously noticed my truck parked out front. *Hey,* he signed.

Hi, I signed back as Archer made a beeline for Bree and his daughter, his face lighting with such open joy that I almost looked away, as though I'd barged in on an intimate moment and had no business being there.

The baby kicked her chubby legs and grinned, two shiny white teeth appearing on her bottom gum. Averie reached for her father and Archer took her from Bree, kissing his wife on the lips, lingering.

"Well," I said, loudly, giving the papers sitting on the counter a tap. "There's the data you wanted. I emailed it to you as well, but was in the area, so thought I'd drop off printouts. Tell the boys I said bye. I'll pick them up Sunday." We had a long-standing after-dinner ice cream date where I fed them too much sugar and then sent them home so their parents could deal with the aftermath.

Archer glanced at Bree, his hands too full to "speak," and as though reading his mind she said, "Travis can't join us for dinner. He has plans with Phoebe."

Ah, Archer mouthed, smiling at me and nodding.

"Good to see you," I said. "Bree." I smiled at Averie whose eyes narrowed minutely. She leaned toward Archer, her tiny fist clutching his shirt the same way she'd held on to her mother. "Okay, then. See you guys later." And with that, I turned and let myself out of the little house on the lake that smacked of home and love and family.

****

The breeze smelled like peaches. I inhaled a deep breath of the air coming in my open window, as my truck idled on the dirt road that ended at the edge of my property. Peace rolled through me. Hope in the future. The sun was just beginning its descent behind an old barn, the light hazy and golden. Unfortunately, I'd have to tear down the structure. It was right in the spot where I intended on building my home. Maybe I could use the lumber somehow though. Beams . . . or flooring, something to pay homage to what had once been but was no longer.

11

My father had bought this land on the very edge of Pelion, technically in the town of Calliope, the more touristy area on the opposite side of the lake. The land wasn't massive, but it was prime lake-front property. It had once been an orchard, and several of the fruit trees remained: apples, cherries, peaches, and plums.

The water rippled serenely as my gaze went toward the place I'd just been—my brother's house, too far to see from this distance. Archer owned and ran the town of Pelion, but I had this. In addition to the town, that eventually—rightly—went to Archer years before, my mother had been willed this plot of land from my father. Because it wasn't part of Pelion, she'd been able to keep it. I'd given my mother every cent of my savings and purchased it from her. I'd received something important to me—something that was *only* mine—and I'd given her a lump sum of cash that she'd desperately needed since everything else—again, rightly—had been stripped from her. Archer might have gotten the lion's share of the Hale inheritance, and it had always been obvious he had the lion's share of our father's heart because his mother had been the love of his life, while my own mother was a conniving manipulator who tricked him into impregnating her, but this plot of land belonged to *me* and no one else. Here, I wasn't second best to *anyone*.

I couldn't afford to build on it yet, but I was almost there. Someday . . . someday I'd raise a family on this land. Someday I'd live the life our father had wanted for himself. He'd loved Pelion, and he'd been the chief of police just like I was, but he'd wanted the distance from his brothers and, as a matter of fact, even though I only had one, I did too. There was only so much *sainthood*, so much look-what-a-perfect-family-we-are moments I could handle.

I sat there in the quiet peace of the evening for a moment, listening to the water lap the shore, and inhaling the fragrance of sweet, summer fruit.

Could I see Phoebe on this land? Pregnant? Walking out onto a dock that overlooked the water? A house with a porch shining in the sunlight rising above the trees behind her?

I squinted, focusing so hard I winced, trying to visualize it but coming up short. The misty image of a woman wavered, faded, and disappeared. I rubbed my temple. Did Phoebe even want kids? We hadn't talked about it. Maybe I needed to start asking. Of course, if I *did* start talking about it, that was a move forward in itself. My breath suddenly felt constricted and I pulled idly at the seatbelt still strapped around my body as though it'd somehow, inexplicably, grown tighter.

When you know, you know.

Bree's assertion came back to me. But what had I *ever* known? The truth was, I still wasn't sure I could trust what I *knew.* The things I'd thought I was sure about had been lies, many of which I'd told myself. In the end, I hadn't really known crap. So maybe *other* people *knew,* but me? In some ways I was still flying by the seat of my pants when it came to being a person others might be proud to know.

The sun dipped further, the sky streaked in orange, the tall grass moving languidly in the breeze. I smiled, the peace of this place, the *pride* that it was mine, cresting inside and helping to dispel the negative direction of my thoughts. I rolled up the window, cranking the air conditioner as I turned my truck and headed toward Phoebe's.

CHAPTER TWO

Travis

Phoebe lived in an upscale neighborhood on the other side of Calliope, mostly consisting of modern condominiums. The citizens of Pelion had almost unanimously resisted this kind of new construction, opting instead for charming B&Bs and quaint vacation cottages that flanked the shore. What they lost in younger tourism and big-money communities, they made up for in the many families and older people who returned year after year, some of them becoming almost as much a part of the community as those who lived in Pelion year-round.

I stopped at a small grocery store and ran inside for a bouquet of flowers, whistling as I got back in my truck.

Evening was just settling in as I approached Phoebe's condo, the flowers clutched in my hand. I drew back slightly when I noticed that her door was opened a crack, my cop instincts causing the hairs on the nape of my neck to bristle. She'd planned on going to a golf tournament on a nearby course with her friends, but she should have gotten home hours before. I pushed the door open very slightly with my finger, leaning to the side and peering in. Phoebe's purse was on the floor of the foyer, the contents spilled across the tile. *Shit.*

What the hell? Soundlessly, I set the flowers on the ground and walked to my truck as quickly as possible with minimal noise and retrieved the weapon in my center console. I returned to Phoebe's open door and slipped inside.

A soft cry came from upstairs and my heart began drumming, moving swiftly to the base of the stairs, my back to the wall as I climbed to the second floor. There was a mirror on the landing between the two flights and I caught a glimpse of myself in my peripheral vision, jaw tense, shoulders held rigid. Another pained cry and the thud of something hitting the floor.

Fuck, fuck, fuck.

I'm coming, Phoebe.

I'd killed for someone I cared about before. I'd do it again if necessary.

The bedroom door was slightly ajar too and I stood next to it, attempting to peer in, my chest rising and falling. A lamp was lit and in the shadows on the wall, I could see what looked like a man holding Phoebe down. Molesting her as she struggled. Adrenalin pumped through my veins and in one swift movement, I opened the door, raised my weapon, and headed straight for the attacker.

"Fuck! Fuck! Fuck! I'm coming, Phoebe!" A male voice. Not my own, although the words were somehow familiar.

"Oh God! You're the *best!* The *best!*" Phoebe screamed back.

In that split second, my fear and reality collided, a harsh internal *smack*. I drew back just in time to avoid putting a bullet in the back of the head of the guy—I blinked, swallowed—fucking my girlfriend in her bed. The room wobbled. The gun did not.

Phoebe's eyes flew open and my gaze locked with hers. Her expression morphed from bliss to horror and she screamed, the guy on top of her jolting and scrabbling off, getting tangled in the sheets so that he flipped out of the bed, dangling over the side naked. As he tried desperately to extricate himself from the tangled bedding, his expression filled with shocked terror, his—now—flaccid penis flopped limply from one thigh to the other. To his credit, he'd worn a condom.

It would have been hilarious if I was someone different, watching the whole scene unfold on a movie screen.

I lowered my gun slowly as he managed to unbind himself, jumping to his feet, tripping over the contents of the bedside table that must have been knocked over during their—evidently—frenzied fucking, but catching himself before he pitched over again.

Ice water was slowly filling my veins, dulling any emotion. The guy, who looked to be barely legal, froze, clapping his hands over his groin.

"Why bother?" I asked. We'd both already gotten an eyeful.

The guy's gaze darted to Phoebe who was now sitting up in bed, the sheet pulled up to her neck demurely, eyes wide, mouth slack, then to the other bedside table where countless pictures of me and Phoebe rested, back to my face, and finally landing on the gun. "Uhhh . . ." he gurgled.

"I think you better go, Easton," Phoebe said softly, her lashes lowering, her skin smooth and tan against the pale pink sheets.

Easton. My humiliation had a name.

Easton didn't hesitate. He dove for his clothing, pulling on his pants, stepping into one shoe, before he again, glanced at me, the gun, and then did a half limping-running gait toward the door, dropping his shirt, scooping it up, and then practically throwing himself out of the room as if he expected a bullet to slam into the back of his skull at any moment.

He thudded down the stairs and seconds later the front door slammed.

I'd been in quiet situations before. Hell, I'd spent several hours in my brother's company, helping with some project or another, the brother who couldn't speak a word. But I'd never, in all my days, experienced a quiet quite like that one.

"Say something," she finally squeaked.

"I don't think I'm the one who should be expected to speak right now."

Her shoulders dropped. "I'm so sorry, Trav."

"Why?" I asked dully, the gun that I'd almost used to kill my girlfriend's lover now held slack at my side.

Phoebe came to her knees, the sheet dropping away as she moved toward me. "Please forgive me," she pleaded.

I looked away. I didn't want to see her nudity. It felt obscene after what I'd just witnessed.

She sank down, pulling the sheet over her breasts again as though she'd read my mind. "It's just . . . I love you. I really do." Her shoulders lowered. "I just . . . we went to the bar to get a few drinks after the tournament, and I met him there and he was so *into* me. The way he stared . . . it made me wonder if you really love me at all." She looked miserable, and despite myself, a twinge of sympathy twisted my stomach. I pushed it down violently.

My gaze caught on a flyer on the floor from the bar they must have been at. It was an ad for dollar drinks.

"You met him at a bar *a few hours ago?*" Somehow that made it worse. Why did it make it worse? Could it *get* worse? My girlfriend had gone home with a stranger after a few hours of discounted day drinking.

I thought back to what I'd heard her screaming as the guy pounded into her—the woman I'd considered having *children* with less than thirty minutes before for Christ's sake: *You're the best! The best!* And damn if I'd *willingly* be second best to anyone again, *especially* some young Romeo likely just passing through town, spending a few bucks—*literally*—and spewing a couple sweet, drunken words to a girl he'd met in a bar.

19

"I didn't realize you were that cheap," I said. Her expression crumbled and she put her hands over her face. I turned, leaving her sex-scented room, walking numbly down the stairs and out the front door. The bouquet of flowers was still on the ground and I raised my leg and stamped on them hard, grinding the blossoms into the dirt.

It appeared Bree wouldn't need to rename her dog after all.

CHAPTER THREE

Travis

My jaw felt sore from keeping it permanently clenched for the past three days. Every time I relaxed it, the vision of the young naked dude pounding into my girlfriend filled my mind and I practically bit my own tongue.

A car drove by in the opposite direction, nearly sideswiping me when it veered into my lane. "Holy shit!" I yelled, barely avoiding it, my tires skidding in the roadside gravel. I pulled a quick U-turn, flicking on my lights and siren, and sped to catch up to the drunk tourist driving the battered-looking Honda Accord with an out-of-state license plate.

The tan car came to a slow, idling stop on the shoulder of the road that led from downtown Pelion to the turnoff to Calliope. The heat of the day had mostly burned off, and as I approached the vehicle, a soft breeze lifted my hair and set it down gently. It was a strange feeling ... almost ... comforting. I relaxed my jaw, a glare off her vehicle casting my gaze downward, over the bumper stickers. One featured a group of cartoon farm animals and ridiculously stated, *Friends Not Food*, and the other proclaimed, *You're Never too Old to Play in the Dirt*, whatever that meant. The back windows were completely steamed up and the driver's window was already down. Either the occupant didn't have AC, or was hoping the breeze in his or her face would help sober them up. It was one of those inebriation tells I'd witnessed too many times to count, but I always kept an open mind.

A head poked out the window, arms folding over the frame as she watched me approach, a hesitant smile on her face, one eye squinted against the sun.

"You almost ran me off the road back there," I said, leaning back, and turning my head toward the rear of her car when her exhaust pipe rattled loudly. The vehicle looked like it was on its last leg.

"I'm so sorry, Officer. I only looked away from the road for a moment. I feel terrible."

"License and registration, please."

A flash of irritation lit her brown eyes, but her lips tipped sweetly and she unfolded her arms, turning and rifling through her glove box and then reaching into her purse on the

22

passenger seat next to a spilled plant. There was dirt scattered over the faded fabric. Another couple of plants lay on the floor, obviously having toppled from the seat as well, and three more sat precariously on the edge of the dashboard.

I took the offered cards. *California.* Of course. It was where all the nuts came from. "Haven Torres from Los Angeles," I read.

"That's me." She smiled brightly, and then reached over, righting the tipped plant next to her. I noticed a drooping cactus wedged between her tanned thighs.

My eyes held on that cactus. I hadn't realized a cactus could *droop.* "What's wrong with your . . . cactus?"

She frowned. "Oh. It's just thirsty. *Very* thirsty."

There seemed to be several inappropriate innuendos I could come back with, and it pained me not to take the opportunity, but this was official police business.

I bent down, lowering my sunglasses and peering into the backseat of her car. I frowned, my gaze sliding over the veritable jungle. "What is this?"

"Plants," she said.

"Yes, I can see they're plants."

"More specifically, two fishtail palms, a pair of dragon trees, one philodendron, a croton, and that one's a Natal mahogany," she finished, lowering the finger she'd pointed into the backseat and grinning at me proudly.

I narrowed my eyes. I had no idea what she'd just said, but it didn't seem important. My God, plants were everywhere. "Anyway, they're obscuring your view. No wonder you almost hit me."

"Oh . . ." Her gaze slid away momentarily. A chestnut curl sprung free of the bun she had secured on the top of her head, bouncing against her cheek. "Well. I would have transported the plants in two carloads, but . . . the nursery was going to throw them away tonight unless I was able to take them all." I noted the hint of outrage in her voice as though throwing away plants was akin to murdering puppies.

Nursery. There was only one in Pelion so it had to be Fern Alley Botanicals, which was about five miles from where we currently were on the side of the road. Who knew how many pedestrians she'd come close to mowing down between here and there?

She was looking at me expectantly, a certain spark in her eyes that might be nervousness, but I suspected was indignation.

I took another minute, considering her and slapping her cards idly on my wrist. "I could let you go with a warning and risk you driving like a maniac again. Or, I could ticket you and protect the residents of Pelion who rely on me to keep their streets safe. Which one do you think I'll choose, Haven from California?"

That spark increased, eyes narrowing just a tad in a way that reminded me of how my niece watched me. "Oooh, a guessing game!" She tapped her finger on her pursed lips as if in deep consideration. "I'm not always good under pressure so this is tough. Hmm. Which one will you choose? Which one will you choose?" she muttered, suddenly raising one finger

24

as her gaze snapped to mine. "I'm going to go with, the one that appeals to your thirst for power?"

I almost laughed but held it back, disguising the sound rising from my throat with a cough, amusement warring with annoyance, and a dash of astonishment.

I removed my sunglasses slowly and hung them on my shirt pocket so I could take my time considering her. "Have you had run-ins with the police before, Haven from California? Experiences that make you hostile toward law enforcement?"

"No. Check my record. I've never so much as received a speeding ticket. If, in your wise and professional opinion, you deem that I deserve one for my crime, it would be my first. I have no negative personal impressions of the police, other than I think it must be difficult having a job where you constantly think the worst of people. You yourself must be perfect, Officer"—she squinted her eyes at my nametag— "Hale."

"Chief."

"Chief," she repeated. Several more riotous curls escaped and fell around her face as if in protest of this entire interaction. I couldn't decide if she was pretty or not. Definitely not the sort I usually went for. Not that it mattered anyway. I was swearing off women for the foreseeable future. What I did know was that she looked as wild as the tangle of leaves and vines fighting for space in her car. For several beats we simply looked at each other and I had the strange urge to smile at this insolent woman. I recognized her sarcasm and sardonic comments. I'd written the book on interactions like these. I knew exactly how to manipulate with words. But this girl was doing it in a way that wasn't cutting but . . . challenging.

And interesting.

I'd only ever managed cutting.

Then again, I'd learned from the very best.

I stood straight. In any case, why was I tolerating this? "You're going to have to offload a few of those plants," I instructed.

Her eyes went wide, expression stricken. "I can't just leave them on the side of the road! I have to go to work. I won't be able to come back and retrieve them until late tonight."

"They're plants. You most definitely *can* leave them on the side of the road if it means being able to see out your side and back windows. Per the law."

She turned her head slightly, crooning something into the backseat.

I halted, turning back. "Did you just say something? To the plants?"

She sighed. "Living things feed off energy. I'm sure they feel my distress. I want them to flourish and live, not inhale my anxiety. Especially considering they have to wait here on the side of the road, all alone, until I return."

"Inhale—" I leaned toward her. "Have *you* been inhaling something? Should I give you a sobriety test?"

"I don't do drugs." She glanced into the backseat again and then her shoulders dropped. For a moment she looked like she'd argue with me about removing the plants, but then

26

she slowly exited her vehicle, looking dejected. I felt oddly sympathetic until I remembered that they were *free* plants that—frankly—looked like they were at death's doorstep. "It's supposed to rain tonight," I said, illogically.

She glanced at me as she extricated one of the pots from the back seat. "I'm going to drive back and get them later," she said, handing me the pot and turning around for another. It only took a couple of minutes to transfer enough of them—five—for her side and rearview windows to be unimpeded.

I handed her cards over. "Consider this a warning. Drive safely, Haven from California."

"Oh I will, Chief Hale from Pelion. Thank you for your mercy." The side of my lip felt like it was connected to an invisible string and someone gave it one strong yank. I brought my hand up, coughing into my fist again until the spasm stopped. And with that, I nodded and walked back to my cruiser.

CHAPTER FOUR

Haven

Gage Buchanan is the best. The best, I thought dreamily, watching as he raised one perfectly muscled arm, his honed body taut as he paused long enough for me to engrave the picture into my brain, forever available to bring forth when I was in the mood to *fantasize.*

"He's *perfect,*" someone sighed just as Gage shot into action, delivering a serve that whizzed toward the player on the opposite side of the tennis court. A *perfect* serve, of course, because well, he was perfect. His opponent dove for the ball, swung wildly, and missed.

I pulled myself straight from the counter where I'd been resting my face on my palm as I'd gazed at Gage playing singles across from the smoothie bar at the club where I worked.

"Sorry," I said, heading toward the two girls I hadn't notice sit down at the bar, hearing another whack as the game continued.

"No problem," the blonde said, turning her head from the tennis court to me.

The other girl, a brunette, didn't bother to look my way, her head going back and forth, obviously following the tennis ball from Gage and the good-looking blond guy he was playing against. "Peach mango flax seed," she said distractedly.

I gave the back of her head a charming smile. "Of course. My pleasure. And for you?" I asked, turning my attention to the blonde.

"An açaí bowl. But make sure to leave the strawberries off. They make me break out in hives." She lowered her Chanel sunglasses, eyeing me over the top of the tortoise frames. "Last time I think you missed one. I felt *itchy* later."

Sounds like a personal problem, likely unrelated to strawberries, I didn't say.

She glared at me accusingly as if I'd deliberately planted said strawberry in the middle of her açaí bowl in a calculated effort to sabotage her flawless skin with an unsightly rash. My smile tightened as I worked to hold on to it. "I am so sorry," I said sweetly. "I'll double-, triple-check that there are no strawberries on or near your order."

"Good," she said, turning away as Gage shook his perfect dark hair, sweat flying out around him as he ran toward the net to shake his partner's hand. He'd won. Of course he'd won.

He was the best.

I sighed, turning away, and began gathering the ingredients for the two orders. I heard the girls whispering animatedly to each other, the inflection in their tones telling me they were gossiping. I didn't bother to attempt to listen in. I didn't care what they were talking about. This club was filled with a hundred more just like them. Rich, entitled brats who thought those who worked here were solely valuable for their ability to meet their every demand.

That was the thing about Gage Buchanan. He was different. He wasn't *only* gorgeous. Perfect. The *best*. He was *kind*. He had impeccable manners, his smile was sincere. He looked everyone in the eye when they spoke to him, and didn't talk down to anyone. Even me, the out-of-towner working at the smoothie bar. I didn't know too much else about him—other than he was a member of the exclusive golf and tennis club where I was working for the summer—but that was enough.

I set the smoothie and strawberry-free açaí bowl in front of the girls, added the orders to their tabs, and began wiping down the counter I'd just used, when the brunette said, "This summer is going to be awesome. Especially since Gage is single."

Okay, now *this* I wanted to hear. My heart fluttered. *Single.* I moved the cleaning cloth slowly along the counter, craning my ears to listen in. Gage was single. Hmm. I paused in my cleaning. Even if he noticed me, it wasn't like he and I

30

TRAVIS

could be anything long-term—I was only passing through this lake town—but what was wrong with a summer fling? What was wrong with finding happiness—even temporarily—with a gorgeous, kind, *single* man?

Nothing, that's what.

Being on the road wasn't always conducive to flings. Or maybe it'd been my state of mind. In any case, it'd been a long, dry spell.

"I heard Travis is single suddenly too."

Ugh, *Gage*. Keep talking about *Gage*.

"Really?" the other girl practically breathed. "I thought for sure he was off the market permanently."

"No, I don't know what happened, but the rumor is someone cheated."

The other girl snorted inelegantly. "We don't have to wonder *who* cheated. Phoebe *worships* him even if he did fall about ten slots socially when he lost Pelion."

"Yup. Apparently Phoebe left town to visit her sister in Florida. My guess is she's completely brokenhearted and there to recover. At least she'll come back with a killer tan."

"Megs! Chelsea!" a girl in a tiny black bikini across the way called, raising her hand and waving wildly to the two at my counter.

They grinned and waved back, the blonde named Megs muttering under her breath, "God, she's such a bitch. And she's gained at least twenty pounds since last summer." After a small snicker, she called, "Hey sweetie! Look at you! You look *amazing,* doll. Be right over."

God, I strongly disliked other girls who made me strongly dislike other girls. The two gathered their things, got up, and pranced toward their "friend."

I sighed, turning back to the prep station and picking up the blender I'd just used. I took it to the small sink at the end of the counter.

"Water, please."

I turned around, my gaze landing on a dark-haired man just sitting down, his head turned, eyes somewhere in the distance, fingers snapping in the air.

Fingers . . .

. . . snapping in the air.

At me.

To fetch him a water.

I growled softly under my breath, plastering a smile on my face and heading his way.

My, but this club was chock full of *charmers.*

"How may I serve you, sir?"

Apparently, he wasn't so dense that he didn't recognize the sarcasm in my tone, because he drew his gaze away from whatever he'd been staring at, and familiar whiskey-colored eyes met my own.

For a moment my confusion—and the impact of those eyes—rendered me speechless. When had I looked into those eyes before?

"Chief Hale," I said, memory dawning.

"Haven from California."

"Fancy seeing you here."

He used his forearm to swipe the perspiration dotting his forehead. He was wearing gym shorts and a loose gray tank that swooped low under both arms, the material darker with sweat in several spots, obviously having just worked out. He set a lanyard with his VIP club pass on the counter.

I'd pegged him as a power-tripping cop.

But apparently, he was a snobby rich guy.

Could one be both?

Unlikely. The two identities didn't exactly overlap in many areas. But perhaps this person was about to prove me wrong. Interesting.

Not everyone can be put into a box, Haven.

I reached behind me and grabbed a water out of the glass-doored mini-fridge and set it on the counter in front of him. "In addition to the water, might I interest you in something designed to help build muscle?" I asked sweetly.

His eyes narrowed ever so slightly as his head tipped minutely, the same look he'd given me on the side of the road after he'd all but murdered the plants I'd been rescuing. He glanced down at his left arm as though considering it. His tanned, beautifully muscled arm I had to concede, but only to myself, as I worked to keep my expression unimpressed. "Are my muscles not adequate?" He moved his arms forward, leaning on the counter and flexing very slightly as though the movement hadn't been designed to do just that.

"Oh no, no. They are"—I paused—"*adequate.*" I laced the word with a heavy dose of disappointment.

His lip gave the smallest quirk. He sat back slowly, assessing me. "Sideswipe any drivers today?"

33

"Not today, no."

"How are your plants?"

"I don't know. When I went back, they weren't there."

He pressed his lips together, nodding. "This is serious. You should file a kidnapping report. The Feds will want to get involved."

"Joke if you want, but those plants could very well be in the hands of a madman—or woman—facing untold hardships even as we speak."

"My God, I almost think you're serious."

I was serious. But I wasn't going to let this person mock me over my love of living things.

"I'm sorry your plants were stolen. Let us cling to the hope that whoever took them is providing a loving home filled with fertilizer and whispered words of encouragement to . . . grow and . . . make leaves and whatnot."

Really? I resisted an eye roll, crossing my arms. "About that drink . . . since your muscles are clearly . . . adequate, maybe you'd like my avocado banana smoothie with leafy greens and turmeric? It aids cognitive function."

Chief Hale paused and then grinned, a slow smile that blossomed from bemused to blinding. Wow. It was unfair that God sometimes gave grins like that to power-tripping snobs. Because it gave them more power. And self-justification to act snobby.

As a general rule.

That grin had probably been getting him cookies from the cookie jar, literally and figuratively, since he was big enough to reach for them.

His gaze moved behind where I stood to the place several pots of grasses and herbs lined a shelf. Those had been *my* contribution, and the woman who'd hired me had seemed enthusiastic about the additional offerings, especially after I told her she might consider raising the prices for fresh supplements.

He then stared at the basket of nutrition bars near where he sat at the counter, grimacing. "Let me explain something to you, Haven from California. Real men don't eat grass and"—he gave the bars another hostile glance—"birdseed."

I laughed. "No? What do real men eat?"

"Burgers. Things with bones." He unscrewed the water bottle cap and tipped it to his lips.

I sighed. "Men and their obsession with boners."

He choked on the sip he'd just taken, using his forearm to wipe his mouth. "*Boners?* I said bones."

I widened my eyes in feigned embarrassment. "I know. So did I."

He put his arm over the back of the stool next to him and chuckled softly. He gave me a slight nod, taking another sip of water, his eyes trained on me over the bottle. "I apologize for being rude. I was . . . distracted." He looked off to the side to the place he'd been staring at before, somewhere around the corner of the covered smoothie bar out of my line of vision, the amusement that had just been clear in his expression suddenly gone.

"Ah. Well, I understand. You were focused on scantily clad women. They're difficult to miss."

"No." His head turned slightly as though following someone's movement. "I was focused on revenge."

"Revenge?" I laughed but he did not. "*Revenge*?" I repeated.

He tapped his fingers on the counter as he looked back at me. "Yes. What's wrong with exacting revenge when a wrong is done to you?"

I considered that. "Well, it depends on the circumstances I suppose. It just sounds so . . . *melodramatic*. But if it's vengeance you seek, I have faith you'll achieve it."

His fingers stopped drumming. "Do you? Why?"

"Because as someone who works for the Pelion Police Department, you *certainly* yield considerable power . . . have weapons of mass destruction at your disposal, friends willing to assist you in making others *disappear*. Your enemy doesn't stand a chance."

He grinned that brilliant grin again. And *again*, it didn't affect me whatsoever. This man was gorgeous, yes, but he was obviously petty, prone to rudeness, definitely on a power trip, and God help the person who had *wronged* him, whoever *that* was. "I'm the chief of police, not a mob boss." He paused. "But you obviously recognize importance when you see it. You're very observant." The corners of his eyes crinkled very subtly, and I resisted a laugh.

"I have to be. It's part of the job description—knowing just what combination of grass and birdseed will benefit my clients the most."

"Sounds tricky."

"It can be. Some cases are harder than others."

"I bet. In that case, I *would* like to order one of your blended concoctions. Surprise me." He held his hand out. "We met on unfortunate terms the first time. I'm Travis Hale."

Travis. I wondered if he was the Travis the two women at my bar had just gossiped about. What had they said? He'd broken up with—and likely cheated on—his girlfriend and that, shamed and heartbroken, she'd hurried off to Florida to . . . tan?

I wondered at the combination of fact and fiction that might be contained in their casual remarks. He wasn't one of those smarmy, cringe-invoking flirts I'd seen here more than once. Although he was clearly self-assured. He was more difficult to peg than most, I'd give him that. Eventually, though, one side or the other would assert dominance. Time would tell. Although I only had a finite amount of that, so perhaps I'd never know.

Whatever.

I wiped my hand on my apron and gripped his. "Haven. From California. As you know. And I think I have just the thing for you, Chief Travis." I walked over to my blender and began adding ingredients. "Protein powder with collagen for those . . . *bones* you're so fond of." I was rewarded with his soft chuckle from behind me. I added some fruit and almond milk and then I used my scissors to snip one of the plants. "Wheatgrass for stealth so that your enemy may never see you coming. Spirulina to give fortitude for when the fight grows difficult, and carrot juice for clear vision so that you might see when this revenge you speak of is no longer worth your while."

I pushed blend, poured the smoothie into a glass, stuck a straw in it, and turned and placed it on the counter in front of Travis. I was rewarded with an amused smile. But his expression dropped when he eyed the—admittedly—murky-green smoothie. "Looks can be deceiving," I reassured. "Try it."

He screwed up his face as he lowered his lips to the straw, squinting one eye as if bracing for the possibility that he might be about to sample sewer runoff. He sucked in the barest amount, his eyebrows shooting up, and his lips tipping. He took a bigger swallow. "That's good."

"You feel stronger already, don't you?"

He raised a brow. "Strangely enough, I do."

CHAPTER FIVE

Travis

"Travis Hale, you didn't eat half of your breakfast. Is something wrong with Norm's cooking all of a sudden? And what about that?" She pointed at the blueberry muffin sitting next to my plate, sugary-cinnamon crumbs covering the top. "Bree brought those over just this morning. They couldn't be any fresher."

I took a swig of coffee and then rubbed at my stomach. "It's not the food. I think I might be coming down with something, that's all."

Maggie frowned, leaning over the diner counter where I sat at my regular seat and putting the back of her hand to my forehead. "You don't feel feverish. Maybe you should go home. When was the last time you took a sick day?" She nodded at my new recruit, sitting next to me, shoveling Norm's O'Brien potatoes into his mouth as if this might be the last meal he'd ever eat. "Spencer can handle things for one day, right, Spencer?"

Spencer nodded, but before he could speak and show us a mouthful of chewed food, I intervened. "No. I'm fine. Just something that needs to run its course." The truth was, my stomach felt fine, but my appetite was still affected by the sour mood I'd been in since I'd walked in on my girlfriend in bed with another man.

The picture was burned across my retinas and there was a strange pinching feeling in my gut that wouldn't recede.

Maggie studied me for a moment and despite being a grown man with a gun strapped to his hip, I almost squirmed under her perusal. "I heard you and Phoebe broke up."

"Where'd you hear that?"

Maggie waved her hand. "Around."

Around. Sometimes I hated living in a small town.

I took another sip of the now-cold coffee, nodding casually. "Things just ran their course."

She narrowed her eyes. "Huh," she said. "Just like that?"

I shrugged. "Relationships fail all the time, Mags. Just because you and Norm have been together since the ice age, doesn't mean everything lasts as long."

Maggie glanced back at Norm scraping grease off the griddle, the bald spot on the top of his head gleaming in the fluorescent lights, his large gut hanging over his belt. "It's true you're no Norm," she said, turning back to me, and giving me a teasing wink. "But you do have your good points. You know I'm here if you need someone to talk to, right?"

"I do, Maggie. Thank you." Maggie had always seen the good in me, even when I didn't deserve it, and had tried her best to take up where my own mother left off. I felt a tightening in my throat and swallowed around it, tapping Spencer on his arm. "We should get going."

"Yes, boss."

"You don't have to call me boss, Spencer. Travis is just fine." Spencer bobbed his head. He was a good guy, just young and a little too eager to please, socially . . . challenged, and he could be so damned *literal* sometimes. But . . . he was the grandson of a couple in town, the Connicks, who owned a number of cottages on the lake, people I'd known all my life. I remembered Spencer as a kid, holding a toy police car in his hands and watching the now-retired chief stroll by in his uniform with a look of awestruck wonder on his face. When he'd applied to be an officer and I'd called and told him he was hired, I'd known I was granting a long-held dream. And it was obvious that Spencer had transferred the hero worship he'd held for the retired chief to me.

Spencer downed the last of his coffee, and I put some money on the counter, said a goodbye to Norm, and smiled at Maggie. "Be safe," she called as the bell sounded over the door and we stepped out into the warm June day.

We turned into the lot where the cruiser was parked, almost colliding with someone. "Oh shit. Sorry, man. I wasn't looking—"

The man stopped talking suddenly, his mouth hanging slack. I pulled back, my blood freezing, eyes narrowing when I saw who it was.

Him.

"Urrr . . ." he choked, his eyes darting from my face, to my gun, and back again as we stood at the side of the diner, staring at each other.

I smiled, a slow, cold tipping of my lips as I reached down and rested my hand on my weapon. I saw Spencer frown in my peripheral vision, stepping back to get a better view of the interaction, his own hand going to his weapon.

The guy—*Easton*—took a step back, his expression filled with surprised terror. "Listen, man, it wasn't what you think."

I tilted my head. "Really? So you weren't fucking my girlfriend when I walked in on you two naked in her bed? You hadn't seen the photographs on her nightstand of the two of us? You must have asked. Did she tell you about me? Did it make it more exciting?"

He swallowed. I could see by his expression that I'd hit the nail on the head. If anything, those pictures had sweetened the deal, upped the challenge. And then there was likely the fact that, because she'd had—past tense—a boyfriend, Phoebe wasn't a girl who was going to demand anything of him after the deed was done.

You're the best! The best!

That pinching again, humiliation cooling my blood several more degrees. Speaking of ice ages. I felt like a walking glacier.

I was cheated on with this . . . *kid?* This pretty-boy club employee, vacationing in *my* town for the summer? I'd seen him the day before when I'd been sitting at the refreshment bar talking to smoothie girl.

The kid opened his mouth to speak then closed it again. "Here for the summer, I assume?"

"Urrr . . ."

"Maybe it's time to call it an early season," I suggested.

His eyes narrowed minutely. "Yeah . . . sorry. I can't do that."

"What's your last name, Easton?"

He hesitated, the wheels of his mind obviously turning. After a moment, having clearly worked out that I could find out his name easily enough if he wouldn't give it to me, he answered, "Torres."

"Torres," I repeated. Why did that sound familiar?

"Yeah. It's really Torres."

For several moments we engaged in a stare-off. Finally, his gaze skittered away.

"This is Travis's town," Spencer interjected.

I shut my eyes briefly and huffed out a breath. Talk about melodramatic. "Listen, *Mr.* Torres, you might have just arrived, but I think we can both agree that you've burned the wrong bridge here in Pelion. I wouldn't expect this to be an enjoyable summer if you stay."

"You should leave before we run you out of town," Spencer threatened.

"Spencer," I said between clenched teeth, not glancing his way. Spencer had obviously watched far too many reruns of Gunsmoke in preparation for the job.

"What are you going to do?" Easton asked warily.

I chewed at my bottom lip thoughtfully, a slow smile unfolding. His gaze widened. "Nothing," I drawled. His chin jerked minutely, eyebrows lifting. "Nothing until you least expect it," I clarified, my smile growing. I stepped out of his path so he could pass by.

He moved to go around me and I stepped in his way, causing him to have to move around the other side. Immature, yet satisfying.

"You're crazy, you know that?" he said, dipping around and glancing back repeatedly as he almost ran to the diner door, ducking inside.

As if he was safe there.

Those were *my* people. And unlike *Phoebe*, they were loyal.

Still, I'd bide my time.

Spencer followed as I walked toward our cruiser.

I pulled out of the lot, heading toward the station. "We could have him roughed up," Spencer offered.

My brows came down and I gave him a glare. "We're not going to *rough anyone up*, Spencer. Jesus." I was many things, but a crooked cop wasn't one of them.

He looked chastised. "Sorry, boss."

I sighed. "This is a *personal* issue. I'll know when the right opportunity comes along." I glanced at him. "And listen, Spencer . . ."

The guy was staring at me so intently, as though I was about to impart the sagest advice he'd ever been given. I was surprised he hadn't taken out a piece of paper to make notes. "Just . . . dial it down a notch, okay?"

His shoulders sagged and he nodded dejectedly. "I just want you to know I got your back, boss."

I sighed. "I know that. I appreciate it." He was a decent guy. He was even a good cop so far, though he hadn't been on long. His main downfall was that his regular ass-kissing got on my nerves.

"She cheated on you," Spencer said. "Phoebe cheated on you." He looked personally outraged and, though it was overkill—an example of him *not* dialing it down—I still appreciated the concern on my behalf.

"And you walked in on it," he said, letting out one long whistle. "Man. That sucks." He dragged out the word, enunciating the u with a seemingly unending number of head bounces, until it was about fifty-seven syllables long and a headache had started at the base of my spine.

As if the word *sucks* needed to be so dramatically enunciated when discussing my cheating girlfriend. I had no doubt plenty of that had gone on before I walked in the room. I didn't appreciate the sudden visual. "I'd want revenge too," Spencer offered. "I mean, you walked right in on it!" he repeated.

God, why had I told him about it? Why?

Temporary emotional insanity, it had to have been.

"Yes, Spencer, I'm aware that I walked right in on it. I haven't forgotten the moment."

Spencer shook his head, staring through the windshield as the sunshine-drenched streets of Pelion streaked by, the blue of the lake sparkling in the distance. "What that guy did?" Spencer went on. "Humiliating you like that? Seducing your girl? Getting under the sheets with her, naked! Sticking his—"

"Spencer," I barked. He looked at me, startled. "Thank you so much for spelling the situation out for me, step by step, as it likely occurred. I was looking forward to considering all the possibilities and reliving the experience all over again."

"Not a problem, boss."

Okay, so he wasn't the most perceptive person. If he was a good cop, it was likely only a result of luck and the fact that the most serious calls we tended to get in Pelion—barring what had happened between my father and uncles decades ago, and what happened to Archer more recently—were for lost dogs, and the occasional drunk and disorderly.

And once in a while, a reckless driver.

Haven Torres from California. *That's* where I'd heard that name before. Could they be related?

"You can do me a favor, though," I said, thoughtfully.

"Anything, boss. Just name it. Anything. No matter what it is."

I glanced at him, thinning my lips. "This is a place where you might dial it down, Spencer."

"Oh. Right. Yeah. Yes, sir. Um . . ." He screwed up his face, looking lost.

The headache moved up my neck and settled at the base of my skull. I looked back at the road, turning into the station parking lot. "I'm going to find out *exactly* where Easton Torres is from and where he's been. Then I want you to dig up everything you can about him. Traffic tickets . . . arrest warrants, illegal activities posted to his social media, anything and everything we might want to know about."

"What are we going to do with it?" Spencer asked, leaning in conspiratorially as though I was about to impart some evil master plan.

"Make flyers. Write it across the sky, of course," I murmured, not able to roll my eyes for the pounding behind my left eye. I sighed, rubbing my temples again. I wouldn't do anything in an official capacity unless it was warranted. But even if melodramatic, Spencer had been right in one respect: this was *my* town. And though I wanted revenge, I also wanted to protect what was mine.

CHAPTER SIX

Travis

"Goddamn it!" I yelled, holding my hands in front of me to shield my face from the geyser of water that was bursting from the pipe. *How the fuck had this happened?* I turned my head as I yanked my T-shirt off, attempting to wrap it around the place where the pipe had busted, but instead, the entire piece of piping came loose, breaking off entirely and falling into the pond of water on the floor of my upstairs bathroom.

I stood, splashing my way toward the door, almost slipping once and catching myself. I made my way to the shut-off valve as quickly as possible, twisting the knob with a yank. And though I'd shut off the water, the sounds of drips and flowing barely diminished. The pipe had to have burst sometime that morning. It'd filled the upstairs of my home and was leaking through the ceiling to the floor below.

My house was ruined.

For a moment I just stood there, dripping, my head down, wondering what else this week was going to have in store for me.

After a few minutes, I went in search of my phone.

Archer showed up just as the insurance agent was leaving and about an hour after the landlady had walked through the place, shaking her head and saying, "Oh noooo," again and again. "These things happen," she'd finally said, sighing. "That's what insurance is for."

I had insurance. I just didn't have a place to sleep, as my mattress was waterlogged and the ceiling was at risk of caving in.

You can sleep on the couch, Archer signed, thinning his lips in a way that told me he wasn't sure whether he meant it or not.

"God, no," I said and even I heard the weariness in my voice. I'd come home wanting to face-plant onto my own couch and instead arrived to a scene from the Titanic. "There's barely room for the five of you in that little gnome cottage."

Archer smiled, not offended in the slightest, instead very obviously exorbitantly happy by the thought of said little gnome cottage, and all his people gathered there. But then his smile turned into a frown. *There aren't many rooms—if any— available in Pelion right now.*

I grimaced. "Oh shit, that's right. That blueberry festival taking place on the other side of the lake. Damn," I murmured. Tourists had begun arriving earlier that day and business had spilled over into Pelion's B&Bs—which was great news for Bree and all the other businesses in town that benefitted, but not so much for me. "I'll figure something out," I said.

He looked at me for a moment. *You sure?*

"Yeah. You know me. There are any number of women who will volunteer to take me in during my time of need." I attempted a suggestive smile, but I could feel that it fell flat.

You're the best! The best!

As if I'd said something that garnered sympathy, Archer pressed his lips together and patted my shoulder. *I was sorry to hear about you and Phoebe.*

"Where'd you hear about me and Phoebe?"

He shrugged. *Around.*

A small pang of humiliation went through me, but I kept my face neutral. "I didn't see us going anywhere, anyway. It was for the best."

He assessed me for another moment and then finally said, *Okay.* He must know I was lying—I'd told Bree the week before that Phoebe and I were serious and I had no doubt Bree and Archer told each other everything. They probably signed all their secrets while snuggled up in their bed in their little gnome cottage. Despite my inner eye rolling, the thought made me feel more depressed than ever. In any case, if Archer knew I was lying—which, again, I was sure he did—he didn't press the issue.

I was grateful.

His shoes plunked in the water as he showed himself out. I stood there alone, feeling unusually . . . well, alone. Maggie and Norm would take me in, but their place was small too, and they didn't have an extra room. Plus, if I became an unwitting witness to any sort of domestic displays of physical affection between the two of them, I'd have to find a therapist, or maybe a lobotomist, and a serious medical procedure wasn't currently in the budget.

I thought of my mother but . . . hell no. I'd had a bad enough week as it was. I wasn't going to make it worse.

I could pitch a tent on my property if I was truly desperate, but I still had to go to work, and getting ready for a shift with no running water would be challenging.

Spencer would take me in. Spencer would give up his bed and sleep in the bathtub or the doghouse if I asked him to. I massaged my temples, the very thought of enduring Spencer for nights and days on end making my head pound. The other guys who worked for the police department were married, but a few of my good friends at the firehouse who were bachelors might be possibilities—but only if all the B&Bs were actually full.

I grabbed my phone and started making calls.

All the B&Bs were actually full.

The rental cottages too.

I looked at the last B&B listed on the Pelion website I'd gone to. I'd disregarded it because it was in a sketchy area, right on the edge of town, a sort of no man's land, that wasn't exactly Pelion, and definitely not the ritzier side of the lake.

The Yellow Trellis Inn.

It was inexpensive compared to the others. And from what I'd heard, for good reason.

It was also run by a woman I'd heard the town refer to as "Batty Betty." I thought I'd gotten wind of a story floating around about a dead husband and suspicious circumstances but couldn't recall anything specific.

I picked one foot up, water streaming from my shoes. It couldn't be worse than this. And definitely better than Archer's well-worn couch where he and Bree had done who knew what in that little gnome home on the lake.

I picked up the phone and booked the last room they had available. "It has a lake view," the woman on the phone promised, enthusiastically.

"Great," I said. Beggars couldn't be choosers, but in that moment, the promise of a lake view buoyed my mood just a tad. Even this rental I lived in didn't have a lake view. Then I packed some clothes, my work gear, and a few accessories into a duffel bag, all of which thankfully hadn't been rained upon by upstairs plumbing, grabbed a dry pair of shoes, and headed to my car.

****

The room definitely didn't have a lake view.

"Right there," the woman named Betty with the frizzy halo of blonde hair said, pressing her face against the glass and angling it to the side. "If you crane your head *just so*, you can see the edge of the lake." She turned and smiled brightly

52

as if having to meld yourself with the window to see an inch of water made it the finest room in the house.

What I *could* see—clearly and directly outside my window—was what appeared to be a headstone. "Is that a *grave?*" I asked.

"Oh *that.*" She waved her hand, dismissing it. "That's where an old barn cat that used to roam the property is buried."

I peered out the window again. The headstone seemed sizable for a barn cat. Not to mention there was no barn in sight.

Batty Betty. Yet she seemed *mostly* normal.

I gave her one more suspicious glance before looking around the room. It wasn't terrible. It was actually what I'd call somewhat . . . charming. Or at least on the verge of charming. Within *range* of charming. More importantly, it had a bed and a bathroom, so I wasn't going to complain about not having a view of the lake, but instead, a cat's tombstone. I'd been looking at that particular lake since I was born.

As far as the tombstone . . . I'd keep the shade closed.

"Well," she said, clapping her hands together, "you've . . ." She frowned, blinking rapidly, finally using her fingertips to tap her forehead somewhat violently, her head snapping up, "*Arrived!*" she declared.

"Yes. I . . . have . . . arrived?" *What was that about?*

She shook her head. "No, you *arrived* just in time for the social hour downstairs."

"Social hour?"

"Right. It's in the room at the back of the house, where guests are welcome to mingle and such. We serve my sister Cricket's homemade hooch."

My brows flew up. "Prison wine?"

"That's right. She perfected it in the toilet inside her cell during her time away, and now it's a family favorite and all the rave at social hour."

I stared. Speechless.

"Of course, *we* don't make it in a toilet, seeing as we have other options."

"That's good to hear."

"That would be unhygienic," she clarified needlessly.

"Among other things."

She laughed faintly.

"Anyway," I went on, shaking myself, as though I'd stepped outside reality for a moment. "Sounds . . . interesting. I'm a little tired though so I'm going to skip social hour for tonight."

"Suit yourself. I'll just get out of your way then."

After the door had closed behind her, I stripped off my clothes and made my way to the shower and then, clad in my boxers, fell back on the bed, the springs making a loud creaking sound. Despite the obvious age of the mattress, the bed was comfortable. I lay there for a few minutes, expecting to fall asleep immediately. Instead I stared up at the ceiling, wide awake. There was a tall potted plant next to the bed and I turned to it. *Living things feed off energy.* "How's it going?" I asked the plant, hitting a new life low.

The soft sound of laughter drifted to me from below.

Social hour.

Complete with *hooch*.

And here I was, alone and talking to a *plant*.

"Why the fuck not?" I muttered after a minute, pulling myself from the bed and dressing in jeans and a T-shirt. If any day called for some hooch, it was *this* day.

I followed the sound of voices to the large screened-in room, coming to an immediate halt in the doorway, my surprised gaze bouncing between Haven Torres and—my eyes narrowed—*Easton* Torres.

Well. This was unexpected. And either more bad luck, or an amazing opportunity.

Haven was in the midst of a conversation with the woman next to her, but Easton spotted me, his shocked eyes widening. I gave him my best evil smile and he blanched.

"Chief Hale?" Haven had noticed me.

I turned away from Easton, approaching the place where Haven sat. She was wearing a pair of leggings and a long T-shirt that fell off one shoulder. Her chestnut hair was pulled back the way it'd been both times I'd seen her, escaped curls haphazardly framing her face, somewhat reminiscent of Medusa. If Medusa had had a heart-shaped face, big expressive eyes, and lips the color of the wild pink roses that grew along the fence on my property. My heart did a strange unfamiliar something. Sort of twisty. Sort of squeezy. Maybe I was about to have a heart attack. It would be the perfect way to end a perfect week, spread out on the floor of The Yellow Trellis Inn, my life in the hands of my nemesis and a group of strangers drunk on hooch.

The woman Haven had been talking to had turned and was now engaged in conversation with an older woman with long, blonde hair liberally woven with white, and sporting a pair of overalls. "Haven from California," I said.

"Are you *following* me, Chief Hale? This level of stakeout seems overkill for the minor crime of reckless driving."

I stopped, glancing back at Easton. His alarmed gaze had followed me, as a rabbit might track a wolf.

"Ha. No. Did you flood my house in a desperate plan to get more viewing access to my . . . adequate muscles?"

She put her hand to her chest. "You *are* a good investigator. I've been exposed." She gave me a look of actual sympathy. "Are you serious about your house?"

"Sadly, yes. It's a rental, but most of my things are ruined."

"Sorry to hear that."

I shrugged, gesturing to the room at large. "This is your summer residence, I assume. It's about as far as you can get from the club without staying in Pelion."

"It was in the right price range," she explained. "You might be shocked to learn that smoothie bar operators must keep to a strict budget."

I smiled. "Though you're rich in personality."

She returned the smile. "This is true."

"I'm surprised *you're* here though. I'd think the chief of police would have plenty of more . . . upscale options."

"The upcoming blueberry festival," I said in explanation. "Most places are booked. I own a plot of land, but I'd have to pitch a tent if I wanted to stay there."

"Ah." She glanced at Easton, her smile dipping, brow wrinkling slightly. "Do you know my brother?"

Her brother. Aha. "We've met," I said smoothly.

"Oh . . . at the club?"

"No," I said, not offering more.

"I'm so glad you made it after all!" Betty said, entering the room and smiling as she approached me with a jug of purple liquid.

"Yes. I've *arrived.* Again," I said.

She laughed. "Indeed. Hooch?" she asked, holding it up as though it was the finest bottle of French champagne.

I glanced at Haven and she gave me a bright smile. I could see the amusement dancing in her eyes.

"It can't be worse than that smoothie you made me drink," I muttered, grabbing a cup from the tray on the table next to me and holding it toward Betty while she poured.

Once she'd turned away, I sniffed at it hesitantly. It didn't smell like a toilet bowl at least.

Haven laughed. "It's actually pretty good. But it does pack a punch. Be careful."

I took the smallest of sips. And grimaced. "Holy hell. It tastes like sweetened battery acid."

Haven laughed again.

I glanced at a potted plant nearby, noticing others flanking the room. I nodded at one of them. "Your refugees?"

She smiled. "Yes. They're doing beautifully."

"Probably because of all the company and stimulating conversation."

Her eyes brightened and she grinned. "Yes," she said. "Exactly." We stared at each other for several beats, that strange feeling flaring in my chest again. I raised my hand to massage it away when Betty approached.

"Everyone, I'd like to introduce you to our most recent resident," Betty said, placing the now empty jug of hooch down and clapping her hands together. "Chief Travis Hale." She waved a hand back to me and I glanced around at the welcoming faces, all except one of course. "And now we have a full house," she said. "All six guest rooms are filled. Isn't it exciting?"

In addition to Easton and Haven and myself, three others made up the guest list. There was the already infamous Cricket—the woman with the blonde and white hair, and sporting the overalls—and next to her, Clarice, a striking woman with jet-black hair and aqua eyes in town as a vendor at the blueberry festival where she told fortunes and sold crystals to fools and hippies (the description of her customers being my—inevitably correct—judgment alone, and not part of Betty's introduction). Admittedly though, it was eerie the way Clarice smiled knowingly at me like she'd read my mind.

And then there was Burt, a blind man in town on a birdwatching expedition. "It's probably more apt to call me a bird *listener*," he said, his deep-brown skin crinkling at the corners of his milky eyes.

Betty put her hand on my arm, leaning closer. "Burt became a bird . . . oh dear, oh dear," she said, frowning, her eyelids fluttering as they'd done earlier upstairs, two fingers hitting her forehead as though trying to shake something loose.

"Enthusiast," Cricket said.

"No, no," Betty answered, looking distressed, tapping harder. "Well, yes, but *no*."

"Aficionado," Burt interjected.

She let out a sharp breath, smiling. "Yes! That's it. Aficionado. Burt became a bird aficionado after the most amazing turn of events," she said. "He'd lost his will to live after losing his sight. You see, it was very unexpected and he wasn't adjusting well."

"Drank myself stupid one night," Burt chimed in eagerly.

"He made his way up to the top floor of his apartment building and climbed out the window at the end of the hall," Betty continued.

"I stood on that ledge, the breeze in my face, nothing but silence all around me," Burt said, seamlessly picking up the conversation. "It was early morning, and not a soul was awake yet on my quiet street. All of a sudden, this bird starts singing. The sweetest song I'd ever heard. It felt like that bird sang just for me. I stepped back inside and a moment later, that birdsong faded and I heard the rustle of wings rising back into the sky." His eyes teared up as though he was hearing it right that moment. "Saved my life," he said quietly. "Saved my life."

Despite the oddity of this whole situation, I felt a small lump form in my throat.

"Burt still hasn't identified what type of bird it was," Betty added. "But he will someday," she said warmly.

Burt smiled in her general direction.

There was a three-legged cat lounging on an ottoman, because of course there was.

"That's Clawdia. C-L-A-W-dia," Betty enunciated, giggling when she obviously noticed me staring at the cat. "Get it? C-L—"

"I get it, Betty," I assured her. "It's . . . clever."

A full house of eclectic misfits. And I was now one of them.

Betty turned and began talking to Clarice, so I leaned slightly toward Haven. "There's a grave beneath my window."

"I know," she said. "I saw it a few days ago when I took a walk down to the dock. Betty says an old barn cat is buried there." She paused and my shoulders relaxed. Betty had told me the same thing. "Who names a cat *Bob Smitherman*, though?"

"This hooch gets better by the glass," Burt said, moving my mind from the supposed barn cat named . . . Bob? . . . Smitherman? . . . with the oversized tombstone below my bedroom window. Maybe I should check the police department's database later and find out if Betty's dead *husband* had been named Bob.

Cricket nodded. "That it does. Of course, not making it in a toilet means it lacks a little something."

"We're all grateful for that, Cricket," Haven offered.

"You think so," Cricket said, turning to her, "but I'm telling you, the flavor is that much better when excess bacteria aids the fermentation process." She tapped her head. "Prison science."

"You should write a book on that," Clarice said, shooting her a knowing wink.

"I am," Cricket said. "It's almost done. Do you want to read it?"

"God, no."

Cricket laughed, slapping her hand on her knee. "You do have to have a tough disposition to seek out certain forms of knowledge. Some don't have a choice though. The knowing of things that no one wants to consider finds *them*," she said, sagely.

That struck me as true, and wise. We all possessed unpleasant truths, based on where life had taken us, and what we'd encountered, whether personally or professionally. Most people didn't mention such topics during social hour. Most people didn't like to think about those things alone in their own head.

Like me. A drowning I'd arrived at years ago came to mind, the way the five-year-old victim's mother had screamed his name until her voice was nothing but a ragged whisper. And then the memory of a coffin flashed, the way my father's lips had been sewn shut, the way I'd screamed for him in my head, begging for him to come *back*. The way I still pictured him sometimes, even in heaven, trying to smile around the tight thread.

Next to me, Haven's face had gone curiously blank as though she too was reliving a painful memory. I wanted to know what she was thinking. I had this strange urge to take her hand in mine.

I took another drink of hooch, this one more a swallow than a sip.

Easton, seeming to take advantage of the fact that everyone was turned toward Cricket, slunk out of the room, glancing back once at me before turning the corner and disappearing out of sight.

"He's acting so strange," Haven said, her brow furrowed, her gaze lingering on the place where her brother had just exited the room. "He didn't even come over and say hi."

I took a sip of hooch. It was true, it got better the more you drank. I could only imagine the headache one would wake up with after drinking too much of this rot gut. I set my cup aside. "Well," I said, "it might have something to do with the fact that I walked in on him in bed with my girlfriend—*ex*-girlfriend now—last week and, thinking he was a sexual predator who'd broken into her apartment, had pulled my gun out and was aiming it at his head. The big one. Not the one stuck inside my girlfriend at the time."

Her mouth had dropped open and she clapped a hand over it, her big eyes round saucers in her face. "Oh my God," she breathed, dropping her hand. She grimaced and then met my eyes. "Your revenge. He's the object. Oh, God." Her face had gone colorless.

"Do you blame me?"

She let out a long sigh, shaking her head slowly. "Not exactly." She paused, her worried gaze moving over my features. "How exactly do you plan on exacting said revenge?"

"I haven't decided yet." I flashed her a devilish smile but she remained serious, finally sighing. But in all honesty? I had to admit I'd lost some interest in my revenge, even since that morning. I couldn't say exactly why, but there it was.

"Maybe he deserves it." She tilted her head, giving me a sympathetic look. "How serious were you about the girl?"

"I was considering marrying her." It was true, wasn't it? So why did that feel like a lie?

"Shit." She reached out and put her hand on my arm. It was slender and tanned, her nails short and unpainted. The nails of a woman who liked to dig in soil. *You're Never too Old to Play in the Dirt.* "I'm sorry. On his behalf." She looked so incredibly sincere and I felt a small knock in my chest.

"You can't apologize on someone else's behalf."

Our eyes locked for several moments and something passed between us. Something I had no idea how to interpret. Sympathy? Understanding? "No," she finally said. "I know. I know that. Sometimes I feel responsible for his behavior, though. I practically raised him. For so long, it's just been him and me. He's . . . well . . . I don't even know what to say."

Haven looked away and I studied her profile for a moment, taking in those runaway curls that definitely had a mind of their own. I wondered what her hair would look like down . . . all that wildness dancing around her face. "What are you two doing here?" I finally asked.

Her gaze found mine again and she gave me a very slight smile. "We left California—where, as you know, we're from—two years ago." She shrugged. "We've been exploring the country together, stopping for a couple months here, a few months there when we got short on cash."

I whistled. "Nomads. How'd you choose Pelion as the place to enjoy the summer?"

She smiled and tilted her head. "Honestly, I'm not sure. We saw the lake through the trees as we came upon the sign for Pelion and we stopped to stretch our legs. Standing there, the roofs of the buildings just within sight, the sound of the lake lapping the shore, and the smell of pine all around . . . it just felt so peaceful, you know?" She glanced at me and smiled. "Well, of course you know." She shrugged. "Anyway, we checked in here, and then found the jobs at the club the next day. It just worked out."

I was mesmerized by her description of Pelion, the way she made it sound so calm and picturesque. Did I see it the same way she did? In some ways, yes, but in other ways, there were so many locations that held painful memories. Why had *I* never jumped in my truck and left town? Seeking something that Pelion could not provide? I loved my job, and the people of Pelion, but I could have been a police officer anywhere. I'd never considered leaving, and that suddenly seemed like an interesting choice I'd never even pondered on.

What kept me here?

There was a whole world of other places where I wouldn't be "one of those Hale boys," or "that asshole

Travis," or "the guy who lost the town," or "the one with the crazy, bitch of a mother," or even "second best."

"When do you plan on stopping for good?" I finally asked. *And how do you know when you've landed in that spot?*

She shrugged. "At some point, I suppose we'll head back west. But for now, we're fully enjoying ourselves."

"That's definitely true of your brother. I saw just *how* fully with my own eyes."

Haven grimaced again.

I held up my hands. "But you, you are here in our town doing the good work of rescuing plants from landfills."

She tipped her head. "Everyone has a part to play." She smiled, playing idly with the fringe on a throw pillow. There were secrets in her eyes and I wondered what she wasn't telling me about this trip they were on. I remembered that Archer's wife, Bree, had ended up in Pelion because she'd been running away, and wondered if Haven was leaving something specific behind as well. "And what about you? What parts, other than *chief*, do you play?" she asked, turning the subject to me.

"Uncle, for one. I have two six-year-old hellions for nephews, and a six-month-old niece who is still suspicious of me."

Haven laughed. "Family," she said, and I detected a wistful note in her tone. "Sounds like you have a close one."

"Oh, I wouldn't necessarily say that. I could tell you some family stories that might curl your toes," I said, attempting to make light of life-changing events that, in all actuality, would follow me—and my brother too, hell, most of the population of Pelion—all of my days. But family dynamics that, at least, would end with my generation. Maybe my half-brother and I weren't the closest siblings on earth, but our relationship had grown over the years, as his trust in me had been rebuilt, and I knew for sure that Charlie and Connor would have each other's backs forever. Bree and Archer would tolerate nothing less.

Haven gave me a rueful smile. "I suppose all families have their issues."

"What about yours? What do *they* think about this two-year-long adventure you're on?"

"Oh, well, it's just Easton and me, which, you know, is why we're especially close, despite that I want to sock him in the gut sometimes. A lot of times, actually."

"No one at all?"

She cleared her throat, looking away momentarily. "No, like I said, just us." She put her hand over her mouth and let out a big yawn. "I didn't realize how late it was getting," she said, beginning to stand.

I stood too. There was no reason I should want more from her, but I felt an almost fundamental need to have answers. *Who were your family? How can you not have roots?* But I wouldn't push. *Yet.* Mostly though, I was disappointed she was ending our conversation because I liked talking to her. "I'm going to get to bed as well."

"I enjoyed chatting with you." She tilted her head, biting her lip. "I really am sorry about what my brother did and well, the repercussions. And you know, just for the record, I'm not opposed to putting a mild amount of fear into him."

She paused. "If you need any help in that endeavor, let me know."

I raised a brow. "What makes you think I don't want *more* than to put a *mild* amount of fear into your brother?"

She smiled and it was soft. "I just have a feeling that's not really you, Chief Hale."

I laughed, leaning in and speaking softly. "Maybe you don't know me so well, Haven Torres."

For several moments our eyes held, breath mingling and a spiral of heat whirled through me. "Maybe," she conceded, pausing. "But maybe not." She leaned away, and held out her hand. "In any case, can I consider you a friend?"

The whirling spiral of heat cooled and fizzled.

I gripped her hand. It wasn't as if I was even very attracted to her. She *was* pretty, I could see that now. But she was far from my type.

I dated prom queens.

This girl was a *plant* lady.

A plant lady with a penchant for pushing horrific things called *wheat germ* on me, an uncontrolled riot of haphazard curls that sometimes likened her to Medusa, and a lone family member—my now sworn enemy—who'd seduced my girlfriend and was apparently *the best*.

"Friends," I agreed.

We said goodnight to the room at large, a chorus of farewell greetings rising as we left—some sober, some not so much—parting ways at the top of the stairs, me turning left, Haven turning right.

I got into bed and this time, whether it be from my crazy-ass day or the barely palatable hooch, I did fall right to sleep.

CHAPTER SEVEN

Haven

The sky was streaked in waves of pink and amber, the sun cresting over the lake and scattering it with diamond shards.

Gorgeous. Peaceful.

I was a city girl, born and raised in East LA, and yet, in some peculiar way, it felt as if my heart had always known this place.

I wouldn't think too hard about it because that felt dangerous. But I would enjoy it while it lasted.

It's the water. Water calms every human soul.

Perhaps, but interestingly enough, I'd lived within a few miles of the ocean and, though staring out at the Pacific had brought a measure of peace, it'd never felt like *this*.

Heavenly.

The crystal-clear water, the soft sound of gently lapping waves, the fragrant pines, air so fresh you could drink it, and all that *quiet.* It spoke to my spirit in the same way caring for living things did.

I turned away from the window on a smile, lifting the watering can and giving the plant nearest the door a drink. "Good morning," I greeted, moving to the next, and the next.

"Good morning."

I whirled around on an intake of breath to see Travis leaning in the doorway that led from the kitchen to the sitting room at the front of the house. "God, you scared me."

He pushed off the wall, walking toward me. He was wearing workout clothes, damp with sweat. "You're up early."

"Yes," I said hesitantly, suddenly self-conscious. I was wearing my sleep shorts and a tank top, not exactly risqué, but not something I would have worn had I known anyone would be up this early. Even Betty didn't rise until seven to get breakfast started. His gaze only flickered over me though before he looked away. I relaxed. Travis Hale was used to seeing girls in thongs and bikinis so skimpy they were barely a notch above nudity at the club. My current outfit was downright puritan in comparison. "I'm an early riser."

"Me too," he said, lifting the hem of his shirt and wiping it over his forehead. I got an eyeful of tanned, defined abdominals. I turned, adding a generous amount of water to the next plant. "I don't meet many female early birds," he said on a smile. "Most women enjoy their beauty sleep."

70

I looked at him sideways. "Well, obviously, I'm full up on that," I said, tucking one of my ridiculous curls behind my ear. It sprang forward in disobedience.

A meow sounded behind us, and Clawdia the cat came limping forward, her gait slow and staggered.

"You're off today?" he asked, glancing away from the off-balance creature, lowering his voice as he followed me from the front room to the hallway, open to the floor overhead where the rest of the occupants of The Yellow Trellis Inn still slept.

"Yes. You?" I asked, plucking a leaf, running my hand over another, taking joy in the health of the plants that had looked wan and lifeless when I'd rescued them from outside the local grocery store where they'd been left to sit in the brutal summer heat. These particular types did best in partial sun.

Or in this case, the light streaming in through the hallway window.

"No, I'm working," he said, sounding almost . . . disappointed? Did he not like his job? He seemed to do it with such gusto. A meow sounded again, the cat staggering in.

Travis's brow dipped as he looked at the cat wobbling precariously over to where we stood. "Oh for Pete's sake," he muttered, scooping the animal up and holding it with one muscled arm. I pressed my lips together to hide my smile.

"What's on the itinerary?" he asked, following as I moved from the hallway to the kitchen, walking over to the bay window where Betty had been generous enough to allow me to place various herbs and flowers.

"Well, I'm going down to the shore to soak up a little sun, and then I'm making a trip into town to see what's been moved to the discount aisle at the nursery." I turned suddenly and Travis's eyes jolted up as though he'd been staring at something . . . below my eyes, and I'd surprised him. "Do you know that the nursery in Pelion is the only one for miles around?"

"It should make your rescue job easier," he said with a wry smile. The cat butted at his chest and he raised his other hand, petting her head, and then her jaw when she tilted it upward.

"Ha. Well, true." I went back to my watering. I'd never performed my morning ritual with someone in tow, but I found I liked it. Chatting idly while I went about my plant duties. It was . . . peaceful. Who would have guessed? "I spent last summer in a town in South Carolina that had four nurseries. I had my job cut out for me," I said.

He laughed softly. "So you've been rescuing plants and making smoothies across the land."

I shot him a smile. The cat was purring loudly in his arms as he scratched her jaw distractedly, carting her along with us as we walked through the lower floor of the house. "No to the smoothie part. I've done a little of everything as far as paid positions." I grabbed the spray bottle hooked on the waistband of my shorts and misted a fiddle leaf that didn't need more than that and moved on. "Here in your lovely town, I just happened to hit upon the perfect job that utilizes *all* my talents."

"Lucky us." He grinned, leaning against the wall. A smile tugged again as I watched this muscled, athletic-looking lawman in sweat-laden workout gear, holding a three-legged cat gently as it very obviously basked in his affection. "Did you like it? South Carolina?"

I thought back to South Carolina, pictured the massive oak trees draped in moss, and the flawless emerald-green lawn of the golf course where I'd worked at the gift shop. "Yes. It's beautiful." I didn't mention the part where we had left early in July after a big, burly man wielding a baseball bat had shown up at our door at three a.m., because Easton *had done things*—Easton's description—with his wife in their pool and been caught on the backdoor Ring video doorbell.

I pushed *that* particular memory of South Carolina aside. This pattern of his *had* to stop. Not only was it immoral—and weren't there enough *single* women out there?—it became dangerous. This time it had been the *chief of police's* flipping girlfriend. *Who next?*

I didn't even want to know.

"How many places have you stopped?" Travis asked, scratching behind Clawdia's ear as her eyes all but rolled back in her head.

I turned, walking to the next room, his soft footsteps behind me. "For more than a day or two? Seven. Arizona, Texas, Alabama, South Carolina, Virginia, Pennsylvania, and of course, Maine."

"So if you're staying on the same course along the coast, you're pretty much at the end of the line. What will you do after this?"

"Head back, I suppose." A tiny ball of fear bounced through me. "Maybe take a longer, more winding route." Out the window, the sun crested higher. Upstairs, I heard the water begin to run in one of the bathrooms.

He watched me for a minute as if considering something. I turned, plucking some dry foliage, using my spray bottle to mist the top leaves, adding some water to the soil, and crooning a few words here and there.

"What's been your favorite stop so far?"

I eyed him. "Haven't you ever traveled, Travis Hale?"

He shrugged. "Not really. A few spring break trips. But I can't recall too much of what happened on those. Every once in a while, I have a vague flash of a wet T-shirt contest and a long line of Cuervo shots, but that's about it." He'd hesitated in his petting as he'd spoken, and Clawdia headbutted him again until he resumed his scratching.

I shook my head, but laughed, as much at his comment as the forward feline female with an obvious crush. "Before this, I hadn't traveled much either." At all, as a matter of fact. "I've liked something about each place, because it's all been new, but if I had to pick one? Here, honestly." I set my watering can down and turned toward him.

He looked mildly surprised, but pleased. Clawdia arched her back, delighting in his fingers raking over her spine. Something tightened inside me as I watched his large, tanned hand trail idly over the animal's fur. "That's a nice endorsement," he said, his voice filled with sincerity. I took in his expression. He had surprised me. I'd had such a different impression of him when we'd first met. But Travis Hale had layers to him. He was a good listener. He had the ability to laugh at himself and take some good-natured needling, which meant he had at least a modicum of humility. He was a small-town cop who obviously took great pride in his hometown, but it was also clearly important to him to be part of the "in" crowd. He was about as masculine as they came, and yet he was currently carting a disabled cat around, because watching her struggle from room to room behind us had compelled him to assist her. Yes, definitely layers. Wonder of all wonders. Not that I had the time to peel them back, but I could appreciate a person who ended up being more than their first impression. I usually pegged people immediately and I was rarely wrong. It had meant my very survival once upon a time.

For a few moments we simply looked at each other, the sunlight streaming in, and the house just coming alive upstairs, the purr of the delighted cat vibrating softly between us. I closed my eyes and relished the quiet for what it was. *Solitude.* Well, with my new friend. My onion man.

"What are you thinking?" he asked quietly.

My eyes opened as I tilted my head. Travis could have shunned me for what Easton did. He could have made me suffer for it too, others had certainly considered me guilty by association after Easton wronged them. But Chief Travis Hale wasn't doing that. It said something about him. And I was grateful. "I was thinking that I'm glad we're friends."

He smiled. "Me too."

CHAPTER EIGHT

Travis

"Who's the new guy?" I asked casually, as if I didn't already know the answer, glancing at Mrs. Hearst, one of the managers of the golf and tennis club.

She looked up from where she was doing paperwork at a table with a large umbrella blocking out the sun and peered toward where I'd inclined my head. Easton Torres lowered a tennis ball hopper over a ball and then moved toward another, collecting it as well.

"His name is Easton Torres. He's a seasonal employee. One who generally has a line of women trailing behind him," she said, smiling up at me. "Why, hello, Chief Hale."

I smiled back. "How are you, Mrs. Hearst?"

"I'm well, thank you. Why do you ask about Easton?" As though he'd heard his name—though that was impossible because the distance was too far and we were speaking quietly—he glanced up, his eyes widening as he looked between me and Mrs. Hearst. I smiled slyly, raising my water bottle. He tucked his head and hurried away, the hopper clutched in his hand, leaving numerous tennis balls uncollected on the empty court.

I tipped my drink to my mouth, giving myself time to consider how to answer her question. Mrs. Hearst was one of the few in the club who hadn't lived in Calliope when the scandal with my mother occurred. Therefore, if she judged us, it was only because she'd heard the gossip, not because she had a personal stake in Victoria Hale's numerous betrayals and ultimate ejection. When I'd seen her sitting alone at the table and Easton directly in view, it'd seemed a good opportunity to plant a seed or two. Just in case. I drummed my fingers idly on the brick column next to me. *Tap, tap, tap.* But what if I did more than plant a seed? What would happen if I told her Easton was under an unofficial investigation— which was true—that might potentially result in a scandal that brought negative scrutiny to the club—which, again, was true. Potentially. The idea knocked around in my brain momentarily. I'd have to word it just right.

A laugh drifted from the direction of the smoothie bar around the corner from where I was standing.

I'm sorry. On his behalf.

If I *did* word it just right, Mrs. Hearst would likely find a reason to fire Easton, that's what. Who needed a potential scandal brought on by a temporary employee?

You can't apologize on someone else's behalf.

No. I know. I know that.

Of course, if Easton got fired from the club, that would affect his sister. I lifted my hand, rubbing at my eye.

What are you thinking?

I was thinking that I'm glad we're friends.

Friends.

That particular laugh met my ears again, my train of thought regarding *Easton* scattering.

At least this way, with him still employed at the club, I could continue to keep my eye on him, both at work and at home. And keep him guessing. Keep him wondering.

I sighed, tossing the empty bottle in the trash. "Never mind. For a minute, I thought he was someone else."

"Ah. Well, it's good to see you looking so well, Chief. Have a nice rest of your day."

"Thanks, Mrs. Hearst. You too."

And with that, I turned away, moving toward that laugh.

"Don't you see enough of me?" Haven asked, putting her hands on her hips as I rounded the corner.

"I'm not here for you. I'm here for the wheat germ."

She laughed and whatever had been on my mind moments before, was suddenly gone. "Ah. The *wheat germ.* Likely story."

I grinned. "Hey, friend."

"Hey yourself. What can I delight your palate with today?"

At her words, a zing of heat shot through my midriff. A zing that didn't exactly feel . . . friendly.

I'd been rising every morning to accompany her on her plant rounds, and we'd chatted about mundane subjects, getting to know each other on a surface level. It was nice. Peaceful. I enjoyed her company. And maybe *enjoyed* was too tempered a word because again, I was following her as she performed plant rounds.

All while carrying that damn cat who just happened to show up each morning just when I did. *And I didn't even like cats.*

In any case, I was pretty sure Haven enjoyed my company too, and the time we spent together talking in the hush of the early morning. But . . .

Again, I needed a *break* from women. And she wasn't staying in Maine anyway so it was really a moot point. Friendship was fine, but anything else was more complicated than I wanted at the moment. She leaned forward to grab something from a shelf below the counter and I caught the slight rounded swell of one breast. My mouth went momentarily dry.

Haven stilled suddenly and my eyes shot to her face, breathing out a sigh of relief when I saw that she hadn't caught me staring down her shirt, but that she was looking behind me.

I turned to see Gage Buchanan approaching, a wide smile on his face. He took a seat. "Haven," he said in greeting.

MIA SHERIDAN

Her cheeks flushed, lashes fluttered. "Hi, Gage," she said, a breathless quality to her voice that made me narrow my eyes. "What can I get for you?"

"I'll have one of those protein shakes you made for me last week, please." He turned slightly. "Travis."

"Hey, Gage," I said, my eyes still focused on Haven whose eyes were still focused on Gage. A streak of annoyance lit inside me.

"One protein shake coming right up," she said, finally tearing her eyes away as she turned and began adding the ingredients to the blender, giving one not-so-furtive glance back at Gage. I resisted rolling my eyes.

"I hope you're coming tonight?" Gage said, turning his stool toward me.

I searched my mind for what the hell he might be talking about, remembering some charity event invitation that I'd stuck to my fridge at home. The one I wasn't currently living at. "Oh, is that tonight? Sorry, I totally spaced it." I noticed Haven lean back slightly as she obviously listened to our conversation over the grinding of the blender.

"Any donation helps," Gage said. "And we'd be honored to have the chief of police at our event."

I felt a muscle in my jaw twitch. Gage was the only one who still invited me to crap like that. The events that I'd attended regularly, as had my mother, before she had moved away and I'd been demoted to "common citizen." Not lakeside royalty like the Buchanan family. The fact that Gage still endeavored to include me made me feel both grateful and embarrassed. "I'll try to make it," I said noncommittally.

80

In front of us, Haven poured the blended drink into a glass, and set it in front of Gage who gave her a wide, genuine smile, held the glass up in a cheers gesture, and then took a sip. "Thanks, Haven. This is delicious."

She noticeably swooned. *For Christ's sake.* I drummed my fingers on the counter. "Anytime," she breathed as he got up, nodded to me, and walked away.

Haven stared after him for a few moments, sighing as she leaned back against the counter.

"You too, huh?"

She looked at me, watching her with one eyebrow raised. "Me too, *what?*"

"One of the hordes who have a crush on Gage Buchanan. How . . . boring."

She flung the cleaning towel over her shoulder. "Maybe. So?"

I shrugged, glancing at my fingernails, attempting a combo of bored and disappointed, when what I really felt was a strange sense of irritability. *I* was the one who engaged her in scintillating conversation while carting a three-legged cat around. And Gage was the one she had a crush on? Which was good, I reminded myself. Because that would be awkward seeing as I was on a break from women and would just have to let her down easy when she inevitably threw herself at me. "I thought you were more *interesting* than that."

"Maybe I don't want to be *interesting.* How well do you know him?"

"I've known him all my life. Our mothers used to be friends." Which wasn't exactly true. Gage's mother had

81

invited mine to all her social functions, and they'd run in the same circles, but they'd never been close. Because Lana Buchanan was decent, and she'd obviously figured out that Tori Hale was not. Haven studied me for a moment as if she knew there was something I wasn't saying, but didn't comment. I squinted at her as I considered the situation at hand. The truth of the matter was that the entire Buchanan *family* was decent—more than that. They were good people. And so was Haven. I sighed. "Come with me to the event his family is hosting tonight. It's at their house, which is about three times the size of this club."

Her breath caught, eyes widening, but she tilted her head as though hesitant to say yes for some reason.

"As friends," I said.

"Of course," she answered, chewing at her lip momentarily. "What should I wear?" she asked. Ah. Was that what she was worried about?

"Strategically?"

"Uh, sure, a good strategy never hurts."

"Agreed." I sat back, allowing my eyes to travel down her slim body and then back up. She held herself immobile as though struggling not to fidget under my perusal. "The women Gage typically date have more . . . skin," I finally said.

"They're in possession of more skin?"

"Hmm." I smiled. "Much more."

"That sounds medically alarming."

"Very alarming," I said, deepening my voice and adding a dreamy note. I felt the muscles around my eyes tightening subtly as I resisted laughing.

82

She was obviously doing the same, her eyes dancing as she stepped toward the front counter and leaned in toward me. As if we were magnetized, I involuntarily leaned toward her, inhaling the clean fragrance of her soap or shampoo or whatever delicately floral scent she wore. I wanted to lean closer, get *more* of it. She drew away. "Might you mean they *show* more skin?"

"Oh. Yes. Maybe that's it." I grinned teasingly, and was rewarded by the small flare of her eyes. I knew the impact of that particular grin—no female could resist it. Even one who was only a *friend*.

"So what you're saying is that if I want to catch Gage's eye, I should remove several pieces of clothing?"

"Now you're getting it."

She laughed, tossing her dishtowel at me. I reached up and caught it easily.

For several moments we grinned at each other across the counter. It felt good but goofy, which was odd since I was seldom goofy.

"Seriously though," I said, ending the weird bout of goofiness. "Get his attention with some skin, and then roll out your sparkling personality."

"Is that what you do? Flash your muscles and then roll out your sparkling personality like some grand prize on a game show?"

"I do know how to get 'em, even if I don't always know how to keep 'em."

She winced. "Oh, God. I'm so sorry. That was insensitive of me. I poked a fresh bruise—"

"I'm kidding, Haven. Sort of." But speaking of *bruises*. I leaned forward. "How's your brother seemed lately?"

She huffed out a small breath. "He's all but disappeared from the inn. I think he might be sleeping in my car. He probably thinks you're going to murder him in his sleep."

Well, that was welcome news. "Good," I said, sitting back. "I owe you one for not saying anything that might ease those fears." *Murder* as a revenge plot wasn't something I'd even momentarily considered, but Easton didn't need to know that. "Come as my guest tonight."

She studied me for a moment, obviously thinking. "Okay yes, I'll take you up on your offer. I'd love to accompany you to Gage's charity event."

"Great. Be ready at seven."

"Meet me at the bottom of the stairs," she called after me. I was still smiling as I walked away.

CHAPTER NINE

Haven

I pulled my room door shut behind me, making my way toward the stairs. I smoothed the short, black cocktail dress over my hips, feeling unusually exposed. Although if I really thought about it, the dress was no skimpier than the shorts and tank tops I wore on a regular basis. Well, other than my almost completely bared back, laced with three crisscrossing string ties.

I'd bought the dress on the sale rack at the back of a clothing shop called Mandy's on Pelion's Main Street. Even on deep discount, the dress was a splurge, but when I'd put it on, it felt both daring and somehow *me* even though I'd never worn a cocktail dress in my life. The only event I'd attended that one *might* classify as a cocktail party was the social hour here at The Yellow Trellis Inn where prison hooch was served in red Solo cups.

The owner, Mandy herself, had laced the ties up for me and when I'd asked her if it was too revealing, she'd smiled and said that no, I looked like a class act. Perhaps she'd just been trying to sell me the dress, but she'd seemed so kind and sincere, and I'd believed her.

My hair was long and loose, the curls tamed by a good amount of mousse, and a diffuser I'd borrowed from Clarice. The ends of it tickled the bare skin of my lower back.

I rounded the curve in the staircase and saw Travis, his back to me. I was stepping slowly in the heels I wasn't used to wearing, and though I was virtually soundless, Travis turned as though he'd sensed my presence. And his body went utterly still. His eyes swept down my body and I saw his throat move as he swallowed. He was even more gorgeous than usual in dark gray khakis, a white shirt, and a blue and gray patterned tie. He'd obviously gotten a haircut, which made him look more vulnerable in a way I couldn't exactly explain. Younger. Eager to impress.

Time slowed, stretching like the sweet, pink taffy I'd watched being spun in the window of a candy shop in a coastal town Easton and I had stopped at for lunch before we'd arrived in Pelion. Our gazes held as I completed the final handful of stairs and stepped down to meet Travis where he stood. His face was so very serious, almost stunned, and my heart kicked. "Enough skin?" I whispered, a strange hitch in my voice.

He smiled almost sweetly, a smile I hadn't yet seen from this man, my friend. My temporary friend. His gaze dropped again and for a few moments he was quiet. When his eyes met mine, he said simply, "You're perfect."

My breath gusted from my mouth. I'd held it for a moment as I'd waited for his answer. Something moved between us, something lighter and hotter than the sweet, slow taffy that had just moved through my mind. It quickened my heart. It scattered fear through my system. "So you think Gage will approve?" I asked.

His face did something funny. He looked away for a moment and when he looked back at me, his lip quirked. "He's a fool if he doesn't. Let's go, Haven from California."

I heard chatter and the sound of others descending the stairs—the other guests staying at The Yellow Trellis Inn coming down for happy hour. "Oh! Bye, you two. Have fun," Cricket said, coming around the corner and spotting us. I smiled at her, and when I glanced back at Betty, Clarice, and Burt, who had stopped near the bottom of the stairs, both women looked enchanted, their eyes glued. It was like we were their children and they were watching us leave for the prom. Betty whispered in Burt's ear as though narrating our departure.

"I thought about getting you flowers," Travis said. "But I figured a plant lady such as yourself, prefers living things keep their roots."

I smiled, charmed by his consideration, and his accuracy.

When Travis opened the truck door for me, I looked over my shoulder to see Easton standing at his room window, watching us leave, looking both shifty-eyed and concerned, the fabric of the curtain gripped in his fist. Travis waved to him, shooting him that overly demonic smile he liked to use to harass Easton. A laugh rose in my throat, but I pretended not to notice.

"So I didn't ask what this charity fundraiser is for," I said when we'd pulled on to the main road, the lake sparkling under the lowering sun and sending glints of light into the cab of his truck.

"I think it's for some animal habitat. The Buchanan family is always trying to save some endangered species or another."

My heart melted. "How kind and generous." Of course they used their—from what I'd gathered—substantial wealth to rescue animals. Gage was perfect. It only stood to reason that his family was perfect too.

Then again, I didn't ascribe to that whole apple not falling far from the tree philosophy. If I did, I'd feel pretty hopeless about my own future prospects. And Easton's too for that matter.

Travis was tapping his hand on the steering wheel distractedly. Finally, he sighed. "You're right about the Buchanans," he said almost begrudgingly. "They are generous. They are kind. Gage himself runs several foundations. He even chairs some kind of rescue habitat for possums."

I laughed and he shot me an amused look. "Possums?"

"I know. Not exactly the sexiest animal, right? It's probably why he doesn't talk a lot about it. But he's got a thing for them, I guess. Kinda weird, if you ask me."

"I'm sorta weird too," I breathed. This was fate.

"The whole plant thing?"

"Exactly. We're perfect for each other."

I bit at my lip for a moment and then pulled my phone from my small evening bag.

"Tell me you're not googling possums," Travis said dryly.

"The more I have to work with, the better," I said, my eyes scanning the information on the website I'd pulled up.

The house was even grander than I'd pictured, a shining white castle on a hill. A fountain splashed and bubbled in the middle of a circular driveway, and lights shimmered and glistened from every corner of the property. It felt magical. An alternate universe. An alternate *life,* certainly from the one I was currently living, but even more so from the way I'd grown up.

A valet service greeted us, opening my door, the valet offering his hand. As I stepped down, I blinked in wonder.

You've aimed far too high, Haven, I told myself. Gage was handsome, kind, *perfect.* And yes, I'd known he was wealthy, but I hadn't imagined *this* level of wealth.

You're not looking to rope the guy into marrying you.

Surely even Gage Buchanan didn't have anything against a summer fling with a girl just passing through town.

He was a guy, after all. He probably *preferred* flings above all else.

89

"Does Gage live here?" I asked. *With his parents?*

"No, Gage lives in his own house nearby. But the Buchanans host all their events here." Travis led me into the house, and my neck craned as I glanced around at all the opulence. "Nice setup, huh?" Travis asked, leaning in toward me. "What do you think?"

"I think the entirety of the apartment I grew up in could fit in this foyer," I murmured, distracted by the jaw-dropping *size* of everything.

When I looked at Travis, he was watching me closely. I fidgeted with my bag, and let out a laugh that felt false even to my own ears.

"What do *you* think of this place?" I asked. "Not overly impressed?"

Travis shrugged, glancing around. "Oh, it's impressive. But I have the feeling a small-town chief of police's salary wouldn't cover the rent." His lip hitched, but there was something in his eyes that contrasted his wry smile.

We wandered through a few of the wide-open rooms. The furniture had obviously been moved to accommodate the guests, with high-top tables covered in white linen placed around the perimeter where drinks could be set as people gathered and conversed.

The bidding items were set up in a room near the back of the house, the windows thrown open to the patio and gardens beyond. A band played in the corner, something crooning and jazzy, or so I thought. Admittedly, I didn't know a lot about music. Books were more my thing.

"Dance?" I turned my head to see Travis holding his hand out.

I laughed. "*Dance?*"

"That wasn't exactly the response I was hoping for," he said, and though he attempted to add a sardonic tone to his voice, he sounded more offended than anything.

"Sorry. Truthfully? I'm not the best dancer." I inclined my head toward the band. "At least, not *that* kind of dance."

"It's easy. All you have to do is trust and follow."

Trust and follow. "I'm not so good at that," I murmured.

He reached his hand out again and this time, I took it. There were several couples already on what had been designated the dance floor and we weaved through them, stopping when we were near the middle. I pulled in a breath as Travis stepped toward me, wrapping his arms gently around my body as I moved in closer. *Closer.* His body was warm and solid, and so much bigger than my own. He smelled like heaven.

My heart was pounding, I realized, and I attempted to slow it, to gather my nerves, to *trust and follow.*

For a few moments we moved stiffly together, our bodies swaying slowly to the music. All around us, the couples smiled and chatted, looking relaxed and casual, while every atom in my body felt frazzled.

"I like this song," I said, swallowing. "What is it?"

He brought his head back slightly. "How is it possible you've never heard of Nat King Cole?"

I breathed out a laugh. "I don't know." Of course I did know. I'd grown up with a mother who didn't offer a wide exposure to the *arts,* unless your definition of the arts was a People magazine she'd swiped from the methadone clinic now and again. And why did referring to her in the past tense still *hurt* so much, even after all this time?

I focused back on the song. It was beautiful and moving, and somehow unbearably sad. I relaxed against Travis, finally getting the hang of trusting and following, and allowing myself to do so.

For a few moments we simply swayed again, a different song starting. "Were things simpler then, do you think?" he asked softly. "These old songs always make love sound so . . . *easy.*"

I thought about that, listening to the man comparing his love's face to a flower. "I don't know if love has ever been simple," I said. But I knew what he meant. The song alone seemed to convey the idea that love was all you needed.

I knew that wasn't true.

And the man currently pressed against me had recently learned that lesson too, if he hadn't known it already.

"My brother left town for a while, eight years ago," he said.

I looked up at him, surprised at the change in subject. "Your brother?"

"Hmm hmm. Archer owns and runs Pelion. The land it's on has been in my family since the town's inception. It passes from one first-born son to the next."

Wow. I had had no idea families owned entire towns. The Hale's roots must be very deep. "Why did your brother leave?" I asked.

Travis shrugged, a small lift of his shoulders. "To find himself, I think. Sort of like you, maybe."

"Did he?" I asked.

Travis was quiet for a moment. His expression was sort of distant and sort of sad and I had the odd feeling that this was a subject he didn't discuss much. He seemed to be choosing his words carefully as though he'd found himself in a conversation he hadn't meant to begin. But why would that be? It was his history. His family. His brother.

"He did," he finally said. "Anyway, there was a party going on right in this very house the night he came back, which is why I thought of it. It's still a thing of legend here. Bree, his wife now, was on the dance floor with someone or other when Archer arrived. The crowd parted, the earth moved, angels sang, and they've been together every day since. They have three kids now—the nephews and niece I mentioned—but they still look at each other the way I imagine they did that night," he finished, almost as if to himself.

I breathed out a sigh. I felt charmed by the vision and the knowledge that since that moment, the two people he'd told me about had created a beautiful family.

Family. Roots. A rich history. My heart gave a sudden squeeze. What must that *feel* like?

The song came to a close and we stepped away from each other, gazes lingering. I felt slightly flushed, my emotions disorganized. I gave my head a small shake, fanning myself. "I should get some water."

We walked to the edge of the dance floor, Gage suddenly appearing before us like a god from the mist.

"Travis. Haven," Gage said, approaching us with a warm smile. "What a pleasant surprise. Thank you for coming."

"Gage." They shook hands.

"Hi," I said, smiling, feeling better already, more on even footing now that Gage was standing in front of us. "Your family's home is beautiful."

"Thank you. Travis has been here a hundred times, but I'd be happy to accompany both of you upstairs where the bar's set up."

"I, ah, actually see someone I'd like to say hi to," Travis said, sweeping his hand somewhere to the right. "But Haven did want a drink. Find me later, Haven?"

"Sure," I said, feeling a strange twinge in my stomach at his departure. Here I was now, alone with Gage.

Which was exactly what I'd wanted, of course.

"I didn't realize you and Travis Hale were dating," he said.

"Oh, no, we're not," I explained as he led me toward the grand staircase. "We're just... friends." As if he'd heard something strange in my tone, he glanced my way, his eyes lingering on my face.

"Gage, darling," an older woman said, sweeping up to us, her dark hair in a sleek chignon, her champagne-colored dress the picture of class and elegance, "have you seen your father? I've lost him again. I swear, I need to keep that man on a leash." Laughter filled her tone.

"He's in the billiards room sampling the cigars Mr. Henderson brought."

Gage's mother managed to make rolling her eyes look refined. "I should have known. It's where he always hides."

Billiards room. I felt dizzy and suddenly had the strange urge to laugh and cry simultaneously. I was with Gage. In his beautiful, perfect, family home.

Where there was a *billiards room.* I didn't even know exactly what that *was* except that, well, it was probably used for billiards and apparently hiding from your wife.

"Mom, this is Haven Torres," Gage said. "She works at the club."

"Nice to meet you, Mrs. Buchanan." I stiffened momentarily, waiting for Mrs. Buchanan's reaction to the fact that I was hired help. But she didn't bat an eyelash.

"Haven, dear, so nice to meet you. Aren't you lovely. My goodness, what I wouldn't give for your *hair.*"

I smiled. There was nothing phony about this woman. She was warm and gracious and her compliment felt sincere. She was perfect. But of course she was. "I better run and catch my husband before he finds another hiding spot. Have a wonderful evening." And with that, she swept off.

Gage and I chatted as he showed me to the bar, set up in a wide-open space on the second floor, where chandeliers shimmered, and heavy drapery adorned individual balconies that flanked the space. "Wow," I murmured as Gage handed me a flute of champagne.

"So where are you from, Haven, and how long will you be staying in Pelion?"

"I'm from California, and I'm only here for the summer. My brother—who I'm traveling with—and I both took seasonal jobs at the club. We'll leave once the season has ended." Why on earth did I just say all of that in such a flat, practiced way? *Was I so used to every aspect of my life being so temporary?* Thankfully, Gage didn't seem put off by it.

We'd wandered out of the grand room and into a hallway. Gage opened a door and led me outside on to a larger balcony featuring benches and potted trees adorned in twinkle lights. Something flowery and lovely met my nose, drifting from somewhere close by.

I wondered vaguely where Travis might be and who he'd gone to find.

Gage gestured to a bench where I sat down and then he joined me. It felt private and intimate and my heart picked up speed. "Tell me about yourself, Haven."

A small jolt of panic flared in my stomach. What a terrible question. For anyone really, but especially for me. I swayed, feeling slightly woozy. What angle should I take? How could I tell someone—anyone really, but especially *Gage Buchanan*—about myself without revealing anything much at all? My pulse jumped. And how would I do that without sounding like the most boring human on earth? I remembered teachers going around the room asking that question when I was in school, recalling the way dread would sit heavy on my shoulders as my turn approached, my cheeks hot, head ringing. But Gage was only being nice. *Kind.* Because he was both of those things.

Of course, *Travis* would know what to say. Travis would have the perfect strategic answer that would convey just the right thing to pique Gage's interest. And why was I thinking of Travis? Travis was the *last* person I should be thinking about right now. I fidgeted slightly, feeling suddenly strange and off-balance, nervous, and twitchy. All over the place.

I took a breath, placed my palms on the cool stone of the bench, and smiled. "Well," I said slowly, "I'm adventurous. It seemed like the adventure of a lifetime to get in my car, and just start driving, see where life took us, you know? Seize the day, that's my motto." My voice fizzled out toward the end of my statement, squashing the enthusiasm I'd intended on conveying. The adventurous spirit. Look at me! I do wild things like hop in my car and just start driving! Like summer flings! I've never actually experienced one of those but I'd like to! How about you? I almost groaned at the pathetic, scattered nature of my thoughts, but managed to hold it back, rallying and again, taking a deep breath and smiling.

I was never nervous like this with Travis. Talking to Travis was fun. And easy. It just flowed. I felt like *myself*, not this anxious, babbling idiot.

That's because Travis is your friend and Gage is your crush.

"What else?" he asked, and I swore I saw a hint of amusement in his eyes as though he was enjoying something. But what I wasn't sure, because I certainly wasn't being enjoyable. "What else? Oh. Um. I'm sort of a health nut— which you probably already knew." I frowned, second-guessing my choice of wording. "Not a *nut.* I'm not a *fanatic* or anything, and my other motto is to each their own, so if you wanted to . . . oh, eat something laden with chemicals and carcinogens, I would say, have at it." I blinked, laying my hand on his arm and leaning in a little. "Not that I want you to eat chemicals and carcinogens. Because your health might suffer, and you are the picture of health."

His lip twitched. "Health is important to me too."

"Clearly, yes." I reached out and gave his bicep a small squeeze, my hand falling immediately, heat flooding my cheeks.

Oh my God. You actually just did that. Stop now, Haven. Stop touching him. And stop talking immediately. Immediately!

"And I love possums," I added.

Gage's face went blank. "Did you say, *possums*?"

I bobbed my head. "Mm-hmm. They're, ah . . . they get a bum rap. They look sort of scary, and they hiss out of fear, but they're not violent."

"No," he agreed, seeming stupefied. "What else do you like about possums?" he asked, almost hesitantly.

What else, what else? My mind searched to recall possum facts I'd learned less than an hour before. *Oh!* Right. "My favorite, of course," I said, because it was really their greatest achievement, "is the way they um, eat up to five thousand ticks a year. Just think of all the Lyme disease they prevent. Little heroes, honestly. They should get more credit."

That's when I noticed Gage Buchanan was trying not to laugh, his lips trembling and his eyes squinting. I peered at him more closely, a sinking feeling in my gut. "Do . . . do *you* like possums?"

He did laugh then, his eyes twinkling. It wasn't an unkind laugh, but it *was* a laugh. "I don't *not* like possums," he said. "But I can't say I've ever given them a lot of thought.

You've convinced me though. I should. Little heroes. I like that."

Oh. My. God. If laughs could sound *limp*, mine did.

I was going to *murder* Travis Hale.

Where was he? I needed to find him right that second.

"Will you excuse me, Gage? I'm sure you have to get back to your guests. I've loved talking to you, and this house is like something out of a fairy tale. Thank you for having me."

And without waiting for him to respond, I got up and stalked toward the door, flinging it open and going in search of my *friend* the lying liar!

CHAPTER TEN

Haven

I made my way through the groups of well-dressed guests, peering into rooms, and checking twice at the bar. Just as I was turning away from one of the small balconies, I spotted a lone figure, leaning against the stone wall of a patio on the floor below. My heart gave a jolt. Anger of course. I turned abruptly, racing down the stairs and moving through the house, out a back door and along the patio, turning the corner to where he stood. He turned, a drink in his hand, a look on his face I couldn't read—something glum. Almost sulky. He *should* be glum and sulky. I was about to *kill* him.

"You double-crossing *rat!*"

He leaned back casually against the stone, assessing me as I approached. "You look . . . upset, Haven."

I stepped closer, socking him on his arm. It felt like I'd struck the wall behind him. He didn't even blink. "You lied so I'd look like a fool."

"Lied about what?"

"Oh quit the innocent act. You made up some ridiculous story about Gage's soft spot for *possums* of all things." I socked him again with the same result as the first time. "I went on and on about *ticks*, for the love of God! In front of *Gage! Ticks!* I sounded like a screwball!" I placed my hands on my hips. "I concede that I said a few other things that didn't put myself in the best possible light, but the possum thing! The possum thing! There was absolutely no coming back from that." My breath came short, chest rising and falling.

"It does sound ridiculous. I'm surprised you believed me."

My mouth dropped open and I stepped closer, toe to toe. "Do you like to humiliate people, Travis? Is that it? Do you like to set people up? Is that what you *do?*"

He flinched slightly. "It was meant as a joke. I didn't think you'd run with it."

"Well I did, you *ass*. I made a fool of myself in front of my crush. Why did you do it? What is *wrong* with you?"

He stood straight, a muscle in his jaw jumping. "You're right. I am an ass. You should know that. It's a good thing to know about me."

I started to agree with him, my mouth opening and then closing, my chest still rising and falling with the emotion I'd exerted as I'd searched this monstrosity of a house looking for him and then subsequently railed and socked him on his immovable arm made of rock.

He was watching me, his own quickened breath mingling with my own, despite that, from what I assumed, he'd been standing nearly motionless on this patio for at least a little while. He looked so damned *wounded,* when *I* was the one who'd been tricked into talking ridiculously about tick-eating-possums with a man I'd wanted to impress. Which . . . did sound . . . well, ridiculous. My lip trembled and then I laughed, a sudden hiccup-sounding guffaw.

Travis regarded me warily, offering a tense, concerned smile.

I clapped my hand over my mouth, laughing again. Oh my God, it was all so ridiculous. Being at this house. The way Travis Hale was looking at me as though simultaneously hopeful my anger had faded and he was off the hook, and also like he was considering making a call to have me committed. This *road trip* I was on was ridiculous. This *dress* that I couldn't afford yet had bought anyway to impress some man who'd likely only ever see me as ridiculous and rightly so, was totally ridiculous.

Hell, my whole *life* had been one ridiculous link in a ridiculous chain of events. I was laughing so hard that tears pricked my eyes.

And there was a *billiards room* upstairs. A billiards room! The apartment we'd lived in the longest had had a homeless prostitute named two-toothed Trina who had slept in our building's doorway. I'd made her sandwiches when we had enough food to spare and sat with her as she'd gummed them.

I laughed and laughed.

And some absurd part of me missed Trina and worried that there was no one to make her sandwiches anymore, because I was here in Maine lying about my love for possums to a man whose family home included a billiards room.

"Haven," Travis said, and there was something in his tone, something so incredibly gentle as if, though I didn't understand what was happening to me and perhaps he didn't either, he recognized the feelings behind it.

How could that be true? It couldn't. Not from Chief Hale, who'd grown up in a virtual Mayberry by the lake with love and family, and history, and freaking *blueberries*, ripe for the picking, all around him.

"Haven," he said again in that same gentle way, stepping even closer, taking my hands from my mouth and holding them down by my sides.

My laughter dwindled, my shoulders dropped.

"I'm an ass," he said.

"I know," I answered breathlessly.

He nodded, something like sadness in his eyes. "Everyone knows," he said. "There's a consensus about it."

My heart squeezed. My laughter became air. *In. Out. In. Out.* He *was* an ass. But he also wasn't.

"Polls have been conducted," he went on. "Graphs have been charted. There are debates about the magnitude of—"

"Shut *up*," I said, pressing my mouth to his.

103

For a moment, we both froze, our eyes open as we stared at one another in shock, as if we'd suddenly and joltingly found ourselves standing on a different planet. And then, like lightning, he groaned, pulling me close, and fitting his mouth perfectly over mine. I met his groan with one of my own, a feeling I could only call relief spiraling through me. The kiss deepened. Every part of the strange, alarming anger and sadness and confusion from moments before vanished as his heat enveloped me, his scent adding to the intoxication of the moment. Our tongues met, testing, and then tangled together as though our bodies already knew one another and were celebrating this long-awaited reunion.

He feathered his fingers down my back, tracing the laces of my dress, causing me to shiver, sensation flowing over every part of my body. *Pull them,* I wanted to say. *Bare my body. Then cover it with yours.*

What was *happening* to me?

He stroked my tongue with his, fire leaping through my veins, every cell *alive. This is what drugs feel like,* I thought. This is why people go back and back and back, doing whatever they must—whatever they shouldn't—to make this feeling last. I squeezed my legs together and Travis let out a growl, low in his throat. I felt the vibration of it and it made my excitement soar higher, on some plane where gravity no longer existed.

I held on to him more tightly so I wouldn't float away. He was hard everywhere—his arms, his chest, his cock that had swollen and was now pressing against my hip. I leaned closer into him.

"Haven. *God.*" He pulled away slightly and I sagged against him, feeling breathless and needy, both out of my body and deeply aware of every part of myself, most especially the parts that were tingling and throbbing and begging for relief.

I'd *never* been kissed like that.

"We shouldn't . . ." he said, his voice hoarse, desperate. He stepped back farther, glancing around. I met his eyes. My God, I'd forgotten where I was. I'd forgotten *who* I was.

And my God, what a relief that had been.

I blinked. *We shouldn't.* Those words were a bucket of water on the flames still licking at my bones. "No, I know. Of course. That was . . . sorry." I took a trembling breath, wiping the wetness from my mouth and smoothing my hands over my dress. No, of course we shouldn't. I'd just been . . . angry and . . . why *had* I kissed Travis?

He gave a short, pained laugh. "I meant, we shouldn't *here,*" he said, his muscles held tight, his expression searching and slightly drugged. Had the kiss affected him too? He'd certainly *participated.*

Here. The *Buchanan* mansion. I closed my eyes momentarily, taking a few beats to get hold of myself. I glanced upward to where one of the balcony windows had a view of the place where we stood. When I looked back at Travis, he had a small frown on his face.

"No," I agreed. "No. We shouldn't anywhere." He had a broken heart, and I'd just practically attacked him. Plus, I was interested in someone else. And the *someone else*'s family owned the house we were currently standing in.

Travis opened his mouth, then closed it, nodded.

I took a deep breath. "I think I need champagne."

"I could use some too."

****

We arrived back at our B&B an hour later, both of us slightly stiff and awkward. We'd mingled for a little while, each having a glass of champagne. Travis had bid on a couple of items for the charity, and then we'd agreed to call it a night.

Gage had been gracious and kind when we'd sought him out to say goodbye, his eyes twinkling when he smiled at me with some form of affection. "I look forward to seeing you at the club, Haven."

I'd smiled brightly at him, hope soaring that I hadn't humiliated myself to the level I'd thought. Maybe he even thought I was . . . quirky in an attractive way. One could only hope. And another one of my mottos—one I wouldn't share with Gage because I'd already done enough damage for one night—was that hope springs eternal.

I'd turned and caught Travis looking at us, that same glum expression on his face that had been there when I'd found him on the patio, and I'd wondered if it could be interpreted as jealousy.

And a different hope soared, one I was too tired and confused to look at in that moment.

We stood awkwardly at the bottom of the stairs. Neither of us smiled.

I wanted to ask him if he regretted kissing me. I wondered if he'd compared it to kissing his girlfriend, the one who'd broken his heart, the one the gossips thought he'd cheated on when it was actually the other way around. I wondered if kissing me had made him long for her. Sometimes kissing someone else too soon after a breakup did more to amplify your sadness than to distract or heal. I wasn't the foremost expert on relationships, but I knew that to be true.

"Thank you for—"

"I really am—"

Travis cleared his throat, inclining his head toward me, saying wordlessly that I should continue. "Thank you for taking me to Gage's party, even if you did sabotage my efforts at coming off as a normal person."

He gave me a half grimace, half smile, lowering his eyes. "I really am sorry about that."

I waved my hand. "It's okay. Maybe it ended up setting me apart." *As a freak.*

Were we going to pretend we hadn't kissed?

We stared at each other for a moment longer.

"Okay, then, goodnight, Travis."

He paused, but then gave me a tight-lipped smile. "Goodnight, Haven."

We shouldn't.

I walked slowly up the stairs. I could feel his eyes on me as I ascended, and once I almost turned back just to see the look on his face, to see if it might tell me anything at all, but in the end, I didn't. I whispered a quiet word of encouragement to the plant I'd first found limp and root-bound at the back of the nursery, that now resided at the top of the stairs, my hand trailing over its lush, green leaves. It'd grown twice the size it was when I first brought it here, and a small burst of pride lit inside. I'd done that. I'd saved it.

Even if I hadn't saved her.

I headed to my room, closing the door behind me and leaning against it, my palms flat against the wood. Outside, I heard Travis's footsteps, heard them pause at the top of the stairs, and then head to his own room in the opposite direction.

I pushed off the door when I heard the quiet click of his closing, wondering how on earth I was supposed to come back from . . . *whatever* tonight was.

CHAPTER ELEVEN

Travis

"Did I *hear* that right?" Deb Bryant, the Pelion Police Department dispatcher asked. "You put out an APB on a number of house plants that went missing from the side of the road?"

"Yup," I said. "They were stolen."

"From the side of the road. Where someone left them."

"Yes."

"And flyers were hung in town? About the . . . stolen plants. Left on the side of the road."

I leaned on the counter. "Perhaps this person didn't know that they belonged to someone else. I'm not looking to convict, only to recover the property."

"Travis Hale. Sometimes you concern me." She smiled affectionately. "And surprise me." I'd take that as a compliment. I smiled back.

"This is for a woman, I presume?"

I grinned. "How'd you know?"

"I *didn't* know. That's where the surprise comes in. This is *very* unlike you." She paused. "I like it."

"She's just a *friend*." I laughed, pushing off the counter and walking back to my office.

Spencer walked in a few minutes later. "You won't believe the information I've found on Easton Torres from California."

I set the phone messages I'd been going through back down on my desk, removed my reading glasses, and looked up at him. "Warrants?"

"No. But—"

"A call just came in about the missing plants!" Deb said, bursting into my office.

"Really?" I stood. "Who called?"

"Marc Hobbs out on Lark Lane."

"Travis, before you leave, I had an important question!" Spencer said urgently.

"What is it?"

"Well, conducting this research got me thinking . . ."

Uh-oh. Spencer doing any sort of in-depth "thinking" never seemed to bode well for . . . pretty much, anyone. He was an excellent rule follower, but I wished he'd leave the "thinking" to others more suited for cerebral pursuits.

"You know, about our community and all the decent, upstanding people who live here in Pelion."

"Uh-huh." I made a gesture of impatience that he should speed this up. I had plants to rescue.

"And I thought, what if we formed a community relations group that might help inform our office about infractions?"

Infractions? That sounded a little bit like asking the public to snitch on their neighbors over minor offenses that the police department didn't need to be involved with. But Pelion citizens weren't like that. We'd only grown closer over the years, and especially since the . . . drama that had ensued eight years ago. People looked out for each other, more than anything. *Good* had come from the shock of events involving the Hale family. But Spencer was standing there, looking so eager, and hell, maybe it would be a good thing for the community and those who wanted to get more involved. "Listen, Spencer, if this community relations group focuses more on neighbors looking out for one another, and reporting on situations that might result in someone getting hurt, you have my approval."

Spencer looked mildly shocked. "Really? Great! Thanks, bo—Travis."

"Think small budget, though."

"Absolutely. I asked, and Birdie Ellis has already volunteered to be on the committee and to donate any printing we might need."

Birdie Ellis. One of the biggest gossips in town, with a penchant toward dictatorship. She was always volunteering for one church or community-focused group so she could boss people around and generally assert her will. But if she was offering free printing from the company she and her husband ran, why not? I moved around Spencer. "You're in charge of this, Spencer. I don't need to be consulted unless necessary. And . . . keep up the good work," I said, patting him on the shoulder and rushing out of the room, glad he had something to occupy him so he wasn't tagging along behind me on runs we both didn't need to be involved in. Namely, this one.

"Good luck!" Deb called with the amount of joyful enthusiasm she usually reserved for cat-in-tree rescue runs. I shot her a smile as the front door swung closed behind me.

As I drove, I allowed my mind to travel back to the kiss of the night before, remembering how, even in her anger, or maybe especially in her anger, she'd been so incredibly beautiful my heart had nearly stopped. Her cheeks had been flushed, those untamed curls bouncing around her face. I'd been both mesmerized and guilt-stricken.

I'd been an ass. It came easily to me.

And I'd been an ass because I'd been jealous. Jealous that she was there for Gage. There to try to impress *Gage*, to get him to notice her. Of course, I couldn't tell her that. I didn't even completely understand it myself.

We shouldn't.

I tapped at the steering wheel, considering the knowledge that she was also clearly interested in Gage. Jealousy wasn't exactly a novelty in my repertoire of emotions. Truth be told, maybe I'd spent much of my *life* being jealous. But this had felt different . . . I didn't know *how* it had felt different, but it had.

Was I being petty? I didn't want to be petty when it came to Haven. I wanted to be better than that.

Why?

I wasn't sure.

But that kiss. The kiss had shaken me. I was *still* shaken.

I was a thirty-two-year-old man who was far from a virgin and . . . God, I'd had no idea a kiss could be like that. If we'd been anywhere other than Gage's patio during a party where anyone might have seen us, I'd have tried to take it further. Undress her. Feel her extremely soft skin against mine. Taste her everywhere. Why? Because I was turned on, and even though maybe Haven wasn't the sort of woman I normally went for, she'd ticked every box in that dress.

I adjusted myself in my seat, a flush of hot arousal at the thought of getting Haven naked and beneath me making me feel in control again.

This, *this* feeling I could identify and understand, even if I'd thought twice about acting on it once my blood had cooled and we'd arrived back at the B&B the night before.

I still felt shaky on why I was on a plant rescue mission, other than that I owed her. Again, I'd been an ass. I'd set her up. I'd upset her. In a way that'd made me want to simultaneously comfort and distract her from whatever was happening in that head of hers. She'd been *spiraling*.

In any case, I'd been the cause of her distress, and I wanted to make it up to her.

Marc Hobbs and his wife, Lynn, had a cottage right on the lake near the one Bree had rented when she first visited Pelion. I knocked on their front door and removed my hat when Lynn opened it. "Oh, Chief Hale, come in. I saw the flyer at the grocery store this morning and texted Marc to call the office right away. I didn't realize they belonged to someone else when I picked them up." She eyed me nervously.

"You didn't do anything wrong, Mrs. Hobbs. It was just a misunderstanding. But the plants were important to the citizen who, er, was forced to abandon them due to circumstances beyond her control, and the police department takes the concerns of all its citizens seriously and steps in where we're able and time allows."

"It just melts my heart the way the Pelion Police Department looks out for its citizens, in matters both big and small. I tell Marc all the time, I say, Marc, we are lucky to be part of this lovely community. The wonders your brother has made happen since . . . well . . . since—"

"I agree," I said softly, knowing the color creeping up her neck had to do with the fact that she'd been about to bring up my mother and how much better the town ran now that Victoria Hale and her selfish motives had moved three towns away.

"I do have some bad news though," she said, hesitantly. "You see, I had good intentions but apparently, I just don't have much of a green thumb. Those plants might have done better if I'd just left them on the side of the road and let the small amount of rain we've had do its thing."

114

She led me to the screened-in porch off the back of the house. Five dehydrated, miserable-looking plants sat near the window, staring longingly out at the water beyond.

Ten minutes later, the plants stuffed in my backseat, a trail of leaves leading from the Hobbs's front door to my cruiser, I waved out my window, peeling off down the street. "Stay with me, guys," I told the plants.

I picked up my cell phone and called Haven's number.

"Chief Hale," she said sweetly.

"Are you home?"

Home. Had I really started thinking of The Yellow Trellis Inn as home?

"Uh, yes. Why?"

"Meet me out front," I demanded. "And bring . . ." My mind searched for the right apparatus or product or tool that might help these sorry suckers. "Bring the hose!" I shouted.

CHAPTER TWELVE

Haven

The screen door swung closed behind me as I stepped outside the house. I frowned in confusion, squinting down the road as I waited to see Travis's cruiser.

What in the world was he up to?

Bring the *hose?*

I glanced back at the house, spotting a wound-up hose near the wide front steps. With a huff, I walked back to it, unwound it, and squatted down next to the spigot.

"What's going on?" Betty asked, her tone laced with concern as she stood on the porch, watching me.

"I don't know," I said. "Travis just told me to be ready with the hose."

"Oh dear." But she looked more excited than nervous now.

"What's happening?" Burt asked, his walking stick clicking on the wood of the porch as he came up beside Betty.

"I don't know, but I'll describe the scene as it . . . as it . . ."

"Happens," Burt said quietly.

"No, no . . ."

"Unfolds."

"No . . ."

"Occurs."

"Exactly," Betty said.

A car appeared in the distance, turning onto the road that led to the B&B and coming to a skidding halt in the driveway.

Travis jumped out of the cruiser, throwing the back door open and removing the saddest-looking plant I'd probably ever seen. I gasped, turning the water on with a flick of my wrist and dragging the running hose to where he stood. "Oh my God!" I said, gasping and then laughing. "You found them? You *found* them?"

"Yes!" he called, his head back in the cruiser as he removed another plant, setting it next to the first one. "Hurry! They might only have minutes left."

I laughed again, but got right to work moving the hose back and forth over their roots and leaves, giving them the drink they so obviously needed, crooning to them while I did.

As Travis shut the doors of his cruiser, I lifted the hose too quickly and accidentally shot a stream of water in his face. "Eek," I said, lowering it and soaking the front of his uniform.

He brought his hands up in defense, running one back through his saturated hair, laughing suddenly, water droplets flying out around him.

I dropped my arm, water pooling at my feet as I stared at him, laughing proudly in front of the plants he'd rescued. For me.

My heart constricted. My muscles felt heavy. It made me feel both energized and . . . afraid.

He ran his hand over his face again, his gaze meeting mine, his smile slipping as he watched me stare at him.

Behind me, I heard Betty's soft voice rise and fall as she narrated the scene for Burt.

"You did this for me. Why?"

He paused, as though the question had caught him off guard and he wasn't entirely sure how to answer. "Because that's what friends do."

I felt a small drop inside me but shrugged it off, the fear from a moment before lifting.

Travis's face went very serious, water droplets catching the sun and shimmering in his thick, dark lashes, highlighting those unusual whiskey-colored eyes. God Almighty, but he was beautiful. "And also," he said softly, "because I wanted to say I was sorry. For what I did . . . with Gage. The possums. Ticks. You know."

I couldn't help laughing. How could my heart not soften at that? "You're forgiven." He'd saved my plants. He'd done it just for me. "How'd you find them anyway?" I asked, nodding to the dripping line of greenery . . . or . . . brownery as the case may be.

118

"I put out an APB. And I hung official police department flyers on bulletin boards all over town."

I grinned and so did he. For a few moments we stood there smiling inanely at each other, my shoes saturated by the running hose, still held at my side.

Behind me, Betty's voice had lowered, almost to a whisper and when I glanced back, Burt had a dreamy smile on his face.

I looked back at Travis. Were we *ever* going to discuss that *kiss?*

Or was it unnecessary? A one-time-deal chalked up to . . . anger stirred up to a mostly incoherent breakdown, that had then flared to some form of passionate temporary insanity?

Travis raised his head and squinted to where Betty and Burt stood, lifting his hand and giving them a small wave and then returning his gaze to me. "So um, I've been meaning to ask you if you'd like to come with me to the blueberry festival tomorrow."

The blueberry festival? Oh right, the one Clarice was in town for, and I'd heard mention of at the club.

"As friends," he clarified, as though my pause may have indicated I was wondering if he was asking me on a date. He'd said that about Gage's party though too. The one where we'd kissed, and done . . . non-friendly things.

I released a small breath, ignoring that. "A whole festival surrounding . . . blueberries?"

He grinned again. *My God, that grin. Those eyes. The dents in his cheeks. That stubborn jaw.*

119

Some insanely ridiculous idiot had cheated on this man . . . with my brother.

He'd been *hers* and she'd let him go.

Right. *Friends.*

He nodded behind me to the house. When I glanced back I saw that Betty and Burt were no longer there. "Clarice will be there," Travis said. "I bet the whole crew will be."

The crew. "We have a crew?"

He laughed. "For better or worse, for now, yeah, I think we have a crew."

I laughed too but something about that made a flush of happiness warm my insides. A crew indicated . . . belonging. Even if temporary.

"Most of the town will be there," Travis said. "My brother will give a speech. In sign language. His voice box was injured when he was a kid."

"Oh." I frowned, adding that small nugget to what I already knew about Travis's family. "How sad."

Travis shrugged. "Everyone is used to it now. Most of the town speaks sign language, as does his family, even my six-year-old nephews. They had this group class at the high school about six years ago. They had to move it into the gymnasium it was so crowded." I smiled softly. He was babbling and I wasn't sure exactly why, but it was very endearing coming from Chief Hale, the picture of masculine law and order, even if he was standing there in a sopping uniform.

"You live in a really nice town," I noted. I'd already experienced the kindness of so many strangers in Pelion, but it told me even more about who they were collectively that they'd all shown up to learn the singular language of one community member.

He almost looked surprised by my comment, pausing for a moment. "Yeah. Yeah I—we, that is—really do."

I nodded and our gazes lingered for another moment. I had this foreboding feeling that attending things like *blueberry festivals* with the town's handsome chief of police and our *crew,* was going to make it that much more difficult to drive out of town in less than two months. I should decline. I should stay in and read. I should clean out my car. It needed a good detailing after weeks of being on the road before we'd arrived in this lake town, not to mention my propensity for transporting things packed in *dirt. And also considering my brother may or may not be sleeping in it.*

"Sure," I finally said. "I'd love to go to the blueberry festival with you."

****

What did one wear to a blueberry festival?

Something . . . summery, no doubt as it was . . . well, summer. The season of blueberries.

I rifled through my suitcase, sitting open on the luggage rack under the window. I had a strict no unpacking policy, a policy that discouraged ideas about settling in or growing too comfortable in one place, but unfortunately, *encouraged* a constantly wrinkled wardrobe.

Would blue make me look like I was trying too hard?

You are *trying too hard, Haven.*

With a huff of frustration at myself, I pulled the blue sundress over my head, smoothing out the creases as best as I could.

A knock sounded at my door and in response, I smiled, rushing forward and then pausing, opening it slowly. "You're—"

It was my brother. "Early." I withered. "Hey, Easton. I thought you'd already left for work."

He came in, throwing himself on my bed. "No, I don't have to work until noon today."

"Oh," I said, closing the door slowly. "Okay." I glanced at the clock. If he was punctual, Travis wouldn't be knocking on my door for ten minutes. "You've been scarce," I said to my brother, leaning a hip against the—empty—dresser. "Where have you been?"

His eyes shifted strangely and my heart sank. What in the world was my troublemaking brother up to now?

He held a hand up. "I'm not causing trouble," he said, as though he'd read my mind, which wasn't difficult as it was usually the question that accompanied the lip-pursed look I was currently wearing. I relaxed my face. "I've been volunteering at the local fire house," he said, an unusually sheepish look on his face.

"What? Why didn't you tell me?"

Easton sat up and shrugged. "Fire . . . you know. Sensitive topic." My heart missed a beat and whatever was on my face made him look down, taking the edge of the throw blanket and rubbing it between his fingers idly. "Listen," he said, lifting his gaze again. "I think you should know something about that policeman. The one who *lives* here now."

I released a pent-up breath. "He's the *chief* of police. And I already know, Easton. He told me."

Easton had the good grace to wince. "He's crazy, Haven. Like bona fide crazy. He pulled a gun on me!"

"You're lucky he didn't shoot you! God, Easton, why? Why do you do those kinds of things? They hurt people. They ruin relationships. *Families.*"

"Maybe he should thank me for exposing his girlfriend for the cheating tramp she is." He shot for bold but came up short, arriving at the intersection of sulky and immature instead.

"I think you're missing the point. And I highly doubt you'll be getting a thank-you from Travis Hale anytime soon."

He looked down again, rubbing the fabric. "I know you've been hanging around with him. Which seems suspicious, considering what he obviously thinks of me."

"He should see me as guilty by association? Because of *your* poor choices?"

Easton shrugged again, which ignited a spark of anger. If he was *aware* that his actions might have a negative impact on me, why did he keep behaving in the same manner, over and over again? God, he'd left a *trail* of mayhem in our path. Thank God we'd left all those places behind.

We'd been *forced* to leave those places behind.

"Just be careful of him," he said. "Seriously. Something isn't right about that guy. There's something very wrong with him." He stood up, and though he irritated and frustrated me regularly, my heart softened when he leaned in and kissed me on the cheek, taking my hands in his, the burns on his palms raised yet smooth, a reminder of how he'd fought to save the only thing familiar to him, and had been—literally and figuratively—scarred.

CHAPTER THIRTEEN

Travis

The door swung open, revealing Haven in a blue sundress and white slip-on sandals, her hair pulled into a braid that trailed over her shoulder.

She looked young and fresh and so beautiful my breath stalled.

Had I really wondered if this girl was pretty?

She was no prom queen, true. She was more timeless than that. Botticelli. Aphrodite. Helen of Troy, sprang to mind.

I was almost *confused*, as though she might have pulled something over on me, and I didn't know what or how, only that my first impression had been wildly off target.

I smiled. "Ready?"

Outside, she climbed into my truck and I turned out of the parking lot onto the road that led to the fairgrounds where the festival was being held.

The morning was bright and sunny, flickers of light dancing on the lake, not a cloud in the clear blue sky.

And a pretty *friend* in a sundress that showed off her slim tanned legs, and her smooth shoulders, sitting next to me, her hands grasped in her lap.

I cleared my throat. "I'm going to go out on a limb and assume you're a *vegan?*" I did my level best to infuse the word with the same horrified contempt with which I might utter the charge of devil worshipper.

I was rewarded with Haven's laugh, a side-eye, and a curl falling loose and bouncing against the side of her neck. "You're almost right. I'm not a vegan, but I am a vegetarian."

"What's the difference?"

"Well a—"

"Never mind." I waved my hand around. "It pains me to discuss the subject in too much detail. My point in bringing it up is to let you know that, despite the topic of the festival, there are very few fruits, vegetables, or plant items available for a festival-goers consumption. Unless the fruit is drowned in sugar. Think pies. Jams. Tarts. Muffins. Pastries of all kinds. And BBQ. Lots of BBQ."

She didn't look my way but I held back a laugh as I still saw her roll her eyes, even from the side. "Don't worry about me. I'm sure I can find a pine cone to gnaw on."

I laughed.

Families strolled toward the entrance to the festival, the parking lot already filled with cars when we arrived. I pulled into a spot and inhaled the—according to me anyway— delicious smells of grilled meat and sweet desserts.

There was something almost . . . old-fashioned about the blueberry festival. It spoke of simple pleasures: good food, family bonding, and the wholesomeness of a town gathering for no other purpose than to celebrate their shared community. I lingered on the feeling. It was the small-town police officer in me—the cop who considered all of these people, his. The part of me that found joy in simplicity.

It spoke of my dad.

"You look like you just realized something immense," Haven said, eyeing me sideways, a gentle smile curving her lips.

Immense. This was who my dad had been. This, right here.

Sometimes I forgot who he really was, at heart, because I was so wrapped up in the hurt surrounding his departure. And *maybe*, because I'd forgotten whole aspects of who *he'd* been, I often overlooked or dismissed those same facets in myself. "Maybe I did," I said, not offering more. But she looked away, accepting my vague answer.

The sun was warm on my shoulders and I had the strange urge to grab her hand, but reminded myself we were only friends, and friends didn't hold hands. God, I wanted to, though. My palm itched to reach out for hers, to revel in one of those simple pleasures: the warmth of a pretty girl's hand in mine.

To remember why those songs had been written, ones like the piece we'd danced to at the Buchanans' home. To remember why I'd kissed her and why I didn't want to stop. Damn the reasons why maybe I shouldn't. The ones that sounded all-too-valid in my mind but somehow weren't.

"Uncle Travis!" Two dark-haired boys shot toward us, Bree and Archer watching from a picnic table as they ran in our direction.

"Are you ready for these two?" I murmured to Haven.

"I . . . I think so?" she said, giving me a wide-eyed look.

Connor arrived first and I scooped him up in one arm, with Charlie fast on his heels. I scooped him up as well, taking the few steps to where Archer and Bree sat.

"Uncle Travis!" Connor said, breathlessly. "I learned about living orgasms at camp today!" Archer choked on the sip of water he'd just taken.

"Are there *other* sorts of—" I began to question curiously before the fact that my nephew was six occurred to me.

"It's pronounced *organisms,* Connor," Bree intervened calmly, spooning something into Averie's mouth where she sat in the stroller parked next to the table. She smiled at Haven. "Hi, I'm Bree, and this is my husband, Archer."

"Hi, I'm Haven," she said shyly. "It's nice to meet you."

"Uncle Travis!" Charlie leaned in as if to whisper but then said loudly, "Averie *farts* when she sneezes."

Both Connor and Charlie clutched their stomachs, peals of laughter ringing out.

I leaned in toward Charlie who'd gotten control of himself. "It's not gentlemanly to discuss a woman's bodily functions. You should pretend not to notice."

Charlie went serious as he appeared to mull that over. "But it's *loud*!" he finally explained.

I looked over at Haven, who was very obviously trying not to laugh, and lost my own battle.

Bree shook her head in exasperation. "Boys, I'm sure Uncle Travis wants to get something cold to drink. Come finish your hotdogs."

I set both boys down and Connor glanced at Haven, going up on his tiptoes in front of me. I leaned down to hear his sure-to-be loud "whisper." "Uncle Travis, what happened to that other girlfriend?"

Haven glanced away, obviously slightly embarrassed, and pretending she hadn't heard. "Well, buddy, I broke up with that girlfriend, but Haven here is just my friend."

Connor glanced at her. "Ohhh," he said. "Do you like *bugs*?" he asked Haven, very seriously. "That other lady didn't like bugs at *all*." I almost laughed as I recalled Phoebe practically jumping out of her skin, emitting a high-pitched *shriek*, when Connor tried to place a ladybug on her arm. A gesture he'd meant as affectionate and welcoming, and one she'd responded to as domestic terrorism. They mostly steered clear of her after that, not that I brought her along with me very often when I spent time with the twins. It seemed to be her preference. And mine.

But Haven's face filled with surprised happiness, eyes widening with pleasure. "I *love* bugs!" Ah, here my nephews were on common ground with a woman. The bug enthusiasts and the plant lady. A match made in heaven. Or the garden of Eden, or whatever paradise welcomed both plants *and* bugs.

She bent forward, putting her hands on her knees, both going down to their level, and getting closer. Archer's mother, Alyssa, had spoken to me that way. A sudden picture of her in front of me filled my mind. Clear. Sharp. My gaze flew to Archer's and he peered at me, his expression registering confusion and mild concern about whatever he'd seen on my face. I relaxed my features, looking away. "One of my favorite bugs is the pirate bug," Haven was saying. "It eats bad insects and keeps plants healthy."

Their identical golden-brown eyes grew wide. "*Pirate* bug!" Charlie repeated gleefully. "Ladybugs eat bad bugs too!" he said. "My mom says they're good luck but I shouldn't put them on Uncle Travis's girlfriends." He looked down, grinding his toe into the dirt, perhaps recalling the piercing rebuke he'd received to his gift.

"Well I'm not Travis's girlfriend," she said, giving me a quick glance, "but I'd like it very much if you gave me a ladybug. I'd call her Bitsy, and make her a home in the ivy on my windowsill. Every night, before turning out the light, I'd say, goodnight, Bitsy. Sleep tight in your bed of ivy."

They stared at her in utter, awestruck delight.

"Another favorite bug of mine is the dragonfly," she went on, cementing their everlasting devotion. "They devour mosquitos and all kinds of other pests. Just suck them right up for dinner like a spaghetti noodle!"

"Hurray!" Charlie shouted while Connor made a slurping sound filled with as much saliva as glee.

Haven laughed, standing straight, her eyes dancing with happiness. For a moment, I couldn't look away. The sun seemed to have grown several degrees hotter, even though we were standing in the shade, somehow warming my insides as well as my skin.

Haven looked off behind me, waving. "Oh! There's Betty and the rest of the crew just setting up a picnic table," she said, placing her hand on my arm. "I'm going to go say hi and see if I can get anything for them." She turned to Bree and Archer. "It was so nice to meet you."

They smiled at her warmly. "You too, Haven," Bree said. "I hope to see you again soon."

Her smile grew as she looked at the twins. "Me too," she said. "Goodbye, fellow bug lovers."

"Goodbye!" they said. "Uncle Travis! Will you take us to get an ice cream? Our daddy has to make a speech."

"I'll be back shortly," Haven said to me.

"Yeah." I nodded. "I'll be waiting." Our eyes lingered for a moment and then she turned, heading toward the place where our *crew* was setting up.

"Uncle Travis! Ice cream! Ice cream!" Charlie reminded me exuberantly.

Bree kissed Archer and he turned to leave, giving me a chin tilt. "Good luck," I said. I knew he didn't need it. He had made hundreds of speeches to the community members at this point, and there wasn't a lot of pressure involved in waxing poetic about the history of the town festival, and the significance of blueberries.

"Is ice cream okay with your mom?" I asked. The twins both looked over their shoulders, and shot nervous glances at their half-eaten hotdogs and then at their mother.

Bree put her hands on her hips, making them suffer for a moment before she looked at me, smiled, and said, "Sure."

"Hurray!" they both cheered, taking my hands.

After the ice cream and the short welcome speech, thanking people for coming to the festival that had been going on for more than two centuries, Archer took his boys in hand and I made my way back to the picnic tables. Disappointment descended when I saw that the table where Haven had gone to greet the crew was empty. I pictured them off playing ring toss, blind Burt's shots going wild and knocking over small children, or getting smashed on cheap beer and smuggled-in hooch, or some other such nonsense, and felt strangely glum that I wasn't there with those ridiculous fools.

Bree was sitting on a blanket near their table, the stroller parked next to her, and I wandered her way, sitting down, stretching my legs out in front of me, and leaning back on my hands.

Bree peeked under the blanket draping the stroller, where Averie had apparently fallen asleep. An electric fan, clipped to the side and making a soft whirring sound, was keeping her cool as she napped. "Beautiful day," I said, scanning the laughing, strolling people in the near distance, moving from one booth to another, my eyes peeled for a walking stick or a halo of blonde hair or maybe a pair of

132

overly large overalls. But mostly, looking for a head of chestnut curls, mostly constrained into a braid. Archer stood nearby, his hands moving briskly in the air in front of him, turned away so I couldn't see exactly what he was saying to the couple he was speaking with. Whatever it was, he was making them laugh, the woman's hands rising in response, though her husband spoke with his voice. The twins ran around Archer's legs, playing tag as their father simultaneously—and expertly, it had to be said—used his hands both to speak and keep his energetic duo under control with a gentle pat here and an arm block there.

I had a vision of him as the quiet recluse he'd once been, shoulders drawn in, shaggy head down, utterly alone and ignored, walking down the streets of Pelion, and a sharp pang of regret burned through my gut.

I'd been one of the people doing the ignoring.

That burn intensified.

What's wrong with you?

What's wrong with you?

"Hmm?" Bree asked, bringing me back to the present, her eyes glued to her husband, that soft, gooey look she still wore on her face all these years later when she watched Archer interacting with others. Or fathering their children. Or breathing air. Just existing.

"Hmm what?"

She glanced at me, a worried frown replacing the look of love she'd just worn. "You just mumbled something."

Had I said it out loud? I gave my head a small shake. The memory had been so shockingly strong, I'd zoned out for a minute there. "I said, what's wrong with you," I answered. "It's what my father said to me the day before he left." I paused. Haven had said the same thing to me at Gage's party after the possum incident and it'd suddenly come back to me, the hurt of those words. I could feel Bree's gaze on the side of my face as I continued to stare—blindly now—into the crowd, my mind cast back . . . back. "My father always seemed so concerned about Archer, gave him all this attention. I was jealous." Another pause. It hurt to say this out loud. It felt *good* to say it out loud.

"You were seven, Travis," she said gently.

"I didn't want to share my dad. He was the only parent that felt stable, the one who didn't confuse me. I didn't want to be second best," I murmured. Even before my mother had given me those words, I'd felt it. I'd known my father's heart was split between the two of us. And why should it be? He was *my* dad. I'd only learned the truth later. "I was mean to Archer. I tripped him and he scraped his knee. My father knelt down and took my shoulders in his hands and gave me this hard, little shake." I sat up and mimicked the action, replacing my hands on the blanket behind me. "He looked so damned disappointed. And he asked, *what's wrong with you?* I still find myself asking that question sometimes, only there's no answer. Just that same *feeling*. The feeling of being a disappointment."

The next day he'd left me without a goodbye. He'd left me and taken Archer with him, the son he really wanted. *Left me behind. Forever.*

134

"Oh Travis," she said softly, "he didn't mean it. He said it in anger and frustration. Believe me, I get fed up with those wild children of mine a hundred times a day." But the way she was looking at them run circles around their father, such open adoration in her eyes, told me everything I needed to know about what kind of mother she was.

"I know," I said, because I did. On some level, I knew that. But I'd still acted on that feeling far too often over the years. *Why?* Had I let the lingering fear of not being good enough in the eyes of the one person who really mattered to me, rule my behavior?

The couple Archer was talking to turned to each other momentarily and I watched as Archer glanced somewhat longingly to the place Bree and I were sitting. The place devoid of people, except those he felt comfortable with, and perhaps that even meant me. The expression was fleeting, his smile returning as the couple's attention focused back on him, but it suddenly hit me. Archer's life wasn't perfect. Sure he'd gained confidence and social skills over the eight years since he'd inherited the town. He had a family now, friends, a full life. But surely he also still carried the part of himself that had once lived as a complete loner, and perhaps he even missed some aspects of that life.

Weren't all of us a compilation of the versions of ourselves we'd once been? Maybe if we were lucky—and insightful—we learned how to extract the good, and leave the bad behind, the parts that hadn't worked for us, and instead brought nothing but pain.

Maybe.

And maybe the things Bree and Archer signed to each other in the quiet of night weren't just words of love and tenderness, but fears, and insecurities, and whatever their worries might be.

Bree and I were both silent for a few minutes as we thought our own thoughts, the whirring sound of the fan and the low din of the crowd beyond creating a peaceful white noise.

"What happened with Phoebe?" Bree asked finally. "If you don't mind me asking."

A small group of people moved from the place they'd been standing and I caught sight of Haven, her laugh ringing out as she listened to something Burt was saying. I felt a smile tilt my lips and a zip of electricity moved from my chest to my midsection and back again.

"She cheated on me. I walked in on it."

Bree let out a small gasp. "Walked in on . . . you mean—"

"Oh yes. The thing you think I mean is exactly what I mean."

She grimaced. "Oh my God. Travis." She massaged her temple as though the image had literally brought her pain. My heart gave a small kick. I'd brought *her* pain once upon a time. Some would say that to witness mine might feel like poetic justice to Bree Hale. Some might be right. "I'm so sorry that happened to you," she said.

I looked at her, noting the pure sincerity on her face. "I know you are." Our eyes met and an understanding passed between us. "And I'm grateful." I took a deep breath, looking away and ending the moment, my eyes finding Haven again. "But, on the bright side, better to know now, than at a point when *breaking up* involved lawyers and the division of assets." Or in my case, *property*, as it was the only net worth of any real significance that I had.

"You don't seem overly upset about it," she noted. "Were you really considering marrying her?"

Her question caused me a moment of pause. Because honestly, I *wasn't* that upset about it anymore. And it suddenly struck me that my distress had been more about my own pride than about the loss of Phoebe in my life. I'd wanted *revenge* because I'd felt humiliated and spurned. Second best. Again. And if I was *really* being honest with myself because, *why not*—an old dog could learn new tricks—there was this ray of relief that I hadn't really looked at since *that day*. But that was a lot to convey, and something I'd have to pick apart and think about later, and so I answered Bree simply with, "I don't know." I gave her a glance. "You didn't like her."

"No, no. I liked her fine."

Fine. She'd liked her *fine.* A ringing endorsement from the woman I'd once heard describe Norm's maple cayenne bacon as, "that which has the power to cast out evil from all the world for all eternity." My lips tipped in amusement.

"Of course, I can't say I like her much *now*, considering what she did to you."

"So you like her less than fine now."

"Much less."

I watched the crowd again as Haven laughed, a few escaped curls bouncing and catching the light, making her hair gleam mahogany.

"What about the girl you're here with?" Bree asked. "Haven. She seems very sweet. The boys are in love."

I looked away from Haven, back to Bree. "We're just friends. I'm taking a hiatus from women right now."

"That's probably a good idea," Bree murmured. "Rebound relationships never work out."

"Plus, she's a vegetarian *plant* lady," I hissed, low and ominously under my breath, glancing around covertly to make sure no one else had heard.

"I'm sorry, did I hear you right? She's a communist spy?"

"Basically."

Bree laughed.

"She's only twenty-three."

"That's how old I was when I moved to Pelion," she mused dreamily. *And fell in love with Archer, and he with her, went unspoken.*

"Her brother's the one who cheated with Phoebe."

Bree's head whipped my way. "You're kidding."

"Nope."

"Wow. That's . . . complicated?"

"Revenge always is." I shot her a cunning smile, more for effect than because I'd given much thought to my plans of vengeance.

"Revenge?" She lifted a brow. "Travis Hale, that sounds very melodramatic." I huffed out an amused chuckle. That's the same word Haven had used. I supposed it did sort of conjure up visions of a sword-wielding Count of Monte Cristo descending in a hot-air balloon.

Still . . . The vision wasn't completely unwelcome. "He humiliated me. Don't you think I have the right to get even?"

Bree sighed. "Maybe with Phoebe." But her tone conveyed she wasn't even convinced of *that.* "But Haven's brother didn't make any promises to you, therefore he didn't *break* any promises to you. And in any case, all that revenge stuff? That sounds like the *old* Travis."

The old Travis. The disdain in her voice told me all I needed to know about how she viewed the *old* Travis. Apparently, it wasn't as a mysterious count who descended in hot-air balloons. Her tone said it was someone decidedly *less* dashing than that.

Did I feel like an updated model from the man she'd met eight years before, this *old Travis?* In some ways, yes . . . in others, I had no idea. I continued to stare at Haven, smiling in reaction to her sudden laugh. *God, she's beautiful.* The unbidden thought hurt vaguely for reasons I couldn't explain.

"Anyway, with Haven, there's the brother thing. But also, we have very little in common," I explained, as though Bree had pressed me further when she had not. "We're simply friends. Temporary friends."

"And yet . . ."

I looked over at Bree to see she was watching me again, a small, secretive smile on her face. "And yet *what?*"

She looked toward the place where I knew Haven was still chatting with our *crew.* "I've seen you around other

139

women enough to know that you're usually the one being watched by *them*."

"Of course." I shot her a smirk.

Bree shook her head. "No, you've never seemed to notice. It's like it's just a *given* to you."

"Again, of course."

"But this girl . . . you can't keep your eyes off her."

I made a scoffing sound in the back of my throat. "Please. She just happens to be standing right in front of the beer tent." I pulled myself up. "And I'm thirsty. Want one?"

She laughed, shaking her head. "No. Thank you." She stood too. "The pie judging contest starts in a few minutes and I have to get over there. I made Anne's recipe." Her eyes got misty when she mentioned Anne's name, but they always did, still, even though Anne had died several years ago when the twins were only toddlers. Bree made Anne's recipe every year for the festival's blueberry pie contest. And Bree won with Anne's recipe every single year. I had an inkling that it was "fixed" as a way to honor the longtime and deeply beloved Pelion resident, but I probably wasn't going to bust anyone for blueberry-tinged corruption anytime soon.

"Okay. Good luck," I said, needlessly.

I headed toward Haven, almost missing a step when she turned my way, her face lighting in a smile to rival the sun.

CHAPTER FOURTEEN

Haven

"Hi." I smiled as he approached. It felt big. *Too* big, probably, but I found I wasn't interested in putting very much effort toward its suppression. The noise of the crowd faded, the world suddenly growing impossibly brighter.

"Hey." Travis smiled back, his dark hair lifting off his forehead as a breeze stirred. I caught the sight of a small white scar near his hairline, an old wound. He would have been young when it bled. "Having a good time?"

"This is the most wonderful day of my life," I said. I couldn't even be embarrassed that my enthusiasm might seem overdone to someone like him. I was too happy. Too bursting with it.

I watched in fascination as several emotions passed over his face, one by one. Surprise, confusion, pleasure, a strange sort of sadness, and then wonder. "You mean it."

I laughed. "We don't have blueberry festivals in California."

He smiled, but I could tell he knew it was a false explanation. There were plenty of *other* events in California where I might have experienced a day like today. Farmers' markets, carnivals, craft fairs. But I never had. Not once. The people, the sweet smell of sugary desserts, the *families*. The warmth. It was all so incredibly *warm*. It glowed, and I felt like, somehow, just being here, I did too. I glanced around and then looked back at Travis whose gaze was still glued to me. "How lucky you are, Travis, to have all"—I waved my hand—"*this*."

Travis's gaze broke from mine, and he looked around. It was as if he'd been looking through a foggy window and the glass had suddenly cleared. When he looked at me again, his eyes were soft. And yes, warm. There were rings of dark green around his golden-brown irises. *Extraordinary, those eyes.* I'd noticed his brother had very similar eyes, but his appeared about a half shade lighter than Travis's. "Yeah," he said after a moment, "I am pretty lucky." Then he smiled at me, lopsided and boyish as though I'd just offered him a gift he hadn't been expecting.

"Clarice is going to read our fortunes in a few minutes. Come with us."

Travis rolled his eyes. "You don't *believe* in that stuff, do you?"

I laughed. "I don't know to be honest. I've never had my fortune told. But I'll keep an open mind if you will."

He grinned that boyish grin again and my stomach flipped at its unexpected innocence. So *many* layers. "Sure."

Cricket appeared, a tray of beers in her hand, the plastic cups sloshing foam, and handed one to each of us. When Travis hesitated, she said, "Come on, Chief, you're off duty and Burt here will drive us home."

I choked on the small sip of beer I'd just taken and Travis's eyes widened as he glanced at the grinning blind man. Cricket let out a boisterous laugh, whacking the side of her hip with the now empty tray. Travis took a sip. "I guess I don't have to drive home for several hours."

Several hours left of heaven. I held up my cup and he met mine with his.

Clarice's booth was near the other side of the festival so we began walking, Travis and me in the rear of the group. "What part of Los Angeles did you grow up in?" Travis asked.

I stalled, taking a sip of my beer and swallowing. "Are you familiar with LA?"

"Not really, other than the famous parts . . . Hollywood, Bel Air, Beverly Hills, Laguna Beach."

"Not those parts," I said on a small, humorless laugh. "Picture the *opposite* of sunny beaches, Louis Vuitton shops, and gated communities, and that's where *I* grew up."

Cricket let out a loud guffaw and Travis squinted toward where the rest of our group walked. She gave a not-very-surreptitious glance back at Travis and then removed what appeared to be a flask and poured a shot in Burt and Betty's out-held cups. "She's a really bad criminal," Travis murmured. "No wonder she served time."

I let out a small laugh.

"So," he said after a minute, "no blueberry festivals in the opposite of a gated community."

"No blueberries, period."

One brow went up and one brow went down and he considered me. "That can't be true."

"Trust me, it is. Liquor and convenience stores don't tend to sell any produce at all, unless it's a basket of three or four bananas at the front counter that usually go untouched. When my mom did bring home food, she tended to pick up chips, soda, and donuts. It's the food pyramid of poverty-stricken neighborhoods. That's true everywhere I assume, although admittedly I haven't been *everywhere*." I shot him what I hoped was an amused smile, but he didn't smile back. I looked away. Why was I sharing this? At the *blueberry* festival? The warm, glowy, sun-drenched blueberry festival.

Because today of all days, it feels good to be known. *Walking amidst all of these people who are connected to other people, feeling like you are too.*

Was it really so wrong to want that, just for one day? In a couple months' time, I'd never see this man again. Did it really matter?

"Is that why health food is so important to you?" he asked softly.

"I suppose. And I don't want to give my mom too bad of a rap. She tried, you know, sometimes more than others, but . . . she was a product of her environment. She brought home food she thought we liked. Food we *did* like, but that wasn't good for us."

"How'd you manage to be different?"

"I stole a cantaloupe."

"Aha. I knew the first time I saw you, you were criminally inclined."

"I confess. Once upon a time, that was true. I was eleven, and one day I took an alternate route home from school, which took me past this Korean grocery store. There was a stand of cantaloupes. Well, of course, I'd seen cantaloupes on TV before, but we'd never eaten one. I lingered around that stand. I *wanted* one." I recalled that moment of wanting. How it'd been a fierce thing inside that I had no way to explain. Maybe I just wanted to be different, to live a life I hadn't been given, if only for a brief time. Long enough to eat a cantaloupe. "I wanted to experience a cantaloupe, just once," I said, leaving out the rest.

I could feel Travis's stare on the side of my face and I glanced at him. His expression was bemused, and something else I didn't know him well enough to name. "So you stole it," he said.

"I did. And I was caught immediately."

"Oh no."

My lips tipped and even I could hear the tenderness in my voice when I said, "Mr. Kim, the store owner, yelled and railed. I tried so hard not to cry, but I was shaking I was so scared. He marched me a block up the street to this door and this woman, all of four and a half feet tall, answered, and he

145

said, 'Here, this little thief tried to steal one of our cantaloupes. You deal with her.'" I smiled softly again. "She led me to the roof of her building and she didn't exactly seem mad, and so I followed her. And there, she had this garden! All these perfectly organized plants and flowers in wooden boxes covering every square inch of that roof. It was a wonder. I'd never seen anything so beautiful. She told me if I spent the next hour digging potatoes out of the dirt, I would have worked off my debt and she'd send me home with a cantaloupe."

"That was kind," he said.

"Yes. Yes, she was kind. She and her husband both." I cleared my throat when the final word of my statement came out scratchy with emotion.

"What happened to them?" Travis asked.

I took a deep breath, surprised that it still hurt to talk about the Kims, that the scar their loss had left behind still pulled tight sometimes. "Mr. Kim died of a heart attack when I was in middle school and Mrs. Kim went back to South Korea where she had family. I send her postcards."

"But she doesn't have a permanent address where she can write back to you," he said.

I didn't look at him. "No. Not right now."

"How old were you when she left?"

"Sixteen."

"And the garden?"

I paused. "The landlord let it remain, even after the Kims left. I replanted a few things in pots and brought them home. And I tried to keep the garden alive, but gardens take a lot of

146

time and a lot of effort, and some money to maintain, and I . . . well, it died. At first it was slow, and I had hope, but then . . . but then, one day it seemed to die, all at once."

"And the ones you brought home?" he asked, his tone gentle.

I paused, a sharp pain cutting through me. "Well those died eventually too." *Later.*

"I'm sorry," he said, and the empathy in his voice was so very clear that a lump formed in my throat.

I managed what I hoped was a bright smile and shrugged. "Anyway, gardening wasn't really a possibility anymore, but I did get this job at a health food store. It was halfway across town, so I had to take three buses there and back for every shift. But . . . like I said, we didn't have stores like that in my neighborhood and regardless, without the garden, we couldn't afford that kind of food. Even with the employee discount at the health food store, I still shopped off the discount shelves. I . . . got that job and I was able to bring home fruits and vegetables . . . eggs . . . so the commute was worth it." Nourishing food. Food that made us healthy and strong, not sick and still hungry all the time. Food that I sometimes went without so my skinny, little brother would thrive.

The group had come to a stop in front of what had to be Clarice's booth, a rich velvet blue curtain enclosing the small space, gold moons and stars sewn onto the fabric. Travis and I joined them.

"Who's up first?" Burt asked, and it had to be noted that his words were markedly slurred.

"I'll go!" Betty said, pulling aside the curtain and heading unsteadily inside.

Travis raised his brows and gave me a look and I laughed, the heaviness of my memories about the Kims and the rooftop garden that died melted away by the warmth of the sun, and the mildly numbing effects of bad beer.

A dark head of perfect hair came into view, moving above the small group he was walking with.

Gage stepped out of the crowd, a woman next to him saying something and laying her hand on his arm. He stopped and listened to her for a moment, his eyes meeting mine.

I smiled and so did he, even as the woman continued to chatter, oblivious of anything except him. Gage's gaze moved to Travis and he gave him a small chin lift, his brows lowering slightly as he looked between the two of us.

I felt Travis's gaze on me too and glanced his way. He appeared to be wrestling with something. But then his expression cleared and he leaned in, his breath at my ear as he said, "Look at me adoringly, Haven."

"What?"

"Look at me like I'm the only man here at this festival."

I blinked, tipping my chin, our faces close, those golden-brown eyes catching the sunlight as he smiled that slow grin. I stared, mesmerized, and suddenly, it *did* feel like he was the only man at the festival. I swallowed, pulling my gaze from those spellbinding eyes to where Gage stood, his brow lowering further as he watched us. The woman talking to him swatted at his arm as if he'd neglected to answer or comment on something she'd said. Gage startled, responding to her and, evidently satisfied, the woman continued talking.

Travis took my hand in his and leaned in again, mock whispering. His hand was warm and enveloped mine. Small sparkles danced up my arm. "Men are simple," he whispered. "Add a little challenge, a little healthy competition, and the interest increases tenfold."

I turned to him, my hand still held in his, "Is that true of you too, Travis?"

"Of course. I'm a man, aren't I?"

"You are definitely a man. I can't argue with that."

He laughed softly and those sparkles danced again.

Gage stepped away from the woman he'd been talking—or rather listening—to, and headed our way. I let go of Travis's hand, feeling a strange loss.

"Haven." Gage smiled, his straight, white teeth gleaming. "Travis," he muttered, not moving his gaze from me. "You look like you're having fun."

"I am."

"We are."

Travis and I both spoke at once, our heads turning toward one another. With a smile I turned back to Gage. "Yes. We both are. Having fun." I gave Travis a grin. "It's been a wonderful day."

Gage's eyes grew warm, his gaze lingering on me. "Good. You look beautiful." His eyes moved from my face to my toes and I felt a warm flush of happiness at the attention from him. My crush. The perfect guy I'd been hoping would look at me in just such a way since the day I'd first seen him.

In a way that suggested he was perfect for some harmless, summer fun.

"Thank you," I said, casting my eyes down momentarily. "How are you?"

"I'm good. I'm supposed to present an award at the grandstand so I should get going." He paused, his eyes lingering on me. "There's a concert in the park next weekend. It's not as big as this event, but it's a nice time, especially if the weather cooperates. Maybe you'd like to go?"

I felt a small thrill between my ribs. Was he asking me on a *date*?

"You too, Hale," Gage said, not looking at Travis.

Okay, maybe a *group* date?

"We already have plans to go to the Crawfordsville Antique Fair next weekend," Travis said smoothly.

Hold up, what? My head whipped toward Travis, but his eyes were glued to Gage. Gage stared back, his lips tipping slowly.

"I didn't know you *antiqued*, Hale," Gage said. "Do you crochet too?"

"Ha. Funny joke," Travis said, glancing at his fingernails as though he was more bored than amused by Gage's humor. "No, no crocheting." He smiled at me. "But, Haven's inspired me to try all *kinds* of new things," he said, pausing for a beat. "Plus, the flimsy bachelor pad furniture I've been living with is getting old in more ways than one. I've decided it's time to invest in more *permanent* pieces."

Gage's eyelids flickered minutely and he nodded slowly. "I agree. Completely."

150

Travis regarded him placidly. I noticed that he didn't add any version of, "You too, Buchanan," in reference to our apparent antique fair outing.

"I was sorry to hear about your breakup," Gage said, and I wasn't entirely sure what was going on between the two of them at the moment, but Gage did sound sincere. Travis merely grunted. "Have things changed . . ." Gage moved his finger back and forth between the two of us.

"No, no," we both said at once, looking at each other and laughing awkwardly. "Still just friends," I murmured.

Gage was looking at me now. "I . . . see." He paused, a smile gathering. "If not this weekend, dinner Wednesday night? I know a great place right on the water."

A breath caught in my throat. A date. Dinner, just the two of us, was *definitely* a date.

"Oh," Travis said, making a low hissing sound between his teeth. "Isn't that the night Betty has the . . . thing?"

I looked at Travis, leaning forward. "The . . . thing?"

"Right, you know, the—" He widened his eyes very slightly.

"Oh right!" I said, looking back at Gage. "Betty has a thing. She needs me there. For the . . . thing."

Gage looked slightly amused, and slightly perturbed. "Friday?" he asked. "What about Friday?"

Before Travis could get a word in, I said quickly, "I'd love to?" My eyes widened at the question I'd added to the end. "I'd love to," I amended.

Gage smiled. "Great. What's your number?" I gave him my phone number and he quickly entered it in his phone.

151

"Maybe you'll tell me more about those possums you love so much."

Oh, Lord. I felt the heat infuse my cheeks but couldn't help smiling.

He began backing away. "See you both later."

"Bye." I watched as he turned and headed in the opposite direction.

"There you go. The perfect day just gets more perfect. Gage Buchanan asked you on a date."

I turned to Travis. His expression was curiously blank. "Antique fair?" I asked.

He shrugged. "It was the only thing that came to mind that's going on next weekend. Anyway, it worked, didn't it? You got a free concert in the park, surrounded by hordes of people, elevated to dinner alone at what I'm sure will be the priciest joint in town."

"What was wrong with Wednesday?"

"Always hold out for a weekend date, Haven. I'm surprised you don't know these things."

"Strategy?" I asked.

"Strategy," he confirmed.

"A date, with Gage."

"Yes, Haven, a date. With Gage. A weekend date with Gage. And I think you have my . . . adequate muscles to thank for giving him that extra push of competition."

I smiled. "Thank you, Travis. You're a valuable wingman."

He nodded but his smile seemed forced.

CHAPTER FIFTEEN

Travis

Each of the crew took a turn in Clarice's booth, stumbling out one by one, their expressions ranging from pleased (Betty), to confused (Cricket), to radiant (Burt).

Haven joined Cricket in the confused category as she ducked out from under the curtain, but her face quickly lit in a grin as her eyes fell on me. "Your turn," she said, laughing and pushing me inside.

The interior of the booth was dim and muggy, the whirring of a large fan in the corner shutting out the festival noise. It smelled like a mixture of pungent herbs and some sort of sweet oil, the same scent I'd picked up wafting off Clarice as she passed me at The Yellow Trellis Inn. Clarice sat near the back, a small, round table in front of her, draped with the same deep blue fabric of her curtain. My eyes adjusted as I took the few steps toward her, sitting down. "I'm being forced to do this," I told her, making sure she understood I was here against my will.

Her laughter was like wind chimes, tinkling and delicate. "Not a believer in the sixth sense, Chief Hale?"

I flashed her a smile. "I tend to be skeptical of anything that requires a cash payment for proof of its existence. No offense."

"None taken. I understand your skepticism, and I can only tell you that though I make a business of my . . . talents, I constantly have one foot behind the veil, unrelated to cash payments. I couldn't shut it off if I tried," she said, leaning forward slightly. "If you look deeply within yourself, you will find that all of us have intuition that can't always be explained by circumstance or evidence. Mine is simply stronger than the average person's. Now," she said, taking my hands in hers. "Let's see what the future holds for you."

I sighed, watching her as she gazed down at our joined hands, her brows taking turns moving up and down, her mouth thinning and then puckering as she apparently listened to whatever message might be coming from beyond the beyond. *Oh for Christ's sake.*

I was sitting in here for *Haven,* doing this ludicrous thing because she had looked so damned excited for all of us to have our fortune's read, and I was—apparently—unwilling to do anything that might take that joyful smile off her pretty face on a day she'd declared *the best of her entire life.*

I'd even helped sway Gage into asking her out on a date. Because dating Gage was her dearest wish come true.

My stomach muscles tightened. Damn cheap beer.

I considered what she'd divulged about the cantaloupe and rooftop garden. I pictured Haven as an eleven-year-old girl with curls springing out around her little face and sighed. She'd said, "when" her mother brought food home. She'd been hungry once upon a time. And it'd killed me to hear that.

She'd traveled halfway across town to work at a store where she could get an employee discount, only to bring home items off the discount shelf. In my mind's eye, she'd morphed from an eleven-year-old to a weary teenager, but with those same runaway curls, lugging bags of bruised apples, and half-wilted spinach home on three buses so she could make meals for her mother and brother that said, *I care for you. I will sacrifice for you.*

I very suddenly understood what fresh spinach, brewer's yeast, chia seeds, and all the other stuff I couldn't even pronounce meant to her and why. And I felt ashamed for the teasing I'd done before I truly understood.

So, yeah, perhaps if anyone deserved their wishes to come true, it was this girl. Even if that meant Gage Perfect Buchanan.

I'd moved my eyes from Clarice to the fabric draped behind her as I thought about Haven, and when I returned my gaze to her face, she was looking at me strangely, head thrust forward. "There are one of two paths for you. Either lose it all. Or lose it all."

'Scuse me?

I waited for more. Only silence came. "Um . . . what?"

Clarice dropped my hands, letting out a loud whoosh of breath, and repeated what she'd just said.

"Yes, I *heard* you. Both potential future paths sound . . . equally terrible."

"Yes," she agreed. "It does sound that way." Her brows did that quizzical thing again, but she offered no further insight. I gave it another moment.

Nothing.

"I don't think things are supposed to work this way." I narrowed my eyes. "Are you messing with me because I expressed doubt in your . . . talents?"

"Oh no, no. Definitely not. I never lie when it comes to my predictions." She peered at me again. "The fog is very dense around your future. Very, very dense. Murky even."

Very, very dense.

"Are you serious? That's what you're leaving me with?" I stayed planted in my chair. Why did I care? I didn't believe in this crap anyway. But even so, shouldn't you be able to expect certain things in these situations? I was under the impression that there was an agreement among shysters like Clarice. They told you your future was bright and shiny and all your dreams would come true. It was vague and silly and you basically knew you'd just thrown away twenty bucks, but even so, you walked out smiling, friends clamoring to know what you'd been told. Clarice didn't get to tell me my future was full of loss and darkness and zero paths that led to happiness. "This is outrageous," I sputtered. "It's not how this sort of thing is done."

Her forehead shot up. "I believe you've been misinformed on how *this sort of thing* works. Sometimes I'm given a word, or a string of words, perhaps a vision now and again, but an understanding is not provided to me. It's up to the recipient to interpret the message. I do have a disclaimer that I share my predictions whether they're positive or negative."

"Where? Where is that disclaimer?"

"Right there." She pointed behind me and I turned, squinting to see a tiny sign with lettering barely large enough to make out unless your nose was pressed against it.

"If anything more comes to me, I'll let you know as we share a residence at the moment." She smiled and despite her assertion that she'd provide more if she could, she wiped her hands together like she was wiping her hands of me completely.

What the actual hell?

I stood slowly, mouth open in offended disbelief.

The glare of the sun felt like an assault as I ducked out of Clarice's booth, and whatever look I was wearing on my face made Haven widen her eyes and bite back a smile. "The future doesn't look bright, I assume. What did she *say* to you?"

"Nothing that makes any sense," I grumbled as we started to walk.

Haven laughed, laying her hand on my arm. "Don't worry so much. She told me I'd plant ten thousand gardens. Obviously, that can't be true."

My mood brightened. "So she *is* a total quack. I knew it." I took in a full breath.

"Or, maybe she speaks in metaphors. Sometimes I swear I've lived in ten thousand places." She gave a wistful smile, twirling the end of her braid idly in her finger.

"I don't think there was a metaphor in my case. She was very clear. There was an either or and they both sucked."

"How about we forget the future and live in the moment with some whack-a-mole?"

My spirits rose. I was in the mood to whack something. If it had to be a plastic mole, so be it. I'd name it *Clarice* in my head. "It's a plan."

We spent a few hours playing games at the game booths and eating sugary snacks. I won her a stuffed dog that she squealed over and cradled as though it was a Ming vase, making me feel proud and happy. One of those simple masculine pleasures. "What's his name?" I asked her.

She considered him for a moment and then said, "Blueberry," almost shyly, followed by a short self-deprecating laugh, "so when I look at him, whenever that may be, *wherever* that may be, I will always remember today, spent in Pelion, Maine, with Chief Hale and our motley crew of misfits."

"Blueberry it is," I said softly.

We drove home mostly in silence, the sun just slipping below the horizon. Haven's nose and shoulders were red, but she didn't seem to be able to stop smiling, even though it was a sleepy smile. I was tired too from the sun, and the beer, and the sugar crash.

For some reason, things felt different between us. Sweeter somehow, but slightly strained too. I helped her down from my truck and pressed a finger softly into her shoulder, and she smiled, both of our eyes lingering on the light tan fingerprint that slowly faded away. I wondered if I'd be like that fingerprint, pressed into her skin briefly, eventually fading to nothing. No trace that I'd ever touched her at all or that she'd ever known me. Maybe our singular kiss would become just as forgettable. I swallowed down the unexpected tinge of sadness.

"I think I'll go to bed early," she said, her voice stilted. "It's been a long day."

"Yes," she agreed. "But a wonderful one. Thank you again for taking me. For winning me a prize." She hugged Blueberry to her chest.

I put my hands in my pockets. I wanted to kiss her. God, I wanted to kiss her. I'd never wanted to kiss anyone more.

Friends.

And she had a date with Gage Buchanan. A much-*wanted* date it was wise to remember. And I'd been called many, many things, but stupid had never been one of them.

I opened my mouth to say goodnight. "You know what would feel great right now?" Because, damn it, sometimes wisdom was overrated.

Her eyes widened slightly. "What?"

"A swim."

She laughed. "A swim? In the lake?"

"Well, I think our crew would be mildly scandalized if we took a swim in that old clawfoot tub upstairs."

159

She snorted softly. "Probably so."

"What do you say?"

She glanced behind her at the lake, shimmering under the lowering sun. "It does look tempting," she said, "except that I don't know how to swim."

I brought my head back. "You don't?"

She shook her head. "No lakes in the inner city."

I regarded her for a moment. Of course, there had to be pools and other ways city kids learned how to swim, but if her mother didn't provide food on a regular basis . . . My gut clenched. "I usually only wade in anyway," I lied. "Mostly for the coolness of the water."

She glanced at the lake again, bringing her hand up and running it seemingly unconsciously over her shoulder, surely hot from the burn. Out in the distance there was a lone kayak, just a speck on the horizon. All the boats had returned to dock.

For a moment I thought she'd say no, and I realized I was holding my breath. I let it out slowly, as her eyes returned to me. *Please say yes.* I wasn't ready to say goodnight. Not yet. This wasn't me. I didn't *wait* for women to say yes. I never had. Yet, here I was . . . *waiting. Hoping.*

"All right," she said softly.

CHAPTER SIXTEEN

Travis

It only took moments to change. I hadn't brought a swimsuit to the B&B, but I'd brought some running shorts that would work just fine. I grabbed a towel and headed back outside to wait on the shore.

The kayaker was still out in the lake, slightly closer than he or she had been before, but still too distant to determine anything specific about who it might be. The breeze was slight, gentle, and the water was still but for the soft lapping of the shore. The sun had burned away into early evening, and the trees to the left of the dock shaded the small portion of private beach so that it felt cool and intimate. The house

161

was far enough away that it was barely visible. A quiet, refreshing reprieve from the noise and heat of the day.

I spread my towel out on a rock and took the few steps toward the sandy shore, staring out at the lake.

"It feels so incredibly peaceful here," Haven said as she approached.

I turned, swallowing as I took her in. She was wearing a black bikini, a pair of jean shorts over the bottoms, and her gaze was trained on the water. It gave me an opportunity to drink her in without her watching me stare.

Her breasts were small-ish, but high and round, her nipples pebbled under the thin material of the swimsuit as though the slight breeze off the lake had chilled her. She'd taken out her braid and piled her hair on top of her head. And her *skin*. I already knew her skin was smooth and olive toned, but there was so much of it. Her arms, her shoulders, and her curved waist. And those legs. Long and slim, darker than that of her flat, bared stomach.

"You don't swim, but you have a swimsuit," I said inanely, mostly to unstick my tongue from the roof of my mouth.

She smiled. "I like to sit at the *edge* of water, I just don't usually go in."

"It'll feel nice," I said, again inanely.

Her gaze lingered on me. "Yes. It will."

There was a slightly awkward pause, broken by Haven stepping to the rock where I'd dropped my towel and depositing hers in the same spot. Her hands moved to the button of her shorts and I took in a shallow breath, turning

162

toward the lake to give her a moment of privacy while she undressed.

I waded into the cool water, listening for her approach behind me, my heart thrumming with anticipation. The moment felt . . . *new* somehow, in a way I couldn't articulate, as if swimming with a pretty girl in a bikini was something I'd never done, when in actuality, that was far from the truth.

The water was especially clear here, and I could see my feet on the sandy bottom as I moved deeper into the lake, until the water touched my thighs. I turned at the soft splashing sounds of Haven stepping into the lake behind me, and oh God, she was beautiful. With her shorts off, I could see the entire shape of her body, and I visualized what was beneath the small triangles of material, my body growing hot.

"God, this feels nice," she said, walking in farther and using her hands to swish the water at her sides. I smiled, squinting at her as she joined me.

For a moment we stood together, looking at the lake, Haven's hands continuing to move serenely. "What a dream this place is," she sighed.

"Not always," I said.

She turned her eyes to me, tilting her head at whatever she'd heard in my tone. *What a dream.* She'd said something similar at the festival about the town, about being lucky to live here, and I'd agreed with her. It was idyllic, the people were warm and friendly. And living beside a lake was picturesque, among other things. But all of that could be deceiving. Who knew that better than the Hale family?

But I didn't want to talk about that. Not now. Not when the setting sun was beginning to make the water around us shimmer like gold. Not when it had been such a good day, barring the incident with the scam-artist known as Clarice. Not when Haven was beside me wearing practically nothing. "I just mean, no town is perfect."

She paused in thought before looking away. "No. I don't imagine it is. *People* live here after all. But whatever *imperfect* events take place, a setting like this sure must soften the blow," she said, attempting lightness. I smiled. True enough.

I took Haven's trailing hand in mine, stepping deeper into the water. She offered a small amount of resistance. "Not too far," she said on a breathy laugh.

"I'm with you," I said. "I won't let you drown."

She paused only a moment and then took the next several steps with me, until the water was lapping at her waist.

"See?" I said. "You can still see your feet on the bottom."

She nodded. "Yes. The water's so clear." She brought some of the water up with the hand not holding mine, running it over her arms and shoulders. "Ah, that feels nice," she murmured.

I tugged her a little farther and she laughed. "This is far enough."

"Just a few more steps. Here I'll help you." I let go of her hand and moved in quickly, slipping my arms around her waist and pulling her to me as I stepped forward, off the small drop-off that had been just ahead. She laughed, pushing at my chest, but then quickly wrapped her arms around my neck

164

when she realized that she could only touch the bottom with her tippy-toes.

Her face registered surprise then a brief flare of fear, her arms bringing her even closer as she held on. "You tricked me, Travis Hale."

No, you tricked me. How and why and when, I wasn't exactly sure. But I felt bamboozled, as though she'd done something on purpose to make things, me, *everything,* seem one way when they were really another. I couldn't even make sense of my own thoughts.

"I did, but only because I wanted you to feel the water all over you. I wanted you to experience what it's like to float. I won't let you go, I promise. I've got you."

She gave me an exasperated stare, but the fear seemed to have faded and after a moment, she leaned her head back, letting the water lap around her shoulders as we bobbed together in the water.

My gaze dropped to her breasts, her slight round cleavage just showing above the water, her stomach pressed to mine. God, it felt good. She was warm and soft and slippery, and it was taking everything in me not to lower my head and kiss that sweet dip between her breasts, to drag my tongue over the swells, to trail my lips along her collarbone. I throbbed, growing harder. My blood coursing hotter.

Haven brought her head forward, her eyes meeting mine. Her face was so close, the way it'd been when we first kissed. Only that had been in dim lighting and so sudden that I hadn't had the chance to look at her up close, to notice the details of her face . . . the almost invisible, fine hairs that made her skin look like velvet, the dark striations in her coffee-colored eyes, the perfect dip of her cupid's bow, and the small beauty mark on her left cheek, barely as large as the tip of a pen.

My breath came shorter, body reacting to the soft press of her skin and the way she clung to me. A curl sprung free and hit me in the eye, making me squint and laugh in sudden surprise. "This hair," I said, bringing one hand up and attempting unsuccessfully to tuck it behind her ear, "is a wonder."

"It's a curse," she murmured. I attempted another ear tuck, the curl obeying this time, but likely not for long. I allowed my fingers to caress the side of her silken cheek. Her eyes flared, and I saw the same heat in hers that must be in my own. I could feel her heart beating against my chest and I noticed when her breath hitched. "It came from my dad I suppose because my mom's hair was as straight as could be," she said, glancing away, "though that could have been any number of men. My mom never really did pin it down."

My hand paused briefly in its journey down her cheek, the statement catching me off guard. She was watching me closely as though waiting for my reaction. When I met her stare without flinching, she released a breath, shook her head, and lowered her eyes. "Sorry," she said, "I'm a little nervous out here."

"Don't be. I'm not going to let you go."

Her shoulders dropped and she relaxed completely in my arms, her body becoming pliant. *She trusts me.* It felt like a deep and sacred honor. Amazing. *Undeserved* even when trust

166

was part of my daily life. This town trusted me. But Haven's trust was different altogether. For a few moments we were quiet, her breath evening, my arms holding her steadily as we both looked toward the setting sun. The world felt beautiful and peaceful. All the worries, all the questions with no answers, all the complications, and the potential pain of the world, none of it existed in this watery refuge under the dipping sun with this beautiful girl in my arms. *Nothing could touch us out here.* It was only us.

This time the kiss began slowly, Haven's eyes meeting mine, our mouths touching gently, the barest brush of our lips. It wasn't clear who'd initiated it, maybe me, maybe her. But it seemed more likely that we'd both moved together simultaneously. For long moments I gloried in the feel of her body against mine, the cool undulations of the current drawing her away and then pressing her near. It was breathless, and it was sweet. I felt a shift. Me. The world. The order of things I could not name, or maybe had misunderstood in the first place. Assumptions long held all suddenly proven wrong.

I drew in a shuddery breath as I moved my tongue languidly over the seam of her lips and she opened for me. The kiss went deeper, yet the pace remained the same. Leisurely. Dreamy. As though to rush things would dishonor this moment.

The kiss was as natural as the lift and fall of the water around us, as essential as the sky above, as searing as the fiery sun.

Our tongues tangled, danced, parried slowly, her mouth angled over mine so that I could taste every inch of her sweetness.

Our breath mingled, and Haven brought her hands from around my neck, holding my face as her legs circled my waist. I gasped out a ragged moan as her core pressed against my erection and for a moment, I thought I might come in my shorts like a teenage boy feeling a female body for the very first time. She fit so perfectly against me. I used one arm to hold her steadily around the waist, and the other dipped, first to the round curve of her ass, down to the silky smoothness of the back of her thigh, pulling her closer yet, torturing myself.

"What are we doing, Travis?" she breathed, slowing the kiss once more, her lips trailing over mine, her hands weaving into my hair, even as she drew her body away from mine so very slightly.

I don't know. I have no idea. "Enjoying ourselves," I murmured, trailing my lips down her throat as she leaned her head back to give me better access. I darted my tongue out, licking the spot where her pulse fluttered under my mouth. I felt an odd feeling just under the intense arousal, and I could only call it fear. But of what? I knew how to do this. I was an *expert* at this.

"*Why?*" She raked her fingernails through my hair and I moaned again at the pure pleasure assaulting every part of me. But I also heard the barest hint of panic in her tone as though her mind was searching for reasons to resist, even if her body was not. Why *what?* I'd lost the thread of the conversation, and I had to force myself back the same way I sometimes pulled myself from sleep when an emergency call came through in the middle of the night.

When had I ever *wanted* to be lost like this? When had I *wanted* to lose control?

"Because it feels nice," I answered. It felt better than *nice*. It felt amazing. Incredibly erotic. *Right.*

"That's all?" She drew back slightly and looked me in the eyes, searching, giving me a moment to get control of the runaway lust pumping through my veins. Was she looking for a reason to stop? A justification to continue?

"Of course," I answered. "You have . . . feelings for Gage, remember?"

Her gaze went a little hazy. "Right," she said. "Oh. Yes. I do. I'd like to . . . keep myself available just in case."

Available. The words felt wrong, as if the ones we were using were conveying something different entirely.

"Just in case," I repeated, leaning back in and running my nose along her jaw, inhaling the sun-drenched scent of her skin.

"And you're . . . you're on the rebound," she reminded me.

"I know," I said. Something sparked in her eyes, her brows lowering even as she nodded.

"But there's no reason we can't enjoy each other in the meantime," she said.

My heart soared and I felt a moment of victory, despite that she'd just re-established the very temporary nature of our . . . *friendship.*

I was going to make the most of temporary. And I was going to be a very good friend.

"Keep our skills honed and all that," I added.

"Exactly. It doesn't have to be complicated," she said.

"No. Simple. Very simple." Lord, but it *felt* simple. So simple I could hardly *think*.

She ran a finger down my stomach and I sucked in another breath, my cock jumping, a flush of heat infusing my limbs. I desperately wanted to pull her swimsuit bottoms aside, push into her tight heat, thrust gently at first, and then harder, faster, the water splashing around us as I sought the sweet relief that only her silken body could bring.

That couldn't happen. Not here. But I could give *her* relief and despite my own raw need, I'd never wanted anything more than to pleasure her, to watch her face as she fell apart, to know that I had been the one to do it. I removed my hand from the back of her thigh and moved it between our bodies, drawing back so I could slip it lower, into the waistband of her bikini bottoms, my finger sliding over her hot, swollen flesh.

"Oh, oh God," she moaned, her head going back, her hands falling from my head and gripping my shoulders. "Travis, yes . . ."

My hand went lower, my thumb trailing that hard bundle of nerves, even as my finger dipped into her wet heat. *Oh God* was right. She was slick and hot, snug around my finger. My cock throbbed with frustrating intensity, a primitive ache so deep it made me dizzy. Haven's head came forward, her cheeks flushed, eyes half shut as she melded her mouth with mine once again.

I circled and slid and in only moments she was moving with me, riding my hand, the kiss growing erotically sloppy as she made a deep sound of primal pleasure in the back of her throat.

"Oh God, oh God, you're good at this," she said, breaking away from my mouth. "Don't stop."

I had no intention of stopping.

I lifted her higher and bent my head, closing my mouth over the thin fabric that covered one hardened nipple, and tugging on it lightly as she cried out, bucking gently, my finger going deeper as a frantic-sounding groan emerged from her throat. Her hands came away from my shoulders momentarily as she reached behind her, untying the strings of her bikini top, the fabric dropping.

My mind went blank, eyes feasting on perfect round breasts, her nipples tight, rosy points. Apparently, I didn't need my brain to figure out what to do because before a lucid thought had formed, my mouth was wrapped around one bare nipple, tongue lapping at it slowly as she let out a long moan of pleasure, hands finding my shoulders once again and grasping.

I moved to the other nipple and was rewarded with more quickened gasps. I sucked and licked, my thumb continuing to circle as she rode my finger.

Her fingernails dug into my skin and I hoped she was marking me. I wanted to look at those red half-moons in the mirror tomorrow and be brought back to this moment. She

171

was going to come, I could feel it in the vibrations of her body, hear it in the frenzied nature of her pants, and the clutch of her hands. I wanted to watch it as it happened. Needed to. I lifted my head from her breasts, nipples gleaming wet from my mouth, and the sight of that alone made my cock throb mercilessly. Her eyes were closed, cheeks flushed with arousal, mouth parted, and more beautiful than anything I'd ever looked upon in my entire life. Her body stiffened and she let out a strangled cry as she came, eyes flying open to meet my gaze right before her forehead touched mine, gasping as she attempted to catch her breath. We both breathed together, her heart slamming against my chest as she fought for breath.

I slipped my finger from her body, pulling her swimsuit bottoms up and wrapping my arm around her again, holding her in the water as our breathing evened, though my raging erection throbbed with both pleasure and pain.

I kissed her temple. She sighed sweetly as she reached up and retied her top. Her eyes met mine, expression open and vulnerable and there was something so incredibly *hopeful* in her gaze. She stared at me for a moment, blinking as though catching herself revealing what she had not meant to. A flash of fear raced across her face right before her features smoothed.

What did you hope for just now? I wondered. *And why did it scare you?*

She leaned back, her expression hesitant, slightly shy. I took a few steps back toward the shore, stepping up the drop-off and placing her on her feet. She teetered slightly, laughing at herself. The sun had set, leaving only a stripe of red far

172

away on the horizon, but providing enough light that I could still see clearly. Overhead, the first stars were appearing in the deepening sky. "You must be tired," I said.

She nodded uncertainly. "You must be . . ." She glanced downward.

I laughed shortly. "I'm fine." I wasn't fine, but I would live, at least until I made it to the privacy of my shower. Then I'd picture the way her face looked as she fell apart, the way her body squeezed and pulsated around my finger, the way her nipples had tasted on my tongue. One stroke and I'd be done.

She turned away and then turned back quickly. "It . . . I mean, I know we said no complications. But . . . that felt sort of complicated."

Was she saying we shouldn't do that again? Touch each other? My chest suddenly felt tight. *Everything* felt tight. I studied her for a moment. I wasn't sure how to read her expression . . . confused, uneasy. It wasn't how I wanted her to feel. I'd never seen confusion or any form of regret on a woman's face after physical intimacy. I was in uncharted territory here. "I'll leave it up to you, Haven. Whatever you feel comfortable with."

Her gaze moved over my face, and then she nodded once, her lips pressing together momentarily before she nodded *again* as though confirming the first nod. "I . . . that was , , , I mean. You're very skilled. Obviously, I enjoyed that. Very much." Her cheeks colored the way they had right before she'd come. She laid her hand on my arm and then just as quickly removed it. "I don't regret it at *all*. It was . . . wow.

173

Very, very wow. I just . . . you know, it sort of muddies the water and all."

"It does," I agreed. "Muddy waters." So why was I suddenly very willing to wade in muddy waters? To swim in them. Hell, I'd be willing to drink them right at the moment.

"And I . . . well, today was . . . special to me. I would hate to do anything to jeopardize more times like that. Me, you, the crew." The words faded into a small, uncomfortable laugh. She gave me a smile, part hopeful, part puzzled.

The crew. I was part of the crew.

And though she was very obviously attracted to me, the friendly part of our relationship was more valuable to her. If I was reading the situation correctly.

I opened my mouth to say something and then closed it. Her eyes were tired. It had been a long day. And though I was incredibly attracted to her, I also wanted her to have other days like today. Uncomplicated. Easy. *Friendly.* I took her hand in mine and pulled her to the shore where we both picked up our towels and dried off, Haven sliding her shorts back over her swimsuit and slipping her flip-flops on once she was dry.

We walked in silence to the house, the quiet of the night and the gentle lapping of the water making it seem almost unreal, as if what had just happened had been nothing more than a fevered dream.

There were voices and laughter coming from the back porch of the house, but we didn't move in that direction, instead walking silently to the bottom of the stairs and then climbing them together.

We both paused at the top landing. Haven's expression was peaceful, though her eyes remained uncertain. Her hair was windblown and in complete disarray, and the corner of my lip tugged in a smile. She bit at her lip. Cleared her throat. "Goodnight," she said. "Thank you again for . . . today."

"My pleasure," I said and her eyes flew to mine, widening slightly. I smiled, saying nothing. I hated that we were suddenly so awkward. It was strange. And sort of amusing in a disappointing way. And frustrating. And I was still semi hard. That shower was calling. Loudly. "Goodnight, Haven. Sleep well."

She nodded, her gaze lingering on mine for a moment. I swore she held her breath as she moved around me, heading for her room.

CHAPTER SEVENTEEN

Haven

"You sound happy," I said. Easton turned around, his teeth flashing as the tune he'd been whistling abruptly ended. "And you *look* happy too." I eyed him suspiciously. "What have you done now?"

He laughed. "Ah, big sis, you always think the worst of me."

"Yes, and you generally give me a good reason to." I crossed my arms as I leaned against the side of the structure that housed the club's pool equipment.

Easton swung a float over his arm, spinning it onto his shoulder. "Okay, okay, I deserve that. Except you're wrong this time." A blade of sunlight split his face as he stepped toward me and squinted one eye, using his hand as a visor, looking every bit the naughty but lovable little boy he'd once been. Only *then* his naughtiness had generally resulted in cracked windows or broken furniture. His own *bones* on two occasions. He'd moved on since then to breaking bigger things, namely lives and relationships. Things not so easily replaced or put back together.

Like Travis's relationship.

At the thought of the *other* person involved in Travis's relationship, broken though it may be, my body had dual reactions. My ribs ached a little bit while something simultaneously eased inside of me. She was the reason he was unavailable for anything more than friendship . . . with benefits. Because he'd loved her. And he likely still did. Love didn't just fade to nothing in the span of a month. And how could you trust someone who loved that . . . *temporarily* anyway?

He probably still thought about her a lot. Maybe even while he was kissing other people.

People such as myself.

Maybe even while his skilled fingers were between other people's legs.

Again, people such as myself.

I waved my hand in front of my suddenly heated face in an attempt to stir up some breeze.

Maybe even—

"How are you wrong, Easton?" my brother mocked, raising the pitch of his voice as my mind had wandered to

177

Travis and I'd zoned out of the conversation, staring unseeing at Easton as he'd waited for a response that didn't come.

"Okay, first," I said, taking a deep breath and attempting to shake myself into the here and now, "that was a terrible impression of me. My voice is throatier. Much sexier. Second, how am I wrong, Easton?"

He grinned again, and his green eyes glinted in the sun. His grin wasn't slow like Travis's. It flashed instantly, like an unexpected streak of lightning, the unfortunate smile that allowed him to wreak havoc wherever he went. The expression that had women bending over backward— sometimes literally from the stories I'd unfortunately heard— to *assist* him in his efforts at being a complete menace to society. Still . . . I was obviously biased because that grin affected me too as far as a softening of my heart and probably offering him too much allowance when it came to his bad deeds. It was just . . . I knew him, I'd known him since he was a baby, and he was not a bad person. He just made bad decisions. Frequently. And with great and focused application.

"I told you how I've been volunteering at the fire department, right?"

"Yes."

He spun the float again. "Well, it's going great. They say I'm a natural. There was a kitchen fire at one of the B&Bs in Pelion yesterday, and they let me put it out myself."

I swallowed. "That's great." If anything positive could distract him from those bad decisions he so frequently made, I was all for it. Maybe we could get out of this particular town without any more scandals or weapons being brandished in our direction.

He nodded enthusiastically. "The senior fireman is retiring next month," Easton said haltingly. "The guys who are there now are all moving up in rank. There's going to be an extra entry-level spot. All you need is a high school diploma to get hired on. It's just a test and—"

"But we're going to be gone by then," I said, understanding exactly where his thoughts were heading.

He held my gaze for a moment and then nodded. "Yeah, I know."

"You *want* to be gone by then, right?" I asked. We'd agreed on that when we'd driven out of California, the visions of *that night* still fresh in our minds. Four months was our absolute max. We wouldn't stay anywhere longer than four months. One season. We wouldn't stay anywhere long enough to watch anything shrivel or die. No destination, no attachments. Just us and the open road. I'd made the initial suggestion—desperate to literally outrun the stench of smoke and burned flesh that'd seemed to hang over LA—and he'd agreed to the idea. Up until Pelion, there had been no talk of staying in one place. *But now?*

"Yeah. I want to be gone by then." He smiled. "It's been fun in the meantime though, you know, doing things right for a change."

My heart dropped. "Easton, you—"

"There you are!" came a voice from behind my brother. He turned and a pretty brunette in a red swimsuit reached her arms out. He rolled the float off his shoulder and handed it to her.

"Sorry I got held up," he said, and by the sudden widening of her eyes, I knew that he'd grinned that grin of his.

"I'll see you later, Easton," I said, and the girl who didn't know I was his sister, the one I prayed was *single,* shot me a hostile glare.

"See ya, sis," he called, to make it crystal clear.

I headed to the smoothie bar to get set up for the day, chopping fruit and re-filling ingredient containers that had been put away for the night.

I went about the prep errands, my mind wandering as I worked. I'd set up enough at this point that I could basically do it by heart. My thoughts insisted on returning to that lake at sunset, the way it'd felt to be held tight against Travis's hard, wet body, the way he'd kissed me, the way he'd slipped his hands down my bikini bottoms and into my body, bringing me to orgasm as if he'd been made to do just that. A deep shiver snaked through me at the memory alone.

A carton of soy milk rolled over my heated skin helped cool the sudden flush.

It hadn't been a good idea.

It was downright *stupid* and I was so rarely stupid.

I made good choices. Rational ones.

I always had.

Because if I didn't, no one would.

So why had I allowed myself to lose control now? To let down my guard?

I couldn't.

I wouldn't.

Not again.

I practically threw the carton back in the mini fridge, losing my balance and going down on my knees, the container of blueberries falling out of my hands and spilling onto the floor.

Damn it!

My shoulders dropped and I took a deep breath. *Get a hold of yourself, Haven.*

Above me, the scrape of at least a couple bar stools being pulled out met my ears. Ugh. It wasn't even time to open yet, and I needed a few more minutes of solitude before it was time to take orders. And to coax my hormones back into submission after pondering Travis's wet skin and hard . . . everything.

"Who is he?" a female voice asked, the voice close yet distant as though the person was turned away from the bar.

"Travis Hale," another female voice said. Travis was here? My ears perked and I went still, listening, as though two girls had somehow slipped into my brain and we were all having a conversation.

Which would make me insane and I didn't think I'd quite crossed that particular road. Yet.

"Damn," the first voice said appreciatively.

"He's the Pelion chief of police like his father was many years before him." She paused for long moments and I pictured them, backs to me, staring across the club to some place Travis Hale stood, perhaps chatting with another member. I envisioned that sure stance of his, the way he tilted his head just slightly when he was listening intently. The way he listened to me, as if every word I said was important to him.

"The *chief of police?* God, he needs his own calendar, every month dedicated just to him. Hale, you said? Don't they *own* Pelion?"

"Yup. And even more interestingly, every Hale generation has some scandal or another. The previous one was *always* wild," she mused. "Hot as sin, and guaranteed to burn you if you got too close. That's what my mom said anyway. There are stories upon stories about them. Some people on this side of the lake called them trash, despite that their family owned Pelion, because they did whatever they wanted and didn't seem to care what anyone thought. And then of course, all hell broke loose the minute Alyssa McCree showed up."

I couldn't move. I was rooted to the spot, trapped. If I stood now, I'd totally embarrass them in the midst of their gossiping.

At least that's what I told myself.

It was definitely *not* because I was hungry to know more about Travis Hale and his family, not because through fate alone I was receiving answers to questions I'd never ask.

"Alyssa McCree?"

"Mm-hmm. She was Archer Hale's mother. Archer owns the town now. And even though Archer and his wife Bree have gotta be rich, they still live in this tiny Lincoln log house, and Archer drives a rusted, old pickup truck that looks like it's about a hundred years old. And despite his hot factor, Travis was humiliated in front of the entire town eight years ago when everyone found out Archer was the older Hale and Travis had to give up ownership of Pelion. He and his mother lost all their money and social standing."

My stomach tightened. Travis hadn't mentioned that part when he'd told me about his brother owning the town. But why would he? It sounded painful. And like none of my business. Obviously it was well-known town fodder though, and a sour taste filled my mouth at the cold-hearted way the girl speaking had just summed up the situation I was sure held far more nuance, not to mention real human emotions.

"So," the girl went on, "Travis is definite calendar material, but *blue-collar* calendar material. His ex, Phoebe, had plans to get him to run for mayor or governor. She said they'd be political royalty by the time they were thirty-five and live in the Buchanans' neighborhood. But now that they've broken up, I'm doubtful he has those same ambitions. Honestly? I'm surprised they still allow him access to this club. Everyone's still kind of embarrassed for him. And it's not like he's one of us anymore, that's for sure. Especially without Phoebe. God, where *is* that weird smoothie girl who looks like she stuck her finger in a socket?"

I dug in my pocket, moving as little as possible as I pulled my ear buds out and stuck them in my ears, dropping the end in my pocket again as if there might be a phone there. I rose quickly and both girls, now turned toward the counter, jumped. I widened my eyes, pulling the ear buds from my ears. "I'm so sorry," I said. "I was stocking and didn't hear you."

The girl who'd been talking, a pretty redhead, scowled slightly. "It's fine. I'll take a berry blast with a shot of wheatgrass."

A couple sat down at my counter and I greeted them. I looked up and smiled as Travis waved at me from across the club, heading for the exit.

****

I shouldn't do this. There is no point in doing this.

I opened the browser, the cursor blinking in the empty search box. I let out a deep breath and typed in Hale Pelion, Maine. *I can't help it.* My desire to know more was like a burning thirst.

And even more interestingly, every Hale generation has some scandal or another.

A long list of links came up and instead of talking myself out of it—which would have been the wiser move, not to mention one that respected the *boundaries* between friends . . . even friends who'd put their fingers . . . well . . .

I opened the first link and began reading. I learned about the town founding, about the Hale family through the generations—Lord, but there were a lot of *boys*. And finally, I read about the car accident that ended in a shootout between brothers on a highway in the middle of a springtime day.

A sharp pang pierced my heart for Archer Hale. I sat back in the chair at the desk in the small room designated as an office that guests were welcome to use at The Yellow Trellis Inn. I pictured what it might have been like that day, surely coming up far short of reality. *Reality* was never just the picture of events. It was the smells and the sounds and a hundred other small details that no one else would ever understand because they hadn't *been* there, standing among the ashes as your world burned down.

My mind moved to the blueberry festival where I'd met Archer and his wife and kids. Travis had told me about his brother's voice box being injured when he was a kid, and so I hadn't been surprised by the scar on his throat. What I had noticed was the peace on his face, the joy in his eyes, the way his wife had gazed at him with such open love, the sweet exuberance of his twin boys and that beautiful baby girl I'd only glimpsed in the stroller.

However it had happened, and whatever strength he'd drawn from, Archer Hale had triumphed over that day.

And maybe I would someday triumph over my own.

I read about how the land had transferred to Archer and about the shooting that had occurred eight years ago, Chief Travis Hale showing up just in time to stop the threat before anyone else was hurt.

I swallowed down a lump in my throat, thinking about everything I knew about Travis.

One of the men who had died on the highway was his father as well. Where had Travis been that awful day? He'd been seven years old too. Who had explained things to him?

Who had helped him grieve?

And after that, he'd been set to inherit the town apparently. Another loss, rightful or not. Had he suffered over it? Did he still?

It was all too much. Too much trauma. Too much pain. Sometimes the world felt so damned *sharp*.

I clicked the browser off and put the computer to sleep, but it was several minutes before I pulled myself from the chair and returned to my room. Because at the end of the day, what did it matter? *I was leaving. End of story.*

So why did that feel like a lie?

CHAPTER EIGHTEEN

Travis

"Where's Spencer?" Maggie asked, topping off my coffee.

"He's with Birdie Ellis. They're setting up a community relations group that will be presenting at the annual meeting," I said, picking up my mug and taking a sip.

"Birdie Ellis," Maggie said, turning her nose up slightly. "That woman needs a hobby."

"So does Spencer," I muttered. "Hopefully the work it takes to maintain the group will keep them *both* fully occupied."

She eyed me. "Found a way to get him out of your hair a little bit, huh?"

"Am I that transparent?"

"To me. Honey, I've known you all your life. I know you down deep. Don't forget it." She leaned forward and looked into my eyes, pinching my cheek affectionately in the way I'd only ever let Maggie get away with.

"I never do, Maggie."

The bell above the door sounded over the low hum of the end of the breakfast rush and a moment later, I saw Gage Buchanan sit down next to me in my peripheral vision. Just the person I had no interest in seeing.

Or thinking about.

Or acknowledging.

"Travis," he greeted, dashing my hopes that he wouldn't notice me, even if I was sitting right next to him.

"Gage." I took another sip of my coffee, not glancing his way.

"Gage Buchanan," Maggie greeted happily. "What brings you to our side of the lake?"

"I missed you, Maggie. It's been too long."

Maggie made a scoffing noise. "Oh please, you charmer."

Gage chuckled. "I'm picking up some trees my mother ordered that couldn't be delivered until this weekend. Our landscaping crew is there today though, ready to plant, so here I am."

Maggie nodded "The nursery is installing landscaping in three new builds this week. Chase Dooley was in yesterday and said they're stretched thin. Coffee?"

"Please. It's fine, it gave me a good excuse to visit. How have you been?"

"Great. We're updating and expanding the kitchen beginning September first. Norm is finally getting the Top Chef setup he's always wanted, just in time to think about retiring." She turned her head and said the last part so Norm could hear. But then turned and winked at us.

"I don't believe in retirement," Norm called back. "I'm going to take my final breath right here standing at this griddle."

"Oh that'll be swell for business." Maggie rolled her eyes as she grabbed menus for a couple sitting at the end of the counter.

"What's new, Hale?" Gage asked when Maggie had walked away.

"Not a whole lot."

We sat in silence for a minute. "What can you tell me about Haven Torres?"

My muscles tensed. I took a sip of my coffee, setting it down slowly. "Why don't you ask her what you want to know on your *dinner date*?" The words felt strangely acidic in my throat.

He paused. "I will. But I wanted to get your take on her. We've always had similar taste in women."

I almost laughed. We'd competed over women in the past, both of us "winning" about as equally. What he didn't know was that he'd already "won" Haven. Or at least, he'd won her interest. I wouldn't tell him that though. I'd told her I'd help her get him to notice her with a faux competition, despite that it made my gut churn.

You're taking a hiatus from women, remember?

189

At least, anything more than an uncomplicated moonlit rendezvous.

I angled my body toward him. "She's . . . different." I let the word hang suggestively, watching Gage to see what he did with it.

"That's exactly what I think," he agreed on an exhale. "God, I've grown so bored with nothing but women who . . . worship me and yet don't really know me at all." He looked away as if considering those poor, worshipful fools who hung on his every word, and yet heard nothing he said. The interesting thing was, I could relate. I understood exactly what he was saying. And I didn't necessarily like that fact.

"She has this weird thing for possums," he muttered, his brows going in opposite directions as though he was still trying to work that one out. "But she's funny and charming and"—he paused, scratching the back of his neck in thought—"that hair. God, can you even imagine?" His expression had suddenly gone sort of dreamy and unfocused and I knew exactly what he was imagining. That hair wrapped around his fist as he—I shut the image down, slamming it hard into the floor and stomping it once for good measure. Unfortunately, he was still talking. "She has this beauty that sneaks up on you. You know, like"—he clapped his hands together suddenly, causing me to jostle the coffee I'd just been bringing to my mouth—"boom! *Ambush.*"

Oh, I knew. I pictured the way she looked in the morning as she cared for her plants, tipping a watering can, peace in her expression, tenderness even. The light of sunrise washing over her, glinting through her curls. The strap of her tank top falling slowly down her shoulder as I watched in quiet awe. I took a slow sip of the lukewarm brew. It was suddenly bitter and unpalatable. *Ambush.* That was a good way to put it. I'd stepped on the bomb that was Haven Torres. In some ways, I felt as though I'd been blown to smithereens. I was desperately trying to put the pieces back together. Or maybe I was lying there, happily scattered. *Stupidly* scattered. Maybe I *never* wanted to be put back together. At least not in the same order. God, I didn't even *know* anymore.

And we were just *friends.*

But I knew what she tasted like. Sounded like. How soft she was.

Hiatus, Hale. Hiatus.

"The problem is," Gage droned on, "she's only here temporarily. And I'm ready for something more long-term. Something that has the potential to become serious."

"You're kidding. *You,* the unattainable Gage Buchanan is looking to get *serious?*" I said it like a four-letter word.

He gave a short laugh that died quickly. "Yeah." He nodded, as if he was still trying to talk himself into what he was saying. "Yeah, it's time. A man can't just screw around—pardon the expression—forever." He looked at me a little sheepishly. "I really was sorry to hear about you and Phoebe. It seemed like maybe you might have been considering settling down too. At least, that's what the rumor was." I glanced at him to see his expression was genuinely sympathetic, the same way it'd been when he brought it up at the blueberry festival.

I gave a small nod, followed by a shrug. "She wasn't the one."

"No, I guess not. Well, there's someone out there for you, buddy." He gave me a slap on the back that made me want to punch him in his face. I gave my head a small shake, trying to dispel the sudden bout of hostility.

"Anyway," Gage went on, putting his elbows on the counter and lacing his fingers, sighing. "Do you think there's any chance she might stick around?"

"Nothing she's said indicates that. Plus, she's traveling with her brother so it's not only up to her."

"Hmm." His face suddenly broke into that grin that had cost me the win with any number of potential girlfriends growing up. "Maybe I can convince her."

I felt a small internal pinch. Part of me hoped he *would* convince Haven to stay because I didn't like to think of her driving out of Pelion. This town seemed to suit her. As she said, she'd found a place that provided peace. But another part of me absolutely did not, because it would mean she was staying for *him* and I'd have to watch them together for the remainder of my days. Maybe I deserved as much.

You either lose it all. Or lose it all.

I suddenly felt sick to my stomach.

I pulled my wallet out and retrieved a ten, placing it on the counter just as my phone rang. I snatched it up without glancing at who was calling.

"Travis?"

"Hi, Mom." I sighed internally, standing up, covering the mouthpiece. "See you around, Gage."

He gave me a tip of his chin. "Travis."

I gave Maggie and Norm a wave as I headed for the door. "What's going on?" I asked my mother because if she was calling, it was always *something*.

"There's a bad leak in my apartment."

I opened the door to my cruiser, getting inside. "Call a plumber," I said. I was up to my eyeballs in *leaks* already.

"I don't have the money for a plumber," she whined, "because of those medical bills I had to pay last month."

Medical bills.

She'd been to her plastic surgeon for something that wasn't overtly obvious and I didn't ask about.

I ran a hand over my face, about to tell her I'd call a plumber for her. It would be yet another expense when I was still fighting with my insurance company over what they wouldn't cover, facing the likelihood that I'd have to buy at least several pieces of new furniture, not to mention the cost of staying at the B&B. And I was saving every penny possible to start building on my land sometime in the next decade.

"And I have something I want to give to you. Something that was your father's."

That old yearning crept over me. *Something that was your father's.* "What is it?"

"Some photo albums . . . papers, things like that."

I sighed. "How quickly do you need me there?"

"Oh, I don't know! I might be flooded by tomorrow! Drowned in my bed!"

I scrubbed my hand down my face again. Melodrama. Christ. I came by it honestly.

"Okay," I sighed. "I'll come check it out after work."

193

****

My mother's apartment was small, but nice. Not the *nice* by which Tori Hale had become accustomed to once upon a time, but nice by any other objective standards. There were hardwood floors, granite countertops, and even some custom molding. I'd helped her out with extras when necessary, but I lived on a small-town chief's salary, without the benefit of the town income my father had enjoyed, and so that's all I could reasonably do while paying my own rent and saving so I could retire before I was ninety-five. Frankly, it could be argued that I shouldn't do anything at all. She probably deserved to live in a homeless shelter after what she'd done, and what might have resulted. But . . . she was my mother, and I didn't have the heart to abandon her completely, despite the suspicions that had lasted eight years, and beyond her fervent denials. She was still the woman who'd read to me before bed, and clapped at my little league games, the only one in the stands after my father had left. After my father had died. She'd shed tears at my graduation, and even looked on with pride when I'd joined the Pelion Police Department, regardless of the fact that she had more lofty ambitions for me. It was confusing and heartbreaking and it made me feel ashamed. Mostly I just wanted to avoid her. The fact that she lived out of town made it easy enough.

She'd vowed time and again that she hadn't meant for anyone to get hurt when she'd alerted a drug addict with a debt to settle about Bree's whereabouts eight years ago. She'd wanted to "persuade" Bree to move away from Pelion, *yes,* but she had never intended for someone to get shot. *"I was protecting you, Travis!" she'd said, tears filling her big blue eyes. "I panicked when I thought everything would be taken from you. Again."*

Again.

Likely, she was more concerned about everything being taken from *her*, but I doubted I'd ever truly know. Nothing had ever been proven, and it was worthless to continue asking her. Whatever she'd say to me was what she'd convinced herself of. Tori Hale had always been a good liar, because she believed her falsehoods.

"Where's this leak?"

"In the kitchen, under the sink," she said, hurrying behind me as I walked to her gleaming kitchen, setting my toolbox on the table.

I knelt on the floor and opened the cabinet, peering inside. There was a small spot on the bottom where it looked like a few drips of water had dried, leaving a water spot, but other than that, nothing. I peered over my shoulder at my mother.

"Do you see the spot?" she asked.

"That's what you were worried about? A spot? It looks old. And dry. And it might have come from anything. A bottle of cleaner, who knows." Irritation skated down my spine. It'd taken an hour to drive here, and now I had to drive an hour home. Still, just to make sure, I stood, turning on the faucet and letting it run, and then kneeling back down to examine the pipes.

They remained dry, nary a drip in sight.

I stood slowly, turning off the faucet. "I don't think you'll drown in your bed tonight."

She laughed faintly. "What a relief."

I leaned on the sink. "How are you?" She looked as put together as she always had, but there were more lines on her face, and her mouth looked pinched. Even Tori Hale couldn't manipulate gravity forever. She'd called me here not for a leak in her plumbing, but because she was lonely. My heart softened just a bit. She suddenly seemed very human to me when, for much of my adolescence and even beyond, she'd seemed larger than life and almost completely untouchable.

She was always working, always strategizing. She'd exhausted me since I was a kid, and *especially* then because I had no way of creating distance from her. I wondered if she'd exhausted herself. Maybe, in some deep corner of her mind, loneliness and boredom felt like a soothing *break.*

I didn't hold out much hope of that.

"I'm okay I guess," she said, followed by a long-suffering sigh. "I joined a pinochle club. It meets every Monday."

My eyebrows rose. "That's good." She'd always enjoyed socializing.

She moved her finger idly along the edge of the counter. "And I'm seeing someone." She waved her hand around as though dismissing the importance of her own comment. "It's casual. He's older. Just someone to pass the time with."

"That's good, Mom," I said. "Finding people to pass the time with is good." I'd bet anything he was quite a *bit* older. And rich.

Possibly hooked up to oxygen, or in hospice care.

Nasty thought, Hale.

Why did I always let my mother bring out the worst in me?

But as long as he was a mentally functional, consenting adult, I'd consider it a positive. Maybe if she got herself more of a life, she'd stop calling me for every little thing that barely needed fixed or replaced in her apartment.

"Yes, yes. Listen, Travis." She walked from the open kitchen to a writing desk in the attached living room area. There was a stack of photo albums and file folders sitting to the side. She picked up the folder on top. "I found these albums and papers in the bottom of a box that I thought was mostly junk. I've been reading through the bylaws from Pelion's founding in 1724. I think there are a couple ways you might challenge Archer's right to the—"

"Okay, then," I said dismissively, picking up my toolbox and walking around her toward the front door.

"Wait!"

I stopped, turning toward her. "Give it a *rest,* Victoria. God, please, for once in your life, just give it a rest."

She flinched slightly at my use of her given name. "I'm only looking out for you," she said weakly. "What happened wasn't *fair* and—"

"It *was* fair, Mom. And more than that, Archer's *good* at running the town. Pelion is thriving. The citizens are happy. I wouldn't take it away from him—or from them—even if there was a foolproof way to do it."

She waved the folder around, looking confused and flustered. "You can't be happy living on a *public servant's* salary alone, Travis, deprived of the things we used to have, privileges that I believe are *rightfully* yours."

I was suddenly weary. She did that. She made me feel tired to my marrow. She obviously saw that I had no intention of answering her questions and so she thrust the folder at me. "Here. Along with the bylaws regarding town ownership and legal paraphernalia I just discovered, there are all *kinds* of things in here that belonged to your father . . . certificates, awards he won. As far as the legal documents, they're all original. Just look it all over. When you see what I've highlighted, I think you'll understand the line of my thought. See if you agree."

All kinds of things in here that belonged to your father.

I took the photo albums and the file folder of my father's papers when she held them out to me, unable to resist that which my father had once touched. Something, anything, that I might have a right to even as second best. His handwriting . . . I couldn't even remember what his handwriting looked like. A scrawled note. A photograph I'd never seen. Something. I held it tightly to me as though a part of him might live inside these dusty pages. "Goodbye, Mom," I said, walking out and closing the door behind me. *And for God's sake, drop this,* I wanted to say, but I had a well-earned feeling that it wouldn't make a difference what I said. Tori Hale still felt wronged. It wasn't about me at all. *It never had been.*

CHAPTER NINETEEN

Travis

The air was still and muggy, not a whisper of breeze off the lake. I rolled the cold beer bottle across my forehead, sighing at the momentary relief. The porch swing creaked under my weight as I used one foot to move it idly, taking a sip of the cheap beer, the only kind Betty offered. It was still welcomed, as was the peace of this front porch, away from the hooch-drunk revelers joined together for social hour. It sounded like they were involved in a rowdy game of charades, although that couldn't be right, because they'd never leave Burt out and blind men wouldn't be a team asset when it came to charades. Whatever it was, there were lots of distant hoots and hollers.

I used my toe to give myself another small push. A fish jumped in the water beyond, its small splash leaving ripples on the deep blue surface of the water.

"Lonely, mister?"

My lips tipped and I turned my head slightly. I didn't need to see her to know who it was. She pushed the screen door open, stepping forward into the dim light of the covered porch. She leaned a hip on one of the columns near the steps and turned my way. "And you look like you're thinking very hard about something," she noted.

I gave a half-hearted smile. "I went to see my mother today. She inspires reflection." I held up my beer. "And alcohol."

"Hmm," she hummed, studying me. After a moment, she looked away, seeming to be wrestling with something. "I . . . uh"—she picked at a splinter on the wooden railing—"I looked up the town today . . . read more about the Hale family history." She paused, finally meeting my gaze. "I hope you don't consider it a breach of privacy."

I looked back out to the lake. "No. It's all public knowledge."

"I overheard a couple of girls mentioning your family at the club today and it . . . it . . . well, I should have asked you . . . I just . . . I wasn't sure, you know, if you would want to talk about your family with—"

"My friend?"

She let out a breathy laugh. "Yes." Her fingers found that splinter again. "Yes, your . . . temporary friend. Well, or anyone." *Temporary friend,* repeated in my head. *With benefits,*

200

went unsaid. Then again, I wasn't sure if she'd allow anything physical to happen between us again. At the thought of never kissing her, never touching her body, something opened inside me. Something empty and hollow.

She'd overheard a couple of girls gossiping about the Hales at the club today. It was very possible the conversation was less than positive. My family garnered mixed reviews when it came to the citizens of Calliope. But whatever she'd heard hadn't caused her to judge me harshly. Because she was kind.

I watched her for a minute. By the way she was fidgeting, I could tell she felt awkward and off balance. We were straddling so many lines, and I had the sense that Haven needed to keep me firmly placed in the box she'd designated. I also had the sense that there were deeper reasons for that than just because she was only passing through town and didn't want to make connections that would be difficult to sever when she left.

Call it intuition. Call it being a cop whose job it was to be suspicious of people.

Call it that my mind moved in her direction more often than I gave it permission to but, it'd been slowly attempting to form the full picture that was Haven Torres with the small puzzle pieces she'd been throwing my way.

I knew so little about her life. Just the few details she'd dispensed, seemingly randomly. She'd grown up poor. She'd been rescued, in some sense anyway, by a kindly couple who owned a rooftop garden. She'd worked at a grocery store so she could bring home healthy food. She had a reckless brother who I could only assume had grown up just like she had, only perhaps without the benefit of a rooftop garden to tend. Or the emotional benefits that that garden had obviously provided to Haven. Responsibility. The gift of trust.

And now she knew a few things about me. I didn't know what the gossips had said, but I did know that what was online barely scratched the surface and definitely wouldn't have given her the full picture.

"You're a hero," she said softly. "You took down a gunman who might have killed so many others."

Case in point.

I *had* done that. But oh, I'd done plenty more too.

I was quiet for a good minute. Haven waited, not saying a word.

"I used to swim way over there," I said, pointing across the lake, squinting one eye slightly as I tried to see the small public beach on the edge of what had been my uncle Nathan's land, and now belonged to Archer. It had been public as far as ownership, but not very many people had known about it and so for all intents and purposes, it had been a private area my friends and I had all to ourselves. "Archer lives on the edge of that beach," I explained, "and he has most of his life, at least since the time of . . . the accident. When he lost his voice. I used to make noise so he would hear me and my friends, and then I'd mock him when he came to watch us from the trees."

I felt Haven's gaze on me but didn't raise my eyes to look at her.

202

"Why?" she asked softly, and I heard the quiet edge of surprised disapproval in her voice.

"Because I was jealous. I wanted him to hurt the way I did." I paused again. Why was I telling her this? I never talked about this. Ever. "The day our dad died, he was leaving town with Archer and Archer's mother to live a new life, away from here." *Away from me.* "I wanted Archer to hurt," I went on, "because no matter what he'd lost, he'd had our dad's love—at the very end, our dad had chosen him over me. It was all I'd ever wanted and there was no way to get it back because he was gone."

It was right, I supposed, that I was the one sitting here feeling sort of sad and lost, and he was the one snug in his cozy house across the lake, the love of family surrounding him, all his dreams had come true.

Cosmic justice and all that. It was no surprise that Karma hadn't smiled down upon me.

Haven was staring out at the lake, the expression on her face sort of sad and sort of thoughtful, but when she turned my way, I saw empathy there too. "I understand that, Travis," she told me, letting out a soft sigh. "More than you might know." She paused for a second, her head tilted in consideration. "Maybe the terrible truth about love is that when it's gone, it leaves a hole in your heart so big it feels like nothing will ever fill it. The idea of risking again feels fatal. A human being can't possibly lose that much of themselves and still survive. And so you try desperately to fill it with things that never quite do the job. Things that sometimes hurt other people," she finished softly.

Her words made my heart twist. And I wondered if she was speaking generally . . . or personally. Or maybe a little of both. "You've been hurt," I said. She'd told me a little, but her words made me think there was much more.

But she smiled and waved her hand as if dismissing the gravity she'd obviously heard in my tone. "Of course. Life hurts us all in ways big and small. But as for you, Travis, Archer and Bree have obviously invited you into their lives for a reason. You apologized and your brother forgave you. And however you downplay it, you *were* a hero that day. Take pride in that."

I let out a chuckle devoid of humor. "You think too much of me. You don't know all the details. If you did know . . ." *If you did know, you wouldn't be sitting out here on this porch with me, speaking softly and kindly because you sensed I could use a friend.* I suddenly realized that I *wanted* this woman to *know* me. But with the realization came fear, because if she *truly* knew me, if she knew all the things I'd said and done, not as a child, not as a teenager, but as an *adult* who should have known and done better, she'd turn away in disgust. And why shouldn't she?

"We've all made mistakes, Travis," she said. "We get to reinvent ourselves. And if the new version is even better, it means we've learned and we've grown."

"That easy?"

"No." She laughed softly. "No, not easy. But . . . but I think it might be worth it."

I eyed her. "You sound like you know a thing or two about reinventing yourself."

"I know about trying. And failing. And trying again. That's mostly what this road trip is about. Reinventing myself. Starting fresh." She looked troubled, as if she doubted the probability of that happening.

A bird dove down over the water, and swooped upward just as quickly, wings flapping softly in the still nighttime air, a spray of water arcing behind it. The bird's talons were empty. Whatever he'd spotted under the smooth surface of the water had managed to get away.

"How do you know what to change, and what to hold on to?" I asked. Were there parts of me that were good and valuable, or did I scrap it all and start completely from scratch? And if that was the case, how in the hell did one go about doing that? Especially in a small town where stories became legend, and every buried secret eventually rose to the surface?

If I wanted a *fresh start*, I'd likely have to change my name and move to Siberia.

Maybe Haven had come to a similar conclusion. Only instead of settling in a deserted arctic tundra, she'd chosen to settle nowhere . . . and everywhere.

There are one of two paths for you. Either lose it all. Or lose it all.

Haven smiled at me. "Well, that's a deep question and I don't know if I've quite figured that out yet. I guess the answer is different for each of us. Maybe it's an ongoing process, you know?"

"Yeah," I said. "I know." When it came to learning and growing in an emotional sense, I'd seldom been quick on the uptake.

We were both quiet for a moment but it was a comfortable silence, broken only by the soft splashes of the wildlife in the lake, the buzz of insects, and the muffled shout of laughter that found us from the other side of the house.

"Can I ask you a question?" Haven asked.

Will I kiss you again? Will I take you upstairs to my bed and put my mouth on every inch of your skin? My body stirred, despite the slightly melancholy nature of our conversation and the mood I'd been in since I'd made the drive home from my mother's. *Will I arrest Gage and lock him up for life? Throw away the key?*

"Sure."

She tilted her head. "Why do you drive all the way over from the other side of the lake to work out at that snotty club?"

"That snotty club? The one that hired you?"

She gave a half-hearted eye roll. "I'm temporary help." She paused. "It just seems like it's a long way to go when you live—usually anyway—and work in Pelion. Don't they have clubs or gyms there?"

I shrugged. "Yeah, but the club in Calliope is the best."

But that felt off. It felt like I was lying . . . to her . . . to myself. Especially after I'd just thought about how my family name was often said in contemptuous tones by Calliope residents. So why *did* I make the thirty-minute drive to the exclusive club when I could have worked out in Pelion? Why did I frequent the restaurants on the other side of the lake? Was it because—as I'd told myself—I wanted something of my *own?* Something that didn't have Archer Hale's fingerprints all over it? Even if I wasn't a hundred percent welcomed or embraced?

Or was it something I hadn't acknowledged?

Talk about straddling lines. Maybe it came easy to me as far as Haven was concerned, because I had plenty of practice.

Perhaps I'd grown used to straddling the line between the old life I'd lived when my mother owned Pelion and I was set to inherit it all—when I'd felt *important* and when Victoria Hale was the toast of the town—and my new life as a small-town chief of police who would never live the high life, at least not on the level I once had.

Certainly not on Gage Buchanan's level.

But was there really anything wrong with still enjoying a few holdovers from the life I'd grown up with? The life that separated me from my brother? The one that was my own? Mine and no one else's? Should I apologize for that?

"Just preference," I answered her. *Or habit?* I scratched the back of my neck. *Jesus.* Maybe I had no idea who I really was. Still. Even after all this time.

She bit at her lip momentarily as if unconvinced by my answer. Why shouldn't she be? Hell, I was unconvinced of it myself. "Any interest in running for political office?"

"Political office? Where did that come from?" I gave her an amused half-smile.

She shrugged but looked away. "Being chief of police is a government position. I just wondered if maybe you'd thought of running for other offices."

I shook my head. "No. I enjoy law enforcement, but I have no desire to go into politics."

She was silent for a moment, watching me. "Hmm," she finally answered. "Then . . . what sort of life do you want, Travis? Where do you see yourself, say, in five years?"

Confusion overcame me. *What sort of life do you want? Where do you see yourself?* What she was really asking me was what were my dreams. No one had ever asked me that question. No one since my father. I'd told him I wanted to be a policeman like him, and I'd seen the light of pride in his eyes. I'd tried so hard to let him go because he'd let *me* go. But I'd held on to that look. I'd carried it with me, and I'd become the chief of police. I'd bought the land that was my father's. I planned to settle there. If I had really let my father go like I'd convinced myself, why was I walking in his footsteps?

What sort of life do you want? My mother had certainly never asked me that question. And none of the women I'd dated—including Phoebe—had wondered. Hell, I'd never asked it of myself. I'd thought about marriage, kids. But after Phoebe's betrayal, that particular idea had been lost. And yet I didn't mourn it. At least . . . not with her. "I guess I *have* everything I want," I said. "This is it. This is the dream."

She studied me for several beats. "You don't sound very sure of that."

I chuckled. "What about you? What sort of life do *you* want?"

Haven fidgeted again, staring in the direction of the lake. "One that's peaceful. Stable. We moved a lot as a kid. Usually in the middle of the night." She let out a small laugh that held a hint of pain and little humor.

Ouch. I took the blow of that one too, watching her for a second. She'd lived a life filled with inconsistency and hunger of at least a few varieties. She'd mentioned several times what a dream our town was. How peaceful. *How stable*, went unsaid. And I'd seen the longing in her eyes for what she didn't have, and maybe never did. "Life on the road doesn't seem very stable," I said as gently as possible.

"No. I guess not."

"What will bring you peace?" I wondered. "Where do you see this journey ending?"

She smiled softly. "At a garden somewhere. I see planter boxes filled with plants. That's as far as I've gotten. But it feels like a decent start."

Do you think that garden might be here in Pelion? I wanted to ask. But I didn't. She'd made it clear she was leaving, and I didn't want to hear her say no.

Something crashed inside to a chorus of laughter and Haven gave a small eye roll, breathing out a laugh. "The hooch is flowing tonight," she said.

"Heavily."

Our gazes held for a moment before Haven stood. "I should get to bed," she said. "It's been a long, eye-roll-filled day. Junie Wellington had a 'wardrobe malfunction' at the pool."

"Again?"

209

Haven let out a short laugh. "Again."

"How many guys got trampled this time?"

"At least four."

I chuckled. *Don't go.* "You probably need some rest then."

I know we said no complications. But . . . that felt sort of complicated.

"Yes, I . . . do."

Don't go. "Goodnight then."

Ask me up to your room. I waited, but she only nodded. "Goodnight."

She passed by me and I resisted reaching for her, stood, and turned just as she disappeared through the door.

****

I stared, mostly unseeing, at the blur of the whirring fan overhead, my mind spinning along with the blades.

I wanted her.

Why had I let her go? Why hadn't I made a move?

I'd felt *shy* for Christ's sake.

Scared.

Doubtful.

Because when it came to Haven, I was always the one making the moves and it made me feel vulnerable and uncertain.

She's right down the hall. Only a handful of steps away.

And she made it clear the "with benefits" part of our friendship was overly complicated.

I'd never gone to a woman in my life. I'd always waited for them to come to me, and I was never left waiting long.

Not with Haven though.

If I wanted Haven, I'd have to go to her.

And face rejection.

Kisses ... even orgasms in a lake in the dark of night, might be one thing. But what I wanted was much more than that. I wanted her in my bed. I wanted her naked. I wanted to perform a slow exploration of every dip and swell of her body and then I wanted to—

I groaned in frustration, forcing away the sensual pictures forming in my mind, and turned onto my side.

I could still taste her. I could still feel the silky texture of her skin beneath my fingertips, recall in vivid detail the way she'd shivered in my arms as she came.

And it wasn't enough.

God, the way she made me *feel*. It was ... I didn't even know what it was, because it wasn't only physical. I liked to *talk* to her. I liked to hear her thoughts and listen to her stories. I wanted more of her kindness, her insight, and the understanding she held in her gaze.

Oh God, what was happening to me?

I rolled onto my back, bringing the pillow over my face and then, as a thought came to me, I removed the pillow, my eyes opening and hope descending.

I'd helped Haven gain Gage's attention by increasing the challenge. Maybe, on some level I hadn't even acknowledged, *I* was responding to that challenge too.

I frowned. That didn't feel quite right. Still . . . this didn't *have* to be complicated. I was *good* at simple. Hell, before I'd decided that maybe it was time to start thinking about settling down, simple had practically been my middle name.

I was making far too much of this. So, I liked her. I liked things about her I hadn't liked about other women before. *Different. Seemingly deeper.*

Which spoke to the fact that we really were friends.

Plus, she was only here temporarily. And suddenly that felt like a relief.

I was swearing off relationships for the time being, but did I have to swear off women? Did I have to swear off *simple?*

Forget that she had feelings for Gage. A mist of red clouded my gaze momentarily and I wondered vaguely if anyone would notice one more "barn cat" grave dotting the property of The Yellow Trellis Inn.

Then again . . . did she really have feelings for Gage Buchanan? She didn't even know him. My muscles unclenched. At least *we* were friends. My lips curved into a slow smile that dropped quickly.

I lay there for a few more minutes, wallowing in the confusion, the self-consciousness of being on unsteady ground. I'd never known what vulnerability felt like—not when it came to a woman. And I'd never willingly gone toward vulnerability of any kind. In fact, I'd gone to great lengths to avoid it. So why was I even considering walking toward it now?

Because I was grasping for certainty. And the *only* thing I felt sure of at the moment was that I wanted her. More than I'd ever wanted anyone in my life.

And that's what propelled me to my feet and out the door of my room.

Down the hall, Haven came out of her room. I halted, our eyes meeting, flaring. But then I saw the relief in her expression.

My heart leapt. I walked toward her, her lips parting as she stayed rooted to the spot, her hand still wrapped around her doorknob as though it was the only thing holding her up.

So many emotions warred in her expression, and we simply stared at each other for a few moments, neither seeming to know what to say.

"Slightly complicated isn't . . . isn't as bad as it sounds," she finally said. "We're making too much of this."

Funny, I'd convinced myself of something along similar lines just a few moments before and yet, hearing it from her *scraped* something inside, the words like sandpaper.

Never mind that . . . I wanted her with a desperation I wasn't sure what to do with and so I nodded, accepting what I'd been offered. "No strings," I said. "No promises."

She visibly relaxed, shoulders dropping. "That's my motto," she whispered, and then she took my hand and led me into her room.

CHAPTER TWENTY

Haven

There was no need for preamble. We both knew why he was here in my room. I'd talked myself out of it over and over, until my desire for him was pitched so sky high, my feet had seemingly taken it upon themselves to put the rest of my body out of its misery.

And then to know that he'd been on his way to me, was like the sweetest relief I'd ever known.

I wasn't going to look too hard at this. I was leaving town soon enough, and he was far from available anyway.

Don't think.

Don't think.

Just be here.

With Travis. With this beautiful, layered man who isn't really your friend, but also can never be more.

He moved in, his fingers weaving through my hair as he took my face in his hands and brought his lips to mine. I reached around his neck and drew him closer and we kissed and tasted each other's mouths for long, drugging minutes.

When our mouths broke, chests heaving, his gaze was shiny with lust and so much focus it made my pulse jump. Wordlessly, he reached down, lifting the hem of my long T-shirt and I raised my arms, watching his face as he lifted it over my head and dropped it to the floor.

His heated gaze raked my bare breasts and my nipples puckered in response. I felt unexpectedly shy, though he'd already seen me wearing nothing but a small pair of bikini bottoms. And he'd touched me in ways that were even more intimate than this exact moment. And yet, the way he was *looking* at me was stirring my senses, and making blood whoosh hotly in my ears.

He was staring at me as though he wanted to consume me.

I shivered. "Please," I said, surprising myself. I didn't even know what I was asking for.

His expression didn't change though. Nor did he look at me. Instead, he lowered his head and brought his mouth to one nipple, sucking lightly, knowing exactly what I needed though I had not used the words.

Oh *God.*

I moaned, a flush of pleasure blooming between my legs as his tongue circled my nipples slowly, erotically. I weaved my fingers through his soft, thick hair, holding his dark head to one breast, and then the other as he drove me wild.

"*Travis,*" I gasped. My body was already primed. My mind had done that as I'd lain in bed, picturing just this.

He stood straight, removing his T-shirt and then the jeans he was wearing. My eyes drank him in. That beautifully muscled chest I'd admired over the weeks. It looked different now somehow.

Because you're going to touch it. You're going to feel it against your bare skin. For now, here in this room, it belongs to you.

Something I could only describe as joy radiated in my chest and I shivered with the cascade of sensation, both external and within, reaching out and circling one finger around the small masculine disc that was his nipple. It tightened beneath my touch and he took in a small, sharp breath.

He was so large and tall and solid and I wanted to touch him everywhere. My hands moved over his shoulders and down his arms, loving the juxtaposition of his hard muscles beneath warm, velvety skin.

There were textures to discover everywhere on his body and I felt greedy to learn them all, to memorize them so they'd always be mine.

My gaze lowered, as did my hand, reaching for his erection, stiff and silken, a tiny drop of moisture leaking from the tip. I wrapped my hand around it and stroked lightly, rewarded by Travis's ragged moan.

"God, I want you," he said, his voice thick. "If I told you how much, you would laugh."

A burst of warmth infused me. "I'm not laughing," I said. "I want you too."

He walked me backward the few steps to my bed and lowered me slowly, coming over the top of me. He leaned up, taking a rogue curl between his thumb and index finger, feeling its texture. His lips tipped. "This hair," he muttered. "This damn hair."

I'd always felt self-conscious about my hair. I'd always tried to *control* it but rarely managed the impossible task. As a little girl, I'd wished on stars to make it straight and fine like the Barbie dolls my mom sometimes let me pick out of the toy bin at the thrift store.

But the way Travis Hale was looking at it in that moment made me whisper a prayer of deep gratitude that those stars had ignored my plea.

He leaned in and kissed me again, his long, hard body covering my own, his chest rubbing against mine, his erection probing my lower stomach. I moved my hips so that I cradled his, wrapping one leg around his thigh and moving it slowly upward in an effort to bring our cores together.

He raised himself by planting one knee on the bed, taking himself in his hand and sliding his erection up my damp slit, once and then again. Our mouths broke, his breath ragged as he touched his forehead to mine, teasing himself and me with long slow glides that were wondrous and blissful and torturous and not nearly enough.

Pleasure took over and things turned dreamy, my brain shutting off completely. I surrendered to the sensation, feeling him everywhere, our kisses going from almost savage

217

in their intensity to slow and deep and languorous. I writhed beneath him, wanting more, more, more, and he broke from my mouth, his breath coming harsh. He said my name as his head dipped lower, stopping at each nipple and sucking gently before moving down, his lips grazing across my ribs and over my belly. "Open for me, Haven," he said and I did, my legs widening as he flicked his tongue over my swollen clit. I cried out, bucking slightly and he did it again, opening my thighs wider and holding them gently to give himself more access. "God, you taste sweet."

I said something unintelligible as he lowered his head, circling his tongue and sucking, and then doing it again and again. Oh God, it was wonderful. I whimpered, weaving my fingers through his hair once again, lifting my hips to his hot, talented mouth.

I felt the moan that vibrated in his throat and the orgasm broke over me, even more intense than the one he'd given me with his fingers, bliss crashing in waves as I bucked and gasped, his name tearing from my lips.

He picked up something from the floor. A wallet? A condom. The fog cleared, but only slightly. I thought I heard him mutter, "Thank God," as he pulled it on, coming over my body again. He made eye contact and there was a question there, his muscles held taught, waiting.

"*Yes*," I said, sliding my foot up his leg, welcoming him in.

A long breath flew from his mouth and the look of relief that filled his expression made my heart clench sharply. He lined his cock up at my entrance and pushed inside, guided by the slickness of my very recent climax, and I gasped out at the delicious invasion, my head falling back, fist grabbing a handful of the quilt beneath us.

"God, you feel . . . you feel . . . it's even better . . ." He didn't seem able to form a coherent sentence, giving up and ending on a long, ragged breath.

He wrapped his hand around my thigh, pulling my leg higher and sliding in slowly. I felt every inch of him as he withdrew and then filled me again, his muscles straining, the bed creaking softly beneath our movements.

"Haven . . . Haven . . . *God*."

He moved slowly, biting his lip and a thrill of pleasure raced through me at the erotic beauty of him moving above me, inside me. The pace accelerated and I watched him, seeing the very moment he gave up the fight for control. I clutched him, wanting to continue watching his face, but feeling another wave of pleasure begin to crest, my muscles tightening until I cried out, bringing both legs around his hips and tilting my pelvis so that he went even deeper, prolonging my orgasm even as his broke and he moaned my name, burying his face in my neck as his hips slowed. Our pants mingled as he pressed inside me one final time.

For a few breathless moments, all was still and then Travis rolled to the side, pulling me toward him as our breathing slowed and our heart rates returned to normal.

I ran a finger idly under his pectoral, spreading my palm over the small patch of scattered hairs in the dip above his stomach.

The curtain lifted from the breeze blowing off the lake, the night outside soft and dreamy with moonlight.

And the world felt somehow both very distant and more beautiful than it'd ever been.

He brought his hand up and placed it over mine, halting my exploration on the small breath of a laugh. "Unless you're ready for round two, you should probably stop that." The twitching between his legs proved his words.

I grinned, twisting, and crossing my arms on his chest, propping my chin on my hands so I could look in his eyes. "Sounds like a challenge."

He chuckled. "And one I'd gladly take on, except I don't have any more condoms."

Well, darn.

"We weren't exactly quiet," I said, my cheeks flushing as I recalled how many times I'd moaned his name and shouted for God, and likely all His heavenly angels, though some of our recent activity was still a blissful blur.

"Do you think we scandalized the crew?" he asked, one finger twisting in a curl. I moved my eyes to the side, watching it for a moment.

"I don't know," I said. "They're a pretty accepting group."

"They'd have to be, I guess."

I breathed out a laugh. "Yes. But do you know what I notice most about them?"

"That they're usually drunk?"

I laughed again as that finger continued to twist idly. "No. I notice that they all know exactly who they are and they make no apologies for it. We should strive to be like them."

His eyes met mine, and he seemed to search my face for a moment, something warm and soft coming into his expression. "You're right." He looked away, back to that twisting finger now completely ensnared in my curl. "*Everyone* should strive to be like them," he murmured softly, but I got the sense he was speaking for himself more so than "everyone."

I watched him for a moment, my eyes moving slowly over the perfection of his features. He was so classically handsome, those vibrant eyes unusual and mesmerizing. I wondered momentarily if he looked like his mother or his father, and realized it had to be his father since he resembled his half-brother—the one he shared fathers with—so much.

The Hale boys were always wild. Hot as sin, and guaranteed to burn you if you got too close.

Yes, I could see that. Oh how I could see that.

Deep breath. Temporary. Friends.

But the benefits were . . . spectacular. I was still seeing stars and my muscles felt as though they'd morphed into jelly.

"Be careful," I said, my eyes sliding toward his finger, now hopelessly tangled in my lock of hair. "It's like one of those Chinese finger traps. The more you struggle, the tighter it gets."

He laughed. "Then I guess I'm trapped for good."

And then he rolled me over, his hand moving with my head so he didn't pull my hair. I laughed, a surprised outburst, right before his lips came down on mine. Right before he proved he was up for a challenge, and there were lots of things you could do without the benefit of a condom.

CHAPTER TWENTY-ONE

Travis

The morning was bright and already warm at eight in the morning, dappled sunlight falling over the porch. The screen door swung shut behind me, as my gaze moved around the railing where several of Haven's plants sat in pots, their leaves green and lush under her patient care. I smiled. Others would have given up on them. They'd once been barely living, but now, they thrived. I moved toward the swing, ready to sit and wait for Haven, who was still showering, when I spotted a lone figure walking along the dock.

Burt.

I frowned, descending the steps and walking toward the lake. "A blind man walking alone on a dock?" I said, when I'd made it there. "That seems highly inadvisable."

Burt turned toward my voice. "Good morning, Chief Hale."

I approached him, careful not to make the dock sway under my movement. "Morning."

"And a beautiful one it is," he said.

God, is it. I swore I was walking on air after a night with Haven that I could only describe as mind blowing. "Yes, sir," I agreed.

"What are you up to this fine day?" he asked.

"I'm taking Haven to an antique fair a few towns over. She's upstairs getting ready."

"Ah. Show me to the edge. Let's sit while you wait for her."

I led him toward the edge of the dock and helped him navigate where to sit, lowering myself next to him, both of our legs hanging off the side. He sighed, taking in a big breath of air, smiling again.

"You seem happy this morning," I said. Though in truth, Burt had radiated happiness since I'd met him. I was glad to have arrived at this part of his story. I was glad for him, that he'd arrived here too.

"I found that bird," he said. "The one who sang just for me."

Surprised, I turned my head toward him.

"It's called a prairie warbler and he sang for me again." His smile grew. "Turns out, he was right outside Betty's window." If a black man could blush, he did just that, though his smile didn't dwindle. In fact, it was so wide, I wondered if his face might split.

"You old charmer," I said, only mildly surprised. I'd noticed their friendship . . . watched them gravitate toward each other no matter where we all were.

He leaned in conspiratorially. "Tell me, is she beautiful? She feels beautiful."

I thought about Betty, about her warm smile and her welcoming heart, about how she flitted around the B&B like a bird herself, attending to everyone, making sure each one of us felt important. "She is," I said. "Honestly, Burt? It's a good thing you're blind because otherwise, you'd never have worked up the nerve to make a move."

Impossibly, his smile widened. "I had the same thought. Damn lucky I went blind; my old self would have fallen over in shock to hear this version of myself say it." He laughed. "Life sure can change quickly and in unexpected ways. Don't you agree, Chief?"

"I do, Burt."

For a few moments we sat in companionable silence, me staring out at the water, Burt staring inward at whatever sights were there.

"Betty used to be a writer," he said.

"Did she? I didn't know."

"It was a long time ago. Stories are her passion." His expression grew solemn and I cocked my head, curious about where this was going and why he'd brought it up. "But she had an accident and suffered a head injury that causes her to

225

lose words." He paused for a moment. "You've probably noticed it happen. It distresses her. Writing became frustrating and upsetting and so she gave it up, turned her family home into a B&B to support herself . . ." He trailed off, the weight of Betty's pain obviously a burden he now carried too.

And I suddenly realized something. "She narrates for you," I said, thinking of all the times I'd watched Betty describe something that was going on so that Burt might picture it, watched the focus and the wonder on his face as he obviously did just that.

"She does." He smiled. "And she does it so beautifully, and with such detail, it's almost like, for those moments, my sight has been returned."

Wow. A fish jumped and the water rippled out around the spot where it'd returned to the water.

"As for me," he went on, "I spent my life as a fisherman. There's no place on a fishing boat for a man with no sight. It was part of the reason I felt my life was over when I went blind."

"I'm sorry, Burt." He'd lost everything that meant anything to him. That's how it must have felt.

"Being a fisherman provides some amount of down time, often quite a bit depending on the weather and other factors. I filled that time with crosswords. I got pretty damn good at them too, moving from one level to the next. I even entered and won a few contests. *Words.* They're all about words. Name six different words that mean congenial."

226

I chuckled. "I don't think I can. Not off the top of my head."

"Affable, convivial, cordial, jovial, pleasant, sociable. If you know enough words, you can solve any puzzle out there."

And it dawned on me.

Betty had lost her words, and Burt had spent years collecting them.

I'd watched her become upset when the one she'd meant to use suddenly became unavailable to her, tapping her head in distress, trying to bring back what had once been hers. *Batty Betty.* No wonder Burt always seemed to provide just the one she wanted. He knew so many words. Right off the top of his head.

And Betty, his storyteller, drew such vibrant pictures in his mind, that in essence, she'd given him back his sight.

I swallowed down a sudden lump.

"It's meant to work that way, isn't it?" Burt asked. "All the things that have brought us pain, carve a distinct hole in our heart, and there's someone else out there with the perfect something that will fill the void. And in turn, we get to do the same for them. And suddenly, it all makes sense. It all *fits.* Because we haven't been *forsaken.* We've been *prepared.*"

Haven's words from the night before came back to me. *Maybe the terrible truth about love is that when it's gone, it leaves a hole in your heart so big it feels like nothing will ever fill it.*

Something expanded inside me, something nameless that made my ribs ache. I moved my eyes and my mind back to the man sitting next to me. "Burt . . . that head injury Betty

227

suffered . . . did it have anything to do with her deceased husband?"

Burt paused. "Well now . . . perhaps. But that part of the story is Betty's to tell."

I nodded, his meaning clear, a sharp pang joining the internal ache. *Batty Betty.* The screen door opening on a squeak broke the moment and a breath whooshed from me, relieving some of the building pressure. I turned, looking behind me to where I could see Haven exiting the house.

"That'd be your cue," Burt said, smiling and bumping his shoulder to mine.

I cleared my throat. "Yes, it is." The dock swayed slightly as I pulled myself to my feet and tapped his shoulder so he knew I was offering a hand.

But he shook his head. "I'm going to sit out here a while longer. I promise not to fall in."

I hesitated. "You sure?"

"Very much so." He nodded in Haven's direction. "Go on now and enjoy this beautiful day with that lovely girl."

****

We drove to the antique fair with the windows down and the radio on, talking about the area, and laughing and fighting over which songs should be turned off immediately, and which ones were classics.

She had terrible taste in music.

But I was willing to look past that, considering she had the smile of an angel and the hair of a goddess. And other

228

things I didn't want to think too intently about at that moment and make it tempting to pull my truck over and do lewd things to her on the side of the road.

"I can't believe you talked me into going to an antique fair," I muttered.

She laughed. "*Me?* You forced me to go! You said we might as well make our lie the truth. That someone who knows Gage might be there and mention it to him. What in the world am I going to do with an antique *anything?*"

Hearing Gage's name caused my mood to sour momentarily, but she was right. I'd used that lame argument, half-jokingly, to convince her to spend the day with me.

She'd seemed to need a justification, even after we'd spent the night together. Naked. Very, very naked. And entwined. I'd never had to convince a woman to spend time with me after sex before. If anything, I'd had to devise ways to shake them loose.

I probably deserved this. To know what it felt like to beg.

It sucked. And now I understood just how much.

The antique fair was already packed with cars, and after finding a spot, we made our way to the gate, entering with the others filing into the large, open area packed with side-by-side booths, and hundreds of rows to wander down.

"Wow," Haven said, her head swiveling. "This place is huge. Have you been here before?"

"A few times when I was younger, with my mom." Whatever she'd heard in my voice made her eyes linger on me for a moment before she looked away, back to the miles of vendors, people chatting and laughing as they moved from booth to booth.

We began strolling, stopping here and there, Haven leaning closely toward this or that, moving past one thing and lingering at another. I stood back, fascinated as I watched her, realizing that it was possible to get to know someone better just by watching the things they were drawn to at an antique fair.

My mother had always headed straight for the Tiffany lamp or the Chippendale desk. Phoebe had never expressed any interest in antique fairs at all, preferring more modern décor over anything used. Preferring to *spend* money rather than save it.

Haven apparently, liked old photos.

I trailed behind her, observing her move from one table of photos to another, bypassing the knickknacks, the furniture, and even the jewelry.

"There are whole lives here," she murmured, leaning forward. "Just left behind." She turned to me suddenly. "Can you imagine that no one at all is left to care for"—she turned, picking up a photo of young girl—"her?"

"Care for?" I asked. It was a photograph.

She shrugged, turning away and putting the picture down. "Appreciate. Remember. Tell stories about."

She turned back toward me as quickly as she'd turned away, holding up a different photo. "I'm going to buy this," she declared. "What do you think?"

My gaze moved to the picture in her hand, an old black and white of an ancient-looking woman with dark hair and pale eyes. "I think it's the thing horror movies are made of."

She laughed. It was sweet. *She* was sweet. Her laugh dwindled. "And no one wants her," she said softly.

"Because she might snatch their soul in the middle of the night."

She laughed again. "Stop." She held the photo up again, her eyes softening as she gazed at the old woman. "Left behind," she murmured.

"Until now."

"Until now," she confirmed.

I raised my chin at the booth's vendor who came over and accepted my dollar bill for the singular photo.

"Thank you," Haven breathed, bringing the photo to her chest, grinning up at me, and officially making that dollar the best dollar I'd ever spent in my entire life, even surpassing the one I'd spent on Blueberry the dog.

We started strolling again, down the row of booths. "I'm going to put her up on my dresser and ask her advice," she said, tilting her head as she studied the old woman.

"This gets creepier by the minute," I said.

She laughed. "She'd give great advice though, don't you think?"

"What would she tell you? About me, for instance?"

Haven glanced at me, her expression thoughtful. I realized I was holding my breath and let it out in a slow, quiet exhale. "She says you're much more than adequate," she said softly, her cheeks flushing lightly.

"I'll take it," I said, giving one nod to the picture. "Thank you, Grandma." My brows rose in unison. "You do realize, you have me talking to plants and pictures of make-believe grandmas."

"Promise me you'll always do it, even when I'm gone. It will be my legacy."

Even when I'm gone. Even when I'm gone. It echoed. I didn't like it.

She walked over to a table of odds and ends, perusing them with some amount of disinterest. This booth didn't offer old photos.

I watched her again, thinking about the night of the Buchanans' fundraiser. I'd hemmed and hawed about getting her flowers for our "date," ultimately deciding that cut flowers would wound her somehow. The thought had felt melodramatic at the time, but in that moment, I realized it was not. I'd been *right* to read her that way. Roots were very, very important to Haven Torres, coveted even. Because she didn't have any of her own, and whether she realized it or not, she longed for them.

No wonder she loved planting things so much.

Needed it maybe.

Do you fear you'll be nothing but a forgotten photo someday that everyone left behind? My chest ached, a need rising up to dispel that fear, to *take* it from her even if it meant suffering myself.

The noise faded, blood whooshing in my ears. She said something to the vendor and he laughed, pointing at various objects.

The world tilted and I reached my hand out blindly, grasping at nothing.

Time slowed, everything fading except for her. She turned her head very slightly and in my mind's eye a dock that overlooked the water appeared beneath her feet, a house with a porch shining in the sunlight, rising above the trees behind her. I swallowed. It was so *clear.*

The vision crashed over me like a dizzying wave. It was *my* dock, *my* house, the picture I'd tried so hard to insert Phoebe into and come up short.

But the image of Haven standing in the spot that was mine, the blue ripples of Pelion Lake fanning out around her was luminous and blindingly bright. I couldn't blink it away. And it was wonderful and it was awful, because she didn't want that with me.

We were friends. *With benefits,* but still just friends.

She was leaving, just passing through town.

And somehow, none of those things dimmed the picture in my mind.

I wanted to laugh and fall to my knees. It was hilarious. And completely tragic.

She turned toward me, flashing her dazzling smile, those wild curls bouncing around her face. My heart squeezed and then dipped, then soared, and seemed to bounce off the inside walls of my chest. My brain felt funny too, both cloudy and clanging. Maybe I didn't picture a future with Haven so much as I was suffering from a cerebral hemorrhage. Perhaps apoplexy was imminent.

I waited to keel over.

No such luck.

She smiled again and my heart did the same dip and soar, the same vision blossoming, brighter than before, dispelling the mist that had begun to creep around the edges of my mind. Oh God. No.

I stared, feeling almost . . . baffled. *How did this happen? I didn't ask for this.*

She tilted her head, concern filling her face, and the world rushed back in an onslaught of sound and light. "Are you okay?" she asked.

"Yes." I let out a long, slow breath, picking up a trinket from the table and pretending to study it intently.

"You seem very interested in that."

"Hmm," I hummed, attempting to get my heart rate under control. I felt sweaty and mildly ill. "Yes. I . . . collect them," I said, bringing it closer. I couldn't look at her. Not right then. Not yet.

"It's a thimble," she said. "With the picture of a . . . donkey on it. It's a donkey thimble."

The thing came into focus. I didn't even know what a thimble *was* but it appeared to be a miniature upside-down cup. And yes, with the picture of a donkey on it.

It wasn't even a very attractive donkey.

Frankly, it was downright ugly.

Haven took it gently from my fingers. "I'll take this," she said to the booth vendor, handing him the fifty cents he quoted her and holding the thimble out to me again. "My gift to you."

I swallowed, taking the thimble and putting it in my pocket. "Thank you," I said, finally meeting her eyes. She gave me a searching look. "Are you sure you're okay?"

Well, I'd live. Apparently. I nodded. *Yes. No. I don't know.*

What I *did* know—suddenly and unmistakably—was that she was capable of shattering my heart. And if she was going to, all I could do was let her.

CHAPTER TWENTY-TWO

Travis

I'd eventually reclaimed my equilibrium, and we'd spent the remainder of the antique fair sampling snacks from the food trucks on the outer perimeter, and digging through what might be treasure or junk depending on the individual.

It was the best day of my life.

And the worst.

I was still mildly shaken, even sitting in my room after having returned hours before. We hadn't made any plans and though I longed to go to her, I kind of wanted to wallow too.

There was this distant feeling of happy satisfaction, combined with confusion and discombobulation, similar to the way I'd felt the morning after I'd gotten really drunk at the annual Cinco de Mayo taco and tequila crawl on Main Street. I'd thrown my back out doing the limbo at the lakeshore, and passed out in the sun.

Good times. *Great* times.

And exceedingly difficult to recover from.

Much less live down.

To this day, I still felt a small twinge in my back if I twisted too far in the wrong direction.

Thank God there was no video evidence this time.

I picked up the thimble and stuck it on my index finger, not able to help the groan of embarrassment that rose in my throat over the ridiculousness of the thing. The tangible reminder of the nervous breakdown I'd had the moment I realized I wanted this woman in my future, and that the chances of that actually happening were slim to none.

Speaking of *twinges*.

The muffled sound of Clarice's laughter came from the hall, combined with the thunk of something heavy. "It's been wonderful," I heard her say.

Was she *leaving*?

Oh no, she wasn't.

Not without providing what she owed me. Answers.

I flung my door open, rushing into the hall to see Betty at the top of the stairs, smiling as Clarice descended, a carry-on travel bag in her hand.

"Wait!" I said, following her.

She glanced back at me, but kept going, only stopping when she'd made it to the bottom, setting her bag on the floor. "Stop accosting me, Chief."

237

"*Accosting* you? I'm not accosting you!" I'd only demanded answers from her twice before when I'd left for work and caught sight of her in the hallway, and both times she'd stealthily evaded me by slipping into a room and flipping the lock.

She was obviously practiced at dodging, likely due to leaving a slew of deeply unsatisfied customers in her wake.

I stood in front of her, reaching out, grabbing her hands and closing my eyes. "Tell me what you see," I demanded.

"I see a man who's wearing a donkey thimble."

"Forget the donkey thimble," I said, flustered, gripping tighter.

"Honestly, it will be difficult to forget that."

I opened my eyes, giving her a glare. Her shoulders lifted and fell in a long-suffering sigh. "I gave you two paths," she said, pulling her hands from mine, picking up her bag and heading toward the front door.

I followed. "They're the same!"

She turned suddenly and I came up short. "I will clarify one thing for you," she said, squinting as though trying to put whatever she was about to say in just the right words. "One of the two paths holds deep regret."

My mouth set. "Wow, so much clearer. Which path will I choose?"

She laughed shortly, turning again and moving away. "Consider it carefully!" she sang over her shoulder, opening the door.

"You're a quack, you know that?" I called.

238

She laughed merrily. "Aren't we all, Chief Hale?" And then the door smacked shut behind her.

I returned to my room where I decided to pace.

I'd never really been a pacer though. Instead, I sank down on the bed. Truthfully, I felt like running away from here whether my house was ready to be inhabited again or not. I scrubbed a hand over my face, realizing I was still wearing the thimble. I removed it with more aggression than was necessary, and tossed it on to the bedside table. It landed perfectly right side up with a soft click, the inane donkey grinning crookedly at me.

My shoulders fell and that instinct to run away intensified. But I'd never run from anything. Ever.

There was a soft knock at my door. I startled, standing quickly and rushing to it, my heart flying in my chest. I pulled it open and Haven stood there, looking shy and a bit uncertain. A breath gusted from my lips.

She'd come to me.

"I wasn't sure . . . well, I wasn't sure whether I should knock on your door. That is whether . . . you might want company tonight." Her cheeks flushed and my heart soared higher to know exactly what sort of *company* she meant. "Well, so"—she raised the picture I hadn't noticed she was holding in her hand—"I asked Grandma for her advice."

I opened the door wider so she could enter, and then closed it behind her. "So that's what my life has come to. The picture of a dead old lady now stands between me and a night of . . . benefits." Happiness expanded. She was here.

Haven laughed, considering the photo. "It's not such a terrible fate. She *looks* stuffy, but she's actually very forward-thinking."

"Grandma likes sex?"

"Very much so."

My lip quirked as she stepped closer. "This conversation is killing the mood," I said, even as my body responded to her proximity.

She placed the photo down on the dresser directly to her left, stepping even closer, her gaze sliding down my body. "All evidence to the contrary," she whispered, reaching down and running her palm over my groin.

I hissed, clenching my eyes momentarily in pleasure. And pain. Knowing that in some way, that was always going to be my reaction to her. "Haven . . ." I uttered raggedly.

Her gaze met mine and she watched me for a moment, the way she looked at all suffering things: with tenderness.

I weaved my hands into her miraculous hair, bringing my lips to hers, tasting her sweetness.

She broke from my lips, dragging her mouth down my throat and nipping softly at my skin. I groaned as she reached under my shirt, running her fingers over my stomach, and splaying her palms over my pecs. Surely she could feel my heart, its tempo swift and erratic. She looked up and met my gaze and for a moment an expression that looked very much like fear flitted through her eyes. Or perhaps it was just my own, reflected in her expression. I was scared. I'd never felt this way.

"Take this off," she said, her voice whispery and thin. I did as I was told, lifting my shirt over my head and tossing it on the floor, arousal ratcheting higher and subduing the emotional turmoil I'd been experiencing since that moment at the fair. Hell, maybe since the moment I'd first laid eyes on her.

She brought her palm to my chest again, kneading the muscles softly, and using her fingernails to feather over my skin, her gaze focused on the movement of her hands. I groaned again. "That feels nice."

Without meeting my eyes, she gave me a soft push and I took the few steps backward to the chair behind me, dropping down onto the upholstery.

She did meet my eyes then, her mouth curving as she stepped forward, leaning in, and bringing her mouth to my neck again. She reached for the buttons of my jeans and with an inhale I leaned back, helping her so she could pull them down my legs.

"You're so beautiful," I said, and her eyes rose to mine, her expression both shy and sultry.

And I want you to stay.

She ran her palm over my now-straining erection and I sucked in a breath, my head falling onto the back of the chair, my body stretched out before her.

She brought her head forward, kissing down my stomach and using her hand to rub me through my boxers.

"Haven," I groaned, a tortured sound that accurately depicted how I felt.

"Shh," she said, blowing on the thin line of hair that traveled from my lower stomach beneath the band of my boxer shorts. "Patience is a virtue."

"Cruel."

I felt the curve of her lips as she brought them to my lower stomach, flicking out her tongue and licking downward as she lowered my shorts. I sank down into the chair, giving in to the hot, drugging pleasure of her hands and mouth on my body and the smell of her shampoo drifting up to me as she went down on her knees.

Haven.

She pulled my boxers off slowly and I opened my eyes, our gazes holding as she brought them down my legs, my erection springing free and standing rigid before her. She inhaled a breath, leaned forward and kissed it. I grunted out a gasp, my lips falling open. "You're beautiful too," she murmured, just before she bent her head, taking the tip of my cock in her lips and sucking.

"Oh God," I moaned. *Please don't stop.*

She wrapped her fist around my base and lowered her mouth farther, slowly withdrawing and then lowering again. I reached up, grabbing a handful of my own hair and giving it a slight pull. I felt like I might come in mere moments, the sensation of her hot wet mouth in addition to the visual of her lips wrapped around my cock too overwhelming. Too good.

She sucked and teased, driving me half out of my head, my chest rising and falling quickly with every delicious stroke of her mouth.

"Haven." It sounded like a moan and a laugh and a prayer for deliverance.

She raised her head, releasing me from her grasp and then stood, my sudden despair turning to joy when she pulled her dress off her shoulders and let it drop to the floor.

She was naked beneath it.

"Hallelujah," I said and Haven laughed.

She reached down and pulled something from what must have been the pocket of her dress and held it up. A condom.

"Hallelujah," I said again. It seemed it was the only thing I was capable of saying at the moment. Because it was the only word flashing in my head.

HallelujahHallelujahHallelujah.

Haven tore the condom open and slid it on, her brow knitted in concentration as she performed the task.

"I stole this from my brother's drawer," she informed me. "There's your vengeance," she said, meeting my gaze, her lip quirking slightly, teasing.

Hallelujah.

She climbed astride me, placing one knee on each side of my hips and leaning forward, bringing her mouth to mine as I reached down, guiding my cock to her opening. She lowered herself at the same time I pushed upward, her tight body grasping me as I groaned into her mouth and she let out a soft gasp. "Oh God, that's good."

For a moment we simply breathed against each other's mouths, our eyes opening simultaneously and meeting . . . holding. A *stillness* passed between us, something that somehow felt both weighty and as light as air. It felt *effervescent* and yet it hit me square in my gut. My heart. Haven's eyes widened and then she blinked, swallowed, as though she'd somehow heard my thought. Her head tilted, hands reaching for my shoulders and clutching as if she was afraid of falling. She looked . . . she looked . . . the way I might have at the antique fair earlier as my world fell from beneath me. She looked like she suddenly wanted to run, but our bodies were connected, eyes held. "What are you thinking?" I whispered.

She sucked in a breath, giving her head a shake as if to dispel whatever thoughts had put that expression on her face—wonder. *Fear.* Her fingers dug into my shoulders and she began to move, her eyes falling shut as I watched her. Through the haze of pleasure, I had the strange sense she was running from me, yet we could not have been any closer. I sat up to meet her, bringing my lips to hers and kissing her deeply. *Stay.* She melted against me, her body relaxing as she continued her slow undulations.

God, it was good. It was sweet and it was hot and I never ever wanted it to end.

She'd said she wasn't a great dancer, but she could *move.* I watched her, awestruck. The visual of her slow, erotic hip rolls. The slight bounce of her perfect breasts. The way her internal muscles clenched and slid.

I was going to die of pleasure.

Her grip tightened on my shoulders and, for a few minutes, she rode me slowly, small, bliss-filled gasps falling from her lips with each downward press.

She leaned back slightly and for a few moments we both watched as the hard peaks of her nipples rubbed against my chest. "Oh, Travis. God. Everything. I just . . ."

Me too. Me too.

Despite the slow rhythm, I felt my orgasm stirring and squeezed the arms of the chair, trying desperately not to come before she did. "Haven," I gasped, and as if she heard my desperation in that one uttered word, she sped up, digging her nails into my skin, and riding me in earnest.

I moved my hands around her body, cupping her ass and taking some of the weight off her thighs, which had to be aching. The pads of my fingertips pressed into the skin around the place we were connected, slick with her arousal, the juices not only assisting in my effortless glide in and out of her body, but running down her thighs. The knowledge of the extent of her lust caused a dizzying swirl of excitement to cascade through my body, tightening my stomach muscles, and sending shock waves to my cock.

I was lost. No longer in control . . . *if I ever had been*.

I could do nothing to stop the rising bliss, had no choice but to ride it as it crested and broke, my hips bucking as I came seconds before she did, her head going back as she let out a small scream.

Haven fell forward, her slick skin meeting mine, both of us shaking in the aftermath. Our hearts slammed against one another's, her breath gusting over my skin and cooling the perspiration that had gathered at the base of my throat. I brought my arms around her and held her close, our bodies still connected. My lips feathered along her hairline as I

245

murmured her name, kissing and soothing her because I sensed that she needed it in some way she would not ask for. We stayed just that way for long minutes, our hearts slowing and reality descending.

"Hallelujah," I whispered, turning my head and kissing her temple. I felt her smile against the side of my throat.

And though I said the word with some amount of levity, it felt apropos in a way I couldn't quite describe. There had been something almost ... sacred about what I'd just experienced. But in the moment, my brain was too clouded with pleasure to think too deeply on that or anything else.

"Hallelujah, indeed," she whispered back.

****

I brought the blanket up over her shoulder and she snuggled in to me. "I love this sexy, green thumb," I said, picking up her hand and kissing the aforementioned thumb, closing my lips around it and sucking gently.

She laughed softly and I smiled, holding it against my lips for a moment, my vision going momentarily hazy as I recalled the bliss of *her* lips around a different part of my anatomy. But despite the arousing picture in my mind, my body was heavy with satisfaction and I didn't think I could have moved if a tornado siren went off, warning of imminent danger.

I could see the news print now.

They were swept away, right along with The Yellow Trellis Inn, paralyzed from too much mind-blowing sex. Or that's what reports from the other guests say it sounded *like anyway, right before the rest of them dove into the storm cellar to save themselves.*

I turned my head slightly, my gaze falling on the plant next to my bed, the one I'd talked to on the first night I'd arrived here. Something about the memory of that night brought a measure of what I could only call melancholy. I both hated and longed for the time before I knew I faced certain emotional disaster. A storm was coming. I smelled it in the air like the metallic tinge of an approaching lightning strike. "How will you bear leaving all your plants behind?" I murmured.

How will you bear leaving me *behind?*

She breathed out a soft breath. "With happiness. I'll know I leave a piece of *myself* behind, and that a small corner of the world is better because of it." She paused. "Maybe you'll check on the ones here now and again . . . make sure they're doing okay."

"I will," I said softly.

I rubbed her thumb idly along my bottom lip, not wanting to consider that time. The time when she'd no longer be here. "You've left your rescue plants everywhere along your path, haven't you? Even in the place you started out." *Your home. The one that puts sadness in your eyes.*

She paused for what felt like a long time. "Yes," she finally said, as though that one word had required her to muster up something, and what, I had no way to fathom.

Part of me wanted to question her until she opened up, and another part of me knew that was a very bad idea. Still, I

247

didn't seem able to stop myself from wanting to know more. "Tell me more about it. Your home."

Again, the pause.

"What's to tell? We didn't have things like plants in my apartment growing up. Like I said before, we didn't even always have food. My mom . . . she struggled with addiction. She'd promise to stop . . . but it never stuck for long. Few of her promises ever did."

"Shit. I'm sorry, Haven," I said, running my hand along her arm, wanting to comfort her from something that had long passed. "I shouldn't have asked."

But she shrugged. She felt different suddenly. *Closed off.* Stiff. And I was sorry my question had done that.

Again, I was conflicted. Part of me wanted the easygoing teasing back. But another part wanted to probe her—*force* her to share herself with me. Let her know I could handle it.

That desperate feeling rose up, the one that had always tried to control when I felt scared or needy.

"It's okay," she said. "I'm fine now. It's fine."

I smoothed a curl back that had fallen over her cheek, but it defied me, bouncing back to where it had just been, resistant.

"Once she went an entire year without using," Haven said, almost breathless suddenly. "Men had always come and gone. A few of them were decent. The one she was with that year—Johnny—taught me to play checkers. He always had orange Tic Tacs. I can still taste them when I think of him. Anyway, I learned not to get too attached to any of them because it never ended well for me." She stopped short, a

248

small cringe passing over her expression, her mouth puckering as though she tasted that long-ago orange-flavored memory of someone who had been kind to her, perhaps made her feel she mattered, and then left anyway.

My throat felt tight. *Stop pressing. She's not staying. You won't benefit from digging up her secrets.* She gave her head a slight shake, turning toward me. "Sorry. I don't know why I said that. Can we rewind a little bit?" She smiled, though it was fleeting.

I hesitated, torn again, but knowing that for whatever her reasons were, she needed to turn away from the memory she'd just dredged up. "Rewind?" I leaned forward, kissing her once on her lips. "To which part? I can think of several moments I'd like to revisit since the moment you knocked on my door."

She laughed softly, her shoulders relaxing, the crease on her forehead smoothing out. I smiled, raising my eyebrows suggestively, the mood lightening once again. And then I rolled on top of her, crushing her momentarily as she laughed and pretended to choke. I rolled off, grinning as I dragged my lips down her stomach, going lower, as her laugher melted into sighs and then turned to moans.

CHAPTER TWENTY-THREE

Travis

Clawdia's purr rose and fell as I scratched under her chin, her body a warm, slight weight in my arms. I trailed behind Haven, my vision going hazy at the edges as she stretched up on her tiptoes to water the plants on the kitchen windowsill, the curve of her ass cheeks peeking out from the cotton shorts she wore.

She turned, her eyes narrowing slightly as my gaze shot to hers. I grinned, and she gave her head a small shake, a mock exasperated look pinching her features. She looked sexy and mussed, her hair a tangled riot around her face and trailing down her back. We'd woken with the sun as usual and, despite thoroughly enjoying our morning ritual, I wanted to take her back to bed and bury myself inside her. Stay there.

It'd been an amazing, pleasure-filled week. But a busy one too as one of my officers was out with a broken leg after he'd attempted some trick on a jet ski that had failed spectacularly and left the department short-handed. I'd had to work several double shifts, hardly able to focus on my job, so eager to return home to Haven, even if the hours we spent together were far too short.

"That cat is going to grieve intensely when you leave the inn."

I looked down at Clawdia's blissful face, scratching the top of her head as she leaned into me and I felt a small twang in my chest. Why, I wasn't sure. Again, I didn't even *like* cats. "Do you blame her?" I asked.

Haven gave a soft laugh but it faded quickly as she tipped the watering can and gave another plant a drink. I watched her profile for a minute. She seemed . . . troubled this morning. Or maybe just introspective. I'd detected the same mood off and on since the night she'd talked about her mother's substance abuse. But each morning it'd seemed to fall away. Until *this* morning.

I opened my mouth to ask her what she was thinking about when a soft knock from the front of the house made both our heads turn. I frowned. Who would be here this early?

Betty wasn't even up.

I walked to the foyer and stopped abruptly, seeing Phoebe's golden head through the upper glass portion of the wide front door.

What. The. Hell?

I glanced back to see Haven standing behind me, a questioning look on her face, watering can by her side, as she blinked at the woman on the other side of the door.

"It's Phoebe," I said.

Haven's eyes widened. "Oh."

I stared at Haven a moment. I wasn't sure what to say. This had been the very last thing I'd expected. Frankly, I'd almost forgotten Phoebe existed. I wasn't sure that said great things about me, but there it was.

I had this strange, out-of-body feeling like two worlds were colliding, and I was having trouble orienting myself.

"You should let her in," Haven said. I couldn't exactly discern what was in her tone, though there was something almost . . . resigned in her expression.

"Right," I said. "I should. Let her in." She obviously *saw* me, was standing there watching through the glass. But my gaze stayed stuck to Haven.

Haven raised her hand, waving it behind her. "I'll just . . . go shower. Give you two . . . some privacy."

Clawdia batted at my hand, the one that had ceased petting her and was currently resting on her head. I let out a sigh. *Fuck.* This was weird. But maybe it was necessary. "Thanks." I'd go to her afterward, tell her what happened.

I took the several steps to the front door, pulling it open. Phoebe stood there in white shorts and a yellow tank top, her

252

gaze going over my shoulder to where Haven had turned and was scurrying away.

"Hi," Phoebe said softly, nervousness dancing over her face.

"Hi," I said distractedly, glancing back to where Haven was just disappearing up the stairs. I wanted to follow her. I wanted to resume the peaceful, easy morning we'd been enjoying.

When I looked back at Phoebe, she was looking at the stairs, a small crease between her perfectly arched brows. Her gaze met mine again. "The maid's up early . . ." Phoebe noted, her frown deepening. "And isn't wearing much."

My jaw tensed. "She's not the maid. She's a guest staying here."

Phoebe looked momentarily confused. "Oh." She glanced at the cat, her gaze landing on its stump of a leg, features contorting as she drew back.

I set Clawdia down gently, running my hand over her head. "How'd you know I was here?" I asked, standing straight.

"I . . . heard."

Irritation snaked through me. Damn this small town.

Phoebe moved from one foot to the other. "I'm sorry to hear about your house," she said, gaze flitting away.

Was she? She'd never liked that house. She thought it was too average. And it was, but maybe—for her—I was too.

And maybe you agreed. Maybe that's why you needed her to worship you.

Ouch. I felt confused suddenly, uneasy, awkward even.

Phoebe was watching me and some of the color had gone out of her face. She was obviously even more uncomfortable than I was. "I know you get up early," she said, speaking quickly as though I might throw her out any moment. "I figured I might be able to catch you before work. I thought . . . well, I thought it was better if I just bit the bullet and came over rather than calling." She let out an uncomfortable laugh that ended abruptly. She hadn't thought I'd take her call. Would I have? Maybe not. She looked down, bit at her lip, looking unusually meek. When she glanced up through her lashes, her eyes were shiny. "Can we talk?" she asked.

"Sure." I led her into the sitting room near the front of the house. She sat down on the couch and I took the chair across from it. She stared at me for a few moments and I detected her nervousness, but I also saw cautious hope.

"This is awkward," she said softly. "But I . . . I know I owe you an explanation."

I sighed. What was there to explain? I didn't really require an explanation. *Now, anyway.* But I was willing to listen to one if she needed to say it. I resisted glancing toward the doorway with a view of the stairs. The ones I wanted to rush toward.

Phoebe nodded once, her hands fidgeting in her lap. "That day . . . I was drinking." She shook her head. "I'm not using that as an excuse. But I was. And I met Easton and, God, he made me feel worshipped. Like I was the only woman in the world. And it was like a drug. I gave in, and I hate myself for it." The last few words trailed off, into nothing.

I hate myself for it. For some reason, her statement brought me no satisfaction. I sat back, considering her, considering *us*. She'd been starved. For someone who worshipped her as much as she worshipped him. It didn't make her actions right, but that's what it boiled down to, didn't it? I looked behind her for a moment, gathering my words. "Listen, I'm not happy about what happened. I wish you'd have talked to me instead of . . . well—"

"I know," she said, color moving up her neck. "I wish I had too. So much."

"But the truth is, we were never right together. You obviously felt that too." I hadn't loved her. I wasn't going to say that because I had no interest in hurting her unnecessarily, even despite her betrayal. And I had my own blame to carry. I'd stayed with her for reasons that were less than noble. I'd taken her emotion for me, and given little of my heart in return. I hadn't realized that at the time, but I saw it clearly now. But there were other reasons we wouldn't have worked out too. "A small-town cop, even the chief of police, would never make you happy in the long run, Phoebe."

I saw the pain that skittered over her face. Maybe she still had some feelings for me, even if she knew what I was saying was true. She sighed, shrugged, picking at a thread on the throw pillow she'd moved into her lap, a hideous cross-stitch attempt that declared *Home is Where the Hooch is.* Whoever had made it had imbibed in more than their fair share. Phoebe looked up at me, her eyes imploring. "I thought maybe you'd want to run for some sort of office . . . there's a senator who lives up the street from the Buchanans." Her eyes moved back to that thread, staying there.

I considered what she'd said, remembering that Haven had asked about that. At the time, it'd seemed to come out of nowhere. But sitting there, I realized she'd brought it up right after she'd mentioned that a couple people at the club had been discussing me. Had they also mentioned Phoebe's aspirations on my behalf? That seemed to fit. And it *sounded* like Phoebe, planning for things that met *her* needs, but not sharing them with me.

I sighed, scrubbing my hand down my face. "You never asked me. You never even asked if I wanted that."

She bit at her lip. "I just figured . . . I could persuade you eventually."

God. It would have been a lifetime of being *maneuvered*, the same way I'd always felt when I was under the control of my mother, and even beyond that. I'd let her continue to do it, because it had been habit by that point. Familiar. I didn't *want* to be maneuvered or manipulated anymore. I wanted to be asked what I wanted for my life.

The way Haven had done.

And then I wanted to be listened to and supported in those dreams.

And I wanted to do the same for someone else.

But that would never be Phoebe. And deep inside, I had felt that. I hadn't seen a future with us. Not really. The truth of the matter was that I had never even really *known* her, because I hadn't wanted to.

I leaned forward, placing my elbows on my knees. "You wouldn't have persuaded me. So you wouldn't have been happy. Or if you had, *I* wouldn't have been happy, and things would have crumbled." I gave her a small smile. "In a funny way, you saved us both a helluva lot more misery."

She breathed out a smile, but the pain was still in her eyes. "Is there any chance you and me—"

"No." I paused. "But I wish you happiness. I mean that."

Tears pricked at her eyes and she nodded, giving me a small, sad smile. "Thank you, Travis. I wish you happiness too. And I hope . . . maybe someday you can forgive me."

I tilted my head, realizing the truth. "I already do, Phoebe. And you should forgive yourself." *Learn from your mistakes, and I'll learn from mine.*

She nodded, a soft smile tilting her lips. She hesitated for a moment but there was nothing left to say and we both knew it.

I stood, and she did too. We both glanced toward the doorway where half a feline face had appeared, singular eye narrowed as it watched Phoebe with cold malice. Phoebe shrunk away, backing toward the other door that led to the foyer. "I'll, uh, let myself out."

I nodded. A pipe rattled overhead, the sound of footsteps coming from the back of the upstairs hallway. The Yellow Trellis Inn was waking up.

Phoebe turned and walked to the foyer and a moment later, I heard the door close behind her.

I inhaled deeply as Clawdia limped into the room, rubbing against my legs. I picked her up and set her on the couch, and then headed upstairs. I knocked on Haven's door but there was no answer. I thought I heard the shower running from inside and so I turned and headed to my own room. I had to start getting ready for work anyway.

As I stepped under my own shower spray, washing my body, I felt cleansed in a different way too. I hadn't thought talking to Phoebe was necessary. But I was glad to get the sense of closure. And I'd meant what I said. I hoped she'd go on to find her own happiness too, whatever that might mean for her.

Dressed in my uniform, I stopped by Haven's room, but again, there was no answer, and when I walked out the front door I saw that her car was already gone.

CHAPTER TWENTY-FOUR

Travis

I stepped out of my truck, unbuttoning the top button of my uniform shirt as I shut the door behind me. The windows of The Yellow Trellis Inn were open, music wafting from inside, the curtains swaying in the breeze and I smiled as I walked toward it.

Haven.

I suddenly felt a burst of energy. It'd been another long day in a very long week. But it was finally over. There'd been a multi-car pileup on the highway just outside town, and two boating accidents out on the lake. Thankfully, no one had been gravely injured, but it'd taken most of my shift before both situations were resolved. Spencer and another officer had gone out on the lake, while I'd managed the highway wreck. In other places, the chief of police might be a desk job, but in a small town like Pelion, that wasn't the case. Frankly I was glad of it as it kept me active, and every day was just a little bit different.

I'd wanted to call Haven all day but I hadn't had the chance. She'd been working too though so I was sure she'd been just as occupied. I'd see if she wanted to go to dinner . . . come back to the inn and engage in . . . other enjoyments. I was off all weekend. No work. Just *her*. Anticipation made me break out in a smile.

I whistled as I jogged up the steps, letting myself in the front door and heading for the stairs. The music I'd heard was coming from the kitchen, and I caught Betty's laughter, followed by Burt's, and decided that rather than interrupt them, I'd head straight upstairs.

I knocked on Haven's room door. "Come in," she called, and when I opened the door, she was standing in front of the mirror that hung on the wall, securing a necklace behind her neck.

I smiled. "Hey, beautiful," I said, coming up behind her and taking the necklace from her hands. I met her eyes in the mirror after I'd hooked the clasp. "What are you getting all ready for?"

Her gaze hung on mine for a second. "I have a date with Gage, remember?"

For a moment her words didn't make sense. I struggled to rearrange them. I took a step back and she turned slowly. "You're still going?" I asked, incredulous.

Her gaze skittered to the side and then back. There were two high points of color on her cheekbones. "Of course," she said, stepping around me.

What is happening?

I frowned. My nerves suddenly felt like someone had lit the ends on fire. "This isn't because Phoebe showed up this morning, is it?"

She slid a bracelet on her arm. "Of course not."

"Because that was just about closure. We talked. That was all."

She smiled distractedly as she slid another bracelet up her arm. "Closure's good."

"Because this week . . . it's been amazing."

"Yes. It . . . has."

I was confused, caught off guard, at a loss. Why was she acting like this? I turned toward where she was picking up a small purse on the bed, giving my head a slight shake. "I thought . . ."

"You thought what?" she asked, not meeting my eyes.

I watched her as she opened the purse, rifling through whatever was inside. Had someone hit me over the head with a sledgehammer? What was I missing?

She closed the purse, stood straight, and took a deep breath. She smiled but it looked forced as though she knew she was upsetting me and it made her uncomfortable.

But she was still going anyway.

I watched her, despair washing through me, an unfamiliar version of the emotion that made me want to beg.

I thought we had formed a connection. I . . . thought you wanted me.

"Didn't we have an agreement, Travis?" she asked as if I'd voiced the thought in my head. "This shouldn't be a surprise. You're the one who *scored* me this date, remember?"

I watched her, my throat tight. Yes, I'd scored her a date with Gage because she'd wanted to have a fling with him. But now . . . Did what we were doing really change nothing? "If you wanted a fling, why not just stick to the one you're already having with me?"

She laughed shortly, but there was zero humor in the sound. "Because I have feelings for *Gage*," she said. My muscles seized. It felt like a dagger was lodged in my spine. And if she was contemplating her feelings for Gage, then why did she look so miserable?

My jaw set and for a moment we simply stared at each other, her chin lifting slightly. What could I do? There was nothing I could do, not in that moment. *You* could *beg. It might work.* I gritted my teeth harder. No. "Have fun, Haven. But if you get your . . . *wish* . . . if Gage wants to take things in a physical direction, I won't share you. You should know that," I said quietly.

No, I wouldn't beg. The only promise we had made to each other was there would be no promises. She'd made it clear we were *friends.* So maybe I *was* the one being irrational. But I wouldn't be waiting here to extend *benefits* to her when she returned.

Her gaze danced away again. "Of course I know that. I'm not . . ." She fidgeted with her purse. "I'm not interested in that either."

I waited but she said no more. *Then why bother going on a date with another man?* That's what I wanted to know. She could have a night with me. She didn't need to see Gage, did she? *For what purpose?* My chest ached. My entire body ached.

Choose me. Say you don't want him at all. Physical or otherwise. Say you won't give me up for him. I felt blindsided. I'd thought . . . *What, Travis? That it's something more than great sex? That because you want her, she automatically wants you too? Hasn't she made it clear from the beginning that she does not? This is what you get.*

God it hurt. It killed me. And I'd put myself in this position. *This is exactly why you never have.* It was so incredibly clear now. In the past, I'd chosen those who *couldn't* hurt me. Because I hadn't truly handed them any portion of my heart.

But now . . . *now* . . .

The doorbell met my ears, ringing distantly from the floor below. Her eyes met mine again, those bright spots deepening before she turned, walking stiffly out the door.

Second best. And second best didn't even deserve a goodbye.

I let out a shuddery breath, clenching my eyes shut and letting the pain roll through me in waves.

I heard her laugh from below, and Gage's deep voice saying something that was surely charming and complimentary.

I didn't move a muscle, just stood there alone in her room where she'd left me, until his car doors shut outside and I heard the smooth motor of his Audi—the car that cost the entirety of two years of my salary—pulling out of the gravel driveway.

Only then could I move, propelling myself out her door, down the stairs and back to my truck where I jumped inside and peeled out of the driveway.

I turned in the opposite direction from the one they would have gone in, toward the lakeside restaurants in Calliope where he'd wine and dine her. He'd probably notice she was tense. She had been uncomfortable hurting me because she was kind.

But she'd done it anyway because she didn't have the same feelings for me that I had for her.

Only when I'd turned down the dirt road that led to my land was I able to take a full breath. I came to a slow stop, rolling down the windows and turning off the ignition, staring unseeing at the faded red barn. It would be years before I saved up for the one thing I wanted. The only thing I had left.

I was spinning. *Spiraling.*

You will lose it all. Or lose it all.

Desperation spiked, a hot flood of despondency, and I leaned back on the seat, the breeze through the window ruffling my hair, but doing nothing to cool my blood.

The pile of things my mother had given me was sitting on the small space of floor behind the passenger seat and I twisted, reaching for them. Why? To torture myself further?

To remind myself that I'd *always* been thrown away by people I cared about? By people who mattered?

The picture album was on top of the folder of documents and I rifled through that, shutting it after only a few pages. It hurt to look at my father in that moment.

I could have used you right now. I could have used you in so many moments.

But even if you had lived, you left. You chose him over me.

You fucking asshole.

Only I didn't hate him. I wished I could. And that's what hurt the most.

Underneath the albums was the file of original documents and I opened it, taking several minutes to read through it, furrowing my brow as I read it again, more slowly.

Holy shit. She was right.

I saw what my mother meant.

I looked up momentarily, drumming my fingers on the steering wheel. *Tap, tap, tap.* This amendment to the original contract regarding the ownership of Pelion changed everything. I leaned back, considering. A legal challenge would almost definitely work with the right lawyers involved.

At the very least, Archer and I would split the town. I considered the documents again. I'd regain the social status among the Pelion and Calliope elite I'd once enjoyed. I'd have the money to build the house I wanted on this land in front of me. The land that had once been my father's but now was mine. *Only mine.*

I'd meant it when I'd told my mother that Archer did a great job running the town, and that the citizens of Pelion thrived under his leadership. But Archer could still keep doing what he did. He didn't have to split the ownership of the town. But I could gently demand that he buy me out.

Why should he have everything when Connor Hale had been *my* father too? Even if he didn't want to be.

We didn't *have* to get lawyers involved.

It didn't need to get messy.

My pulse slowed and I felt more in control. *Tap, tap, tap.* Relief descended.

Why not? Even if there was a small possibility of Haven staying, she had walked away from me tonight, showing me that I meant little to her. I had simply been her friend with benefits . . . *temporarily* . . . something I had done to others many times if I was honest. All over Pelion, women would be—justifiably—laughing their asses off if they knew the pain I was in. Despite what Burt said, Haven would not be the one to fill or complete me. The hope of that potential future had died. If I was going to lose it all—again—this time, why not grab what I could before *all* of it was gone?

CHAPTER TWENTY-FIVE

Travis

"I'm glad you made it. But you should have taken the time to change into something more comfortable," Bree said, eyeing the uniform I was still wearing and handing me a fistful of skewers as we walked down the hill toward the bonfire I could already see dancing on the beach below. "Your uniform is going to get all smoky."

As I'd sat in my truck, holding the documents and considering what I was going to do, I'd remembered that Archer and Bree had invited me to roast marshmallows with them and the kids down by the lake. I'd been so wrapped up in Haven that I'd completely forgotten. *Perfect timing,* I'd thought, tossing the albums and the paperwork onto my passenger seat. And I'd driven right over.

"I'm off tomorrow," I said. "I have time to wash it."

"All right. Well Archer's getting the fire going, so go on and join him. I need to change the baby and then the boys and I will gather the supplies. We'll be down as quickly as possible." She paused, considering me. "Are you okay?"

"Yeah. Yeah. I'm fine." I didn't want to look at her. She'd be disappointed in me once she found out what I wanted. *Oh well.* I'd handled it once, and I could handle it again. "I'll see you all in a bit."

Archer looked over his shoulder as I approached, raising his chin and using a poker to adjust a piece of firewood. Firewood I knew he chopped himself even though he could've easily afforded hiring someone else to do it.

Maybe old habits died hard.

I sat in one of the Adirondack chairs flanking the fire, across from Archer, setting a file folder and one of the albums on a rock next to me.

Archer tilted his head, his gaze flicking over my uniform. *Is this an official visit?* he asked.

"No. I came straight from work."

He looked at the items I'd placed on the rock questioningly. *What'd you bring?*

I cleared my throat, going for the file, but instead, sliding the album out from underneath and handing it to Archer. He took it with two hands, frowning slightly as he held the photo album up and then set it on his knees.

I saw him swallow, the scar on his throat raising as he turned the page slowly. The scar that had taken his voice and submerged him in a world of silence. An odd hollow formed between my ribs. He looked up at me and I recognized the emotion in his eyes: surprised wonder. *These are pictures of my mother.*

"Yeah. My, uh, mother gave it to me. It was with our father's things. Alyssa must have given it to him at some point. I'm surprised my mother didn't burn it." I attempted a rueful laugh but it petered out.

Archer looked back down to the photos, flipping a few more pages, his gaze moving from one picture to the next. He ran his hand gently—lovingly—over the plastic-covered page. *I only have one photo of my mother,* he said, raising his hands but not his gaze, seemingly unwilling to look away from the treasure in his lap.

The expression on his face reminded me of the way Haven had looked as her eyes had moved over the antique photographs of someone else's family. Yearning.

"I know," I said. I'd seen the picture of Alyssa Hale in a place of honor on the mantel in Bree and Archer's home. I knew his mother hadn't had much family to speak of, if any. Archer had his memories of her, good ones, I assumed, and the knowledge that she'd loved him, but no tangible items other than the one lone photograph.

I remembered how beautiful I'd thought she was. I remembered how she'd kneel down to my level when she spoke to me, and that she'd always listened closely to what I had to say, even though I was only a kid. She had loved my father and I was the child of another woman, his wife. She had to have had mixed emotions, and even pain, regarding my presence, but she'd never once treated me as though she did.

And I remembered my mother's raging fury at her very existence, the woman who owned her husband's heart no matter how many tricks she deployed or whatever manipulative plans she devised.

I remembered that I wished Alyssa Hale was my mother, instead of the one I was given.

Archer spent a few minutes turning the pages, his gaze falling from one photo to another.

Thank you, he said, and by the look on his face, I sensed the gravity of his appreciation.

"Yeah, of course. It's yours."

He closed the book, but kept it in his lap. He nodded to the file folder I'd placed on the rock. *What else did you bring?*

I began reaching for the folder of papers, but pulled my hand away. I ran my palms over my thighs.

"How long did it take for you to fall in love with Bree?" I blurted out, instead of the, *my mother found some interesting documents,* that had sat cold and heavy in my mouth like a handful of pebbles from the lake's floor.

An amused smile twitched the corners of Archer's mouth. He raised his hands. *Five minutes? Maybe less.*

I chuckled softly. "That long, huh?" I paused. "I guess it really does happen that way sometimes," I murmured.

He considered me for a moment, leaning forward. *Honestly? You'd probably know better than me.* He smiled. *I was a special case.*

270

I breathed out a smile, a flicker of sadness causing it to die quickly. *I was a special case,* he'd said. But by the look on his face, that particular description of who he'd once been didn't cause him any distress. He even looked more than a little proud of it.

Even more profound—and somewhat gutting for reasons that made me feel deeply humbled—he'd answered my question honestly and without rubbing my nose in the fact that I, the supposed legendary Travis Hale, was asking the once-upon-a-time town hermit for relationship advice, whether he realized that's what I was doing or not.

How the tables had turned.

In so many ways.

"I think I'm a special case too when it comes to women," I murmured. And probably regarding many other subjects too lengthy and complicated to bring up at the moment. As far as women though, I either picked the ones who were too available, or not available at all. *Apparently.* Archer eyed me curiously, but waited for me to continue. "How did you know you were in love?" I asked, more curious about Archer now, than my own situation. We'd never talked about these things, about his story once Bree Prescott had come to town and changed everything for him. "Especially considering you were a *special case?* How did you trust yourself?"

He tilted his head, his eyes moving to the lake in front of us. *At the time, I didn't completely trust myself. I knew how I felt, but I questioned whether I had anything to offer her.* He paused, his eyes returning to me. *But she made me want to become the man she deserved. She made me braver, and stronger. Because of her,*

271

I wanted to be the best version of myself. And that, I think, is what love does, if it's really love.

I nodded, feeling strangely choked up, wondering if I even knew who the *best version* of myself might be. *Could* be.

He leaned forward just a bit, his gaze unfocused, as if staring into the past. *I had this vision of what a future with her might look like . . .* He paused, his hands hanging in the air for a moment. *Kids. A family. Things I'd never dared dream of before.* His eyes met mine. *It was so clear in my head, but the reality . . . well . . . I had no idea how we might get there, but I knew I wanted it more than I'd ever wanted anything in my life. And I'd spent my life wanting.*

I swallowed, looking away. *I'd spent my life wanting.*

When I saw Archer raising his hands in my peripheral vision, I looked back at him. He had a teasing glint in his eye. *And then there was the sex—*

"Don't tell me about the sex."

His grin was slow. It was a Hale grin. I saw our father in it. I laughed, the awkward, overly emotional moment ending, something for which we were both—I could tell—grateful.

His smile dwindled, expression going thoughtful. *Uncle Nathan told me once that when Hale men fall in love, it's quick and it's forever. It was true for me.*

It'd been true for our father and uncles too.

And because of it, things had gone so terribly wrong.

The weight of that thought hung heavy inside me.

"Uncle Nate was kind of a nut, though," I reminded.

Yes. He absolutely was. Archer smiled, but there was deep affection in his eyes.

I chuckled softly. We sat in silence, but it was comfortable.

I should go see what's taking Bree so long, Archer said after a moment, standing. *Do you want anything while I'm up at the house?*

"No, I'm good. Thanks. And, Archer . . . thanks."

He nodded once, turned, and headed toward the cottage where I could hear the distant rise and fall of the boys' exuberant and constant commentary as Bree did whatever Bree was doing.

The fire had died down a bit. I picked up one of the logs sitting next to the fire pit and added it gingerly, watching as the flame leapt and licked at the new piece of wood, the kindling having no choice but to let itself be consumed.

Things had gone so terribly wrong for our father and uncles.

My brother had offered me insight I hardly deserved from the generosity of his heart. And what I was considering doing would deftly lodge a wedge between us again, reversing any sense of brotherhood we'd gained over these last eight years.

You either lose it all, or lose it *all*.

Maybe there were many different sorts of losing.

And we each had to weigh our choices.

Choose which hand to discard so that we might win the bigger pot.

Something stirred inside me, a feeling of rightness that I had no way of describing other than that.

Before I could overthink it, or talk myself out of it, I leaned back in my chair and grabbed the file containing the original copy of the amendment to the town bylaws that might have resulted in Archer and me facing each other down in a courtroom. I dropped it on the fire and watched as it curled and blackened and moments later, turned to nothing but ash. Gone forever. *Lost.*

I swallowed, sensing some form of breakthrough, but feeling the familiar hopelessness too. The feeling that meant I'd given up control, that I might fall—*hard*—and no one was going to be there to catch me when I did.

A light caught my eye and I tipped my head, watching as a shooting star moved swiftly across the darkening sky.

"Uncle Travis! We got peanut butter cups!" Charlie yelled, running toward me, his hand proudly outstretched, holding forth the candy. If I'd only heard his tone, and not his words, I'd have thought he was rushing forth with the keys to some magical kingdom.

"Let's make the best s'mores *ever!*" Connor declared, right behind his brother.

"Ever?" I asked. "In the history of the world?"

"Ever! In the history of the world," he confirmed, proving that he'd inherited his mother's enthusiasm for pleasures of the palate.

Bree and Archer were only a few steps behind them, Bree holding Averie, Archer carrying the cooler and a paper bag.

"Sorry we took so long," Bree said, huffing out a breath. "There was a catering emergency," she said, drawing out the word in a way that told me the emergency was less than dire, but still needed to be addressed.

Next to me, the boys were busy skewering marshmallows, spilling graham crackers on the sand and generally making a holy mess. Per usual.

"It's no problem," I said, turning my attention back to Bree. "From what I hear, these s'mores are going to be amazing."

She looked over, raising a brow. "And sandy," she mouthed.

Archer intervened with the boys, rescuing most of the graham crackers and setting things up on a towel near the fire.

Bree sat down and Averie, her solemn eyes on my face, reached her arms out to me, as though she'd just recognized something different about me that she could trust. A feeling not unlike awe wound through me and I reached back, taking her from her mother and bringing her to my chest. I lowered my nose to her hair, inhaling her sweet, pure scent, tenderness rendering me mute. Averie tilted her head back, staring once again into my eyes, gathering the fabric of my uniform shirt in her small fist, claiming me as one of hers.

Finally.

CHAPTER TWENTY-SIX

Haven

I closed the door softly behind me, leaning against it for a moment as I collected myself. Outside, I heard Gage descend the steps and get into his car, the motor purring as he started it up and drove away, the soft crunch of gravel growing more and more faint until it faded completely.

A bird called out. There was a distant splash. And somewhere overhead, a pipe clanked in the wall. I'd already begun to learn the noises of this house. They'd somehow branded themselves on my heart and I was going to have to work to forget them, not to feel an internal piercing whenever I heard a floorboard squeak in some particular way that reminded me of the planks in the hall outside my bedroom door, or the way *his* footsteps sounded on the porch right before he opened the front door.

Right before he arrived *home.*

Oh, I'd made a mistake. I'd gotten attached, and now I would suffer for it.

But I hoped . . . God, I prayed there was still time to save myself the worst of what it might have been.

The date with Gage had helped. At first, I'd worried it wouldn't, but it had. Gage's smile had been beautiful. His *car* was beautiful. The restaurant he'd taken me to was beautiful, the food incredible, the twinkle lights strewn along the railing overlooking the lake romantic. Of course, Gage himself was kind. Sensitive. He'd seemed to know I was troubled and, while he hadn't brought it up outright and made me feel uncomfortable, he'd done his best to make me laugh. And succeeded.

He really was perfect.

"You're home early."

I gasped, jumping, and bringing my hand to my chest as Travis exited the sitting room, leaning a shoulder against the doorframe. "God, you scared me."

"Fun date?"

I swallowed, standing straight. "Yes. It was . . . perfect."

"Naturally. Gage is perfect."

I nodded. "He is. He's perfect." I suddenly felt breathless, shaky. *Awful.*

Travis raised one dark eyebrow, his expression carefully blank. He was gorgeous. And *those eyes.* Those damned eyes.

277

How was I ever going to forget them? I looked away. "I'm leaving in the morning," he said.

My gaze flew to his. "Leaving?"

"My house is officially cleaned up. No reason to stay."

My heart dipped, squeezed. That's good. Better. *Easier.* He watched me as I gave a slow nod.

"I thought I'd wait up and say goodbye. I'm glad I'm leaving on a good note. It seems like our plan worked. Hallelujah." The last word came out slightly choked and I barely resisted going to him. He sounded vulnerable, hurt, and my heart constricted so tightly I feared it might stop beating.

It's better this way. You know it is. "Yes," I whispered. "Hallelujah." I managed what felt like a weak smile. "My feelings for Gage might yet be returned."

Travis let out a long breath, stepping toward me, seeming to have made some decision. "Haven."

My heart slammed between my ribs. "Yes?" *Don't, please don't.*

He stopped a few feet away from me. "Have you considered that you really have *no* feelings for Gage and that's why he's safe?" He stepped closer and I caught his clean, masculine scent. "Have you considered that you're *using* him to keep me emotionally at arm's length because your feelings are for *me* and that terrifies you because when you leave Pelion, when you leave Maine, you'll be facing yet another loss?" He stepped even closer and I turned my head as though by looking away, I could tune out his voice and what he was saying too. "You didn't mean to involve your heart, I know.

But you did. We both did. And one of us has to be brave and say it. One of us has to be the first to lay their heart on the line," he finished, gaze beseeching.

Oh no. No. Not that.

Promises.

Promises.

I couldn't trust promises.

"I know something about keeping people at arm's length, by only letting those in who pose no risk to your heart. I understand the need. I've done it all my life. But I'm telling you now that I don't want to do that anymore. Give us a chance, Haven."

"I can't. And you don't want me, Travis. Not really."

He laughed shortly, his brow knitting. He looked upset and affronted. "You can't tell me how I feel."

I shook my head, denying his words, denying him. He might think he had feelings for me but he didn't. It was good sex, that was all. And maybe he'd fallen victim to some of that competitiveness that he'd said would work on Gage. It would fade though. Sooner rather than later, it would fade. I'd seen Phoebe. She was the most beautiful woman I'd ever laid eyes on. Silken smooth hair, eyes as blue as the summer sky, legs that went on forever. *She* was the sort of woman he'd end up with eventually. Naturally. It wasn't *only* that she was beautiful, *perfect* in every single way. He'd been ready to *marry* her less than a month before. How dare he say he wanted a chance with me, when it was obvious that he'd lose interest when he came to his senses? And I couldn't bear it. I couldn't. "You're . . . on the rebound. You might think you have feelings for me, but you don't. You *can't*."

"Who says?"

"Everyone," I breathed. "Everyone says."

He crossed his arms over his chest, regarding me. "So I don't get to want you—to see a future for us—because of some arbitrary rule about so-called rebound relationships being destined for failure?"

"Yes. And . . . it doesn't matter anyway. We can't have a *relationship* because I'm *leaving*. I have to *leave*."

"You don't have to."

I nodded, a jerky movement. "I do. I do. It's part of the plan." *Don't stop. Keep moving. Outrun the hurt. Don't tempt additional pain. Keep your distance. Keep leaving before others leave you.*

I deserved that, didn't I? After a lifetime of not being able to run? *I* was in control now. Me.

He let out a small rueful laugh. "Yeah. I had a plan too, Haven. Plans don't always work out. You're not a rebound relationship."

"No. I'm not. Because we're not in a relationship. We're *friends*."

I saw how that word cut him and I looked away, taking a deep breath as I gathered myself. I smiled, looking back at Travis, reaching my hand out to him, but bringing it back before it made contact. "Let's not prolong this, Travis. I care for you. I don't want either of us to hurt. That was never the point. We've had fun, right?" I gave him a smile I was sure looked as shaky as it felt. "It's been a good time and I'll remember you . . . fondly."

He winced.

The backs of my eyelids burned.

You're awful, awful, awful.

Better this way.

Better this way.

Better this way.

I could see his mind turning, considering what to say. And so before he could say something that would weaken my resolve, I turned away. "Goodbye, Travis."

I didn't wait for him to reply as I practically flew up the stairs to the safety of my room.

CHAPTER TWENTY-SEVEN

Travis

Go to her now?

> *Wait until tomorrow?*

I sat in the darkened sitting room, plotting.

Tap, tap, tap.

There were a hundred things I could do to delay what she planned as the inevitable. Take the spark plugs out of her car . . . set up a roadblock for some trumped-up "criminal on the run" who didn't really exist . . .

I'd seen the indecision on her face. The way it hurt her to hurt me.

Once my emotions had settled and I'd stopped spiraling, I'd realized what I knew to be true. She cared about me, I knew she did. To what extent, I wasn't sure, but she did. I'd seen it. I'd *felt* it.

She was scared. And I understood that. I longed to comfort her, to convince her that I wouldn't hurt her. And maybe she'd be most receptive tonight. Or perhaps a night alone—missing me—would do the trick. Then, if not, I'd move to plan B. C, if necessary.

Tap, tap, tap.

I stilled my fingers, drumming distractedly on the wooden armrest of the chair I was sitting in.

Was I plotting again after I just had a breakthrough?

Confusion descended.

Okay, yes, but this was different. *This*—letting Haven go without a fight—hurt in a way that giving up material things did not. I could handle certain types of losses in the face of more important goals. But this . . . surely there was something I could *do*, something to make this pain stop, to twist things back in my favor.

The front door opened, then closed, the soft sound of drunken singing meeting my ears. The person stumbled, swore, and commenced singing, entering the living room where I sat.

"Hello, Easton."

"Holy fuck!" He tripped, catching himself, jumping upright when he spotted me, reaching blindly for—I assumed—the nearest weapon and coming up with an umbrella in a stand by the door. He held it out in front of him comically, stabbing it at the air.

"Relax. You don't need to defend yourself."

Easton, seemingly unconvinced, stared suspiciously at me, only weaving slightly.

"I heard you're doing well at the firehouse." One of my best friends worked there and he'd told me the kid was a hard worker. A quick learner. Diligent.

The suspicion in his expression mixed with fear, and some amount of surprise, his drunkenness not allowing him to conceal his every emotion.

He tried though. "So?" He stood straight, feigning nonchalance.

"So that's good."

He squinted at me as if trying to determine what trick I was playing on him. "You're not going to do anything to ruin it for me?"

"No, I'm not going to do anything to ruin it for you. Though you're leaving soon, so what does it matter?"

He watched me for a moment and then let out a long sigh, swaying and sinking down into the chair next to him. He ran his hand through his hair. It was wavy, not curly like Haven's. And his eyes were a different color, but the shape was the same.

"Listen . . . Chief." He looked up at me, and though he was obviously drunk, to his credit, he was barely slurring. He obviously held his alcohol well. "I'm sorry, okay? I knew about you right from the start just like you said. Your girlfriend—" He squinted one eye as if trying to recall something.

"Phoebe."

"Yes, right. Phoebe. She had a picture of you in your uniform as the screensaver on her phone. I saw it."

I regarded him. "It added a little challenge for you?"

"I guess." He looked slightly dejected as if the admittance brought him no joy.

Good.

I sighed, leaning forward, and placing my elbows on my knees. "You hurt your sister when you do things that reflect poorly on her, Easton. Don't you think you owe her more than that?"

His shoulders sank and he was quiet for a moment. "Did she tell you why we're on this road trip?" His eyes met mine and despite his drunkenness, they gleamed with emotion. "Did she tell you our junkie mom accidentally dropped her pipe and almost burned us all to death? The whole place went up in flames like some goddamned inferno that represented the *hell* that was our lives."

He let out a breath, his head dropping. I stared, my muscles clenched tight.

"I dragged Haven out of there," he said, as he massaged the back of his neck, his palms facing outward so I saw the raised and twisted skin. Melted. Burned. *Healed.* But not the same. Never the same. "And I managed to get our mom out too. But she was already dead. She'd died of an overdose before the flames even started spreading." He let out another long breath. "We're better off, you know? Haven spent her *life* trying to help her . . . cooking food for her, cleaning up after her, attending the things *she* was supposed to attend. I would have been in foster care a thousand times over if it wasn't for

Haven." He leaned forward. "Once, our electricity had been turned off, and she asked for help from one of the guys she thought might be her dad." His face twisted in distaste. "There were a few possibilities. I think Haven had this idea that one of them might be decent. Anyway, instead of helping, the dude hit on her. She came home sobbing her eyeballs out, and our mom just looked right through her like she wasn't even there. And she *still* can't manage to hate the worthless bitch. I can. Most days I can. And if I forget, I just remind myself what it looked like, our mom lying there, dead on the street, her skin burned, track marks littering her arms, our building in flames and Haven trying to run back inside for those fucking *plants*, trying to save them like they were her children."

Oh God. The plants from the Kims' garden. The ones she'd nourished and cared for after they'd left.

Not her children. A representation of the only stability she'd ever known. Before it, too, went away.

Just like everything and everyone that had ever meant anything to her. Whether they'd earned it or not.

I couldn't breathe.

Haven Torres had been hurt and abandoned by the people who were supposed to care for and protect her. All her life. But instead of lashing out at others, she'd sought to be a protector, a *rescuer*. She'd remained good and loving despite all that she'd endured.

Unlike me, who'd turned my pain in the opposite direction.

I knew what it was like to lose someone a part of you wished you could hate. I had turned that hate outward. But Haven had found a way to love around it. And it was honorable and brave and beautiful. But I knew better than anyone that it was still there, inside, that ball of complex emotion that festered and *hurt*.

And so she'd run.

She'd cared for others, even to her own detriment. And she'd given every last ounce she had to give until she couldn't do it anymore. And even then, her loving spirit demanded that she rescue *something*, and so she'd rescued *plants*.

She was a goddamn miracle.

How could I demand more? If I truly cared for her, and I did, *God, I did*, then I could not ask for more than she was willing to give. If I cared for her, I could not manipulate or plot, or try to *control*, the way I'd always done.

That was my fallback. Always. Manipulate. Position myself. And when I took a moment to consider this, I knew why. It was familiar and it made me feel artificially powerful because I was doing *something* to attempt to lessen my hurt. My feelings of being less-than. Second best.

Grasp. Hold. Attain for *myself* what no one else would give me, because I wasn't worth the effort.

And it'd brought nothing but unhappiness. Loneliness. Even when a crowd of people surrounded me.

I shut my eyes, pain winding through me at the mere idea of just . . . letting go.

For her.

The way I'd done with Archer and that amendment, but harder. Infinitely harder.

The lessons just kept on coming, didn't they?

Life testing whether I'd truly *gotten it.*

Archer's words came back to me. *She made me braver, and stronger. Because of her, I wanted to be the best version of myself. And that, I think, is what love does, if it's really love.*

The best version of myself wouldn't try to *force* Haven to choose me. The best version of myself would let her keep her fear because, for now at least, she needed it. It was helping her survive, and only she got to decide when to let it go.

Bree had given Archer the time he needed to overcome his fear once upon a time. And I'd give Haven hers. Despite that it killed me.

I wouldn't *plot.* Not with Archer, and not with her. Not with anyone. I'd made my case. I'd bared my heart and it was all I could do. All I *should* do. I laced my fingers, clenching my joined hands, because I'd thought it earlier, and I thought it now: old habits died *hard.*

My eyes remained fixed on the kid in front of me. He carried things too. And he was all she had. Whatever his reasons, he'd turned his pain outward.

I was no better, and probably worse.

"Go to bed, Easton," I said, my voice thick. "You're probably going to have a hangover in the morning."

"Yeah." He ran his hand through his hair again and pulled himself to his feet. He stumbled toward the doorway, stopping and turning his head back toward me. "Goodnight, Chief Hale."

"Goodnight."

I sat there for a few more minutes, letting the suffering wash through me, over me. And then I stood, making my way to my room and packing hastily. I left the key on the dresser and then I exited, looking down the hall at Haven's closed door, longing to go to her, but resisting.

I walked quietly down the stairs, stopping only to write a brief note to Betty before I left.

CHAPTER TWENTY-EIGHT

Haven

My eyes cracked open, light seeping through the edges of the blinds. I was surprised I'd slept at all. I had been sure sleep would be virtually impossible, that I'd stare at the ceiling, the picture of Travis's face front and center in my mind, the way he'd looked so *broken* as I'd turned and walked away.

My ribcage felt hollow, empty. I sat up, swinging my legs over the side of the bed.

Have you considered that you really have no feelings for Gage and that's why he's safe?

I sighed, my shoulders sagging.

Have you considered that you're using him to keep me emotionally at arm's length?

Yes, of course he was right. I could see that now, all too clearly. I'd been using Gage to keep Travis at arm's length. Because it meant my survival. I couldn't risk it again, not now, just when I was finally feeling stronger, just when the sharpest edge of agony over that horrifying night had begun to fade, when finally, *finally,* the smell of smoke and ash wasn't the first thing I swore I smelled when I woke.

I propelled myself off the bed, heading for the bathroom. I'd found peace out on the road, stopping only long enough to fund another stretch, forming no attachments, none at all. It'd been a *relief.* I couldn't go backward. I didn't have more heart to risk.

But right from the beginning, I'd sensed a kinship with Travis that defied words. It had scared me. *Concerned* me. And so I'd done what I thought I had to do to keep him in the box I'd carefully constructed for him.

Friends.

Then—though riskier—friends with benefits.

At first, I'd thought he wanted those things too.

How could he want more? His rebound status would ensure that he'd keep things casual. And in a way that had hurt, but in a way, it had also comforted me.

And so I'd let my guard down.

Give us a chance, Haven.

The joy—the *possibility*—in those words still caused my heart to gallop, but they terrified me too, because chances were risky. Chances could go either way. *Chances* offered no guarantee.

I'd been *forced* to grieve. What kind of fool would I be to *willingly* put myself at risk of that again?

And the scariest part of all was that I saw a future with him too. The beautiful way it might look. I'd pictured it, clear as day, our bodies connected and our eyes locked as visions of wildflower meadows under a setting sun and a myriad of *other* visions—dreams—I wouldn't think about *now* had flashed through my mind. Each time we were together and I was wrapped in the protective cocoon of his arms, the visions grew stronger and stronger until I could no longer shut them out.

And as I'd learned more about Travis, the question I'd asked as I'd sat reading about the terrible way his father had died, was answered.

Who had helped Travis grieve, I'd wondered.

And the more he divulged about himself, about the shames and the burdens he carried, the more I realized that my hunch was correct: no one had. And so he'd tried to heal on his own and gone about it the wrong way. Maybe the hurt part of me that had never received any closure, recognized the same wound in him.

And that had scared me too, because it had made my heart reach for him, wanting—*needing*—to soothe, to care for, to love.

And so *yes,* I'd used Gage like a wooden child's sword, held up against a monster looming out of the dark. A useless shield against something too mighty to fight.

And all a moot point because we were *leaving.*

I rinsed my toothbrush, setting it on the sink just as a knock sounded at the door. I stilled, meeting my own eyes in the mirror.

"Haven, open up."

I huffed out a breath. *Easton.* Simultaneously, my heart sank and relief carried me quickly to the door.

I'm leaving in the morning.

He was really gone.

I pulled it open to see my disheveled brother, sporting a serious case of bedhead, his eyes bloodshot. "You look awful."

"Thanks," he said sarcastically, entering the room and sinking down onto the edge of the bed. I took a seat next to him, pulling my legs beneath me.

"Rough night?" I guessed.

"Nah. Good night. I went out with the guys from the firehouse. We had a few too many, but nothing worse than that."

I sighed internally, watching him for a moment. "So what's up?"

He paused, running his hand through his hair before meeting my eyes. "What do you think about staying here a little longer?"

"*Staying?*" My eyes widened. "What? In Pelion? No. Our plan—"

"I know what our plan is. But . . . I like it here. I fit in here."

"You burned bridges here, Easton."

"Chief Hale? No . . . I think . . . I mean, I don't think he carries a grudge." He looked away as if considering something he wasn't saying.

Fear licked at my heart like the flames that had decimated our building, our life. I swallowed. Picturing a future with Travis was one thing. Knowing he might want one with me too, if that wanting could be trusted, was another. But staying to find out? Well . . . that would take a certain measure of courage I just didn't have, nor could I afford to gather.

"No. We have to keep moving."

"What happens if you stop, Haven?"

My gaze snapped to his. "What?"

"What happens when you stop moving?"

My breath came short, heart picking up speed. Easton stood, walking to the bed where he sat on the edge next to me. "Haven, what happens?"

"It catches up to me!" I blurted. "It all catches up." And then I'd have to start over, risk again, care again. No more excuses. No more *temporary.*

I wasn't *ready.* Was I?

He laid his hand over mine. "It's time to stop, Haven. You have to stop running. You're dragging me with you and I don't want it anymore."

My head swiveled his way, a ball of despair dropping inside me. "Oh, Easton," I breathed, my face collapsing as a sob moved up my throat. I put my hands over my face. "I'm trying to protect you too!"

Easton reached over and gently removed my hands. "But you don't have to. You already did. A thousand times over." He turned more fully toward me, shifting closer. "Listen, I've been guilty too. I acted in ways that ensured I *couldn't* stay anywhere even if I'd wanted to. I burned bridges so it wouldn't hurt to leave."

I let out a shuddery breath. "You didn't want to come on this road trip, did you?"

He shook his head slowly. "No, but I knew you needed it and I wasn't going to let you go it alone." He gave me a small weary smile. "I admit, I didn't think we'd still be on the road two years later." He paused, tilting his head as the smile dropped. "You sacrificed for me all your life, sis. And it was my turn. But we've been on the road long enough now. Let's stay, Haven. For once, let's stay. I like working at the firehouse. I think I might have a future there. I can *see* it, can you? Let's stay," he repeated softly. "Even if it means facing the past."

"I hated her, Easton." It burst from my mouth like a grenade that had been detonated two years before and only now exploded. "I hated her," I said, my voice choked with tears. "I kept waiting for her to be more, to do better, for *us*, and she never would."

"I know," he said. "I know, Haven. But you loved her too, and that's the worst part. It's time for us both to let it go now though. We have to try."

I nodded miserably. I had loved her. Deeply. And though she couldn't care for me, I'd tried to care for her. And it'd never mattered.

Sometimes I wondered if I had a form of PTSD.

Maybe from the fire. From seeing our mother dead—the reality of a lifetime of fearing just that.

Maybe just from our *life.*

The incessant struggle, the hurt, the never-ending *trying* that didn't seem to amount to much. Maybe I'd thought if I could have just *saved* her it all would have been worthwhile. But I couldn't. Perhaps nobody could have. And I had to start accepting that and letting myself off the hook if I was ever going to be truly happy. If I was ever going to stop running.

"I'm afraid," I admitted. "Anyone I hoped would love me left. Eventually, they always did."

So how did I start trusting *now?*

Maybe by believing in myself.

By trusting a man I believed might be trustworthy.

Easton reached out and grabbed my hand, squeezing. "*I'm* not leaving," he said. "You're stuck with me for life."

And then my little brother opened his arms and I fell forward, face-planting into his chest and grasping the fabric of his shirt in my fist, holding on to what felt solid. Easton held me as I cried, releasing some of the long-held pain and the deeply lodged fear.

Finally.

CHAPTER TWENTY-NINE

Haven

A buzz of voices welcomed us as we pulled the door to the town hall open. A few heads turned, some smiled, some looked mildly curious as they sipped from Styrofoam cups. I took a deep breath of the air redolent with coffee and baked goods, running my hands over my thighs. "Come on," Easton said, leading me toward the table where three large silver urns sat beside platters of cookies and baked goods.

"Are you sure this is a good idea?" I asked under my breath.

Easton picked up a donut, taking a big, sugary bite and not bothering to chew or swallow before answering, "Yesh." He paused, gulped. "The Pelion firehouse guys will all be here. There's the captain right over there," he said, lifting his chin and giving a small wave to the stern-looking man near the stage. The man gave a head nod in acknowledgment. "Might as well jump right in if we're going to join this community."

Easton moved from one foot to the other. His tell. He was nervous. He'd never admit it but he wanted to be accepted. He'd always been the odd man out, the kid who couldn't invite others over.

The one whose mother never showed.

The one who'd waited anyway.

He deserved this. To make friends. To be accepted.

I was doing this for him. But I was also doing this for *me.* My nerves felt frayed, heart quickening with both excitement—*hope*—and trepidation. It had been two long years, and I was about to take my first big risk.

You can do this. It's time.

I helped myself to a cup of coffee, sipping tentatively at the scalding liquid. All the seats were taken, but Easton and I stood against the back wall, watching as the community members chatted and laughed, enjoying each other.

You can be part of this. That hope soared in my chest again, and yes, fear accompanied it, but wouldn't that always be the case? Easton was right. I couldn't wait for the doubt to disappear entirely, because that might never happen. I had to make the choice to embrace it and lean in to what I wanted, despite the worry.

I deserved to have dreams.

And how would they ever come true if I wasn't willing to stop, face my past, and then move on, unencumbered, into my future?

And I wouldn't be doing it alone.

My heart gave a jolt and then soared as Travis came into view, standing near the low stage, taking a stack of papers from a younger man who was also wearing a police uniform. Travis took a portion of the stack of papers off the top and handed them to a short, slender woman with a brunette bob haircut who began handing them to the people at the end of each row to pass down to the others.

For several minutes I simply watched him in his element, listening as people passed by and said a word or two, laughing along with them, squeezing one man's shoulder, and patting him on the back as he gave Travis a grateful look and walked away.

Give us a chance, Haven.

Yes. *Yes.*

The man next to him—the young cop with the buzz cut— elbowed Travis and leaned in, speaking in a hurried manner. Travis froze, frowning, glancing down at the papers in his hand for several seconds, squinting, holding it away slightly, and then blinking in what looked like confusion, before his head shot up and he met my eyes. The young cop was staring at me too and even from the distance, I saw his throat move in a swallow.

Travis stared in shock as I bit my lip, shy, happy, and hoping to God he understood why I'd come. Vulnerability made me feel breakable, shaky, and yet that hope continued to flutter inside.

I'm going to stay.

I saw him take in a quickened breath, his expression morphing into . . . horror.

My heart dipped and distractedly I took the papers that had made it to us, handing one to Easton as well.

Why was Travis *looking* at me like that? A buzz started in the back of my head. Was he not glad I was here? A tremor took up inside me, those excited nerves taking a sudden nosedive.

"Oh God," I heard Easton say, his voice choked.

I glanced at him to see he'd started to read the flyer we'd been handed and, confused, looked down at my own, everything inside me going frigid as I saw what it said, my heart plunging lower and lower as I read.

The newly formed community relations committee, along with the Pelion Police Department, will be putting out this monthly bulletin in an effort to protect the safety, well-being, and happiness of our fellow citizens. It has come to our attention that a seasonal employee of The Calliope Golf and Tennis Club has hurt and disrespected our very own chief of police. For that reason, Easton and Haven Torres are listed on this edition of PELION'S MOST UNWANTED. Encourage these individuals to move on from our close-knit community as quickly as possible. When one citizen is hurt

by an outsider, all citizens are hurt. Pelion is a family-friendly town, and the community relations committee vets all residents, both permanent and temporary.

And there were *pictures* of us below the caption, photos I recognized as ones Easton had posted on social media, only blown-up and made into close-ups of our faces.

A small strangled sound came from my throat as I felt eyes turning toward us.

These individuals.

I kept reading. I couldn't stop. I was glued to my spot, unable to lift my head, my eyes refusing to stop taking in line after line after line of Easton's exploits and my own enabling of his behavior. All the destruction left in our wake. Arrests, divorce filings, public altercations.

"How did they . . . how did they . . ." I choked.

"My social media," Easton said, and his voice sounded flat, devoid of emotion. "I've posted from every community we've stopped in since the day we left LA."

I felt numb, confused, sick with distress, my mind reeling with how much work had gone into compiling a list like this. I felt all the eyes on me. Judging.

Most unwanted.

Most unwanted.

Most unwanted.

Some of the information was mostly accurate, and some was wildly off-base. Not that it mattered. Whoever had done this, had put in a lot of time and much effort contacting local townships from California to Maine.

Why?

I was focused on revenge.

Revenge?

Yes. What's wrong with exacting revenge when a wrong is done to you?

The Pelion Police Department, along with the newly formed community relations committee . . .

He'd done this. Travis had done this. I felt hot, woozy. Whispers picked up, people murmuring. I heard my name, the person's tone full of scorn.

"Well, they *don't* seem like people we'd want here permanently," someone said.

"It seems kind of mean," someone else answered. "But I agree," they amended softly.

"Can you imagine the trouble they'd cause?" someone else asked. "It seems like they've already started."

"What trash."

I dared a glance at Easton to see his gaze focused in the direction of the firehouse captain, whose head was bent as he read over the paper outlining all Easton's sins. My brother's gaze lowered. I'd seen that expression before. He'd worn it as he'd sat on the sidewalk, two fingers pressed to our mother's wrist, her track marks glaringly red in the light from the raging fire.

This was killing him. I was watching his soul slowly die. Again.

My gaze flew to Travis's stunned face and he seemed to suddenly remember how to move, dropping the remaining flyers and moving toward me.

Run.

Only I didn't seem to be able to.

I stood, trying desperately to sink into the floor as Travis approached. "Haven," he said, his voice a mere whisper as though he was having trouble breathing. "I didn't know you'd be here."

"No, evidently not," I said, and my voice sounded dull and lifeless even to my own ears. I held the flyer up, my hand trembling. "Did you do this?"

He swallowed, his eyes clenching shut momentarily. "I . . . no. I did not have this flyer printed, but it's my fault. I asked my recruit to look into Easton." He glanced at my brother, then away. "I take responsibility for this. But I didn't think . . ." He breathed out a sharp breath, running his hand through his hair as my heart slowly shriveled.

"Your . . . revenge," I said.

His shoulders dropped and he looked at me pleadingly. "Yes. My revenge."

Voices began to rise as more people gossiped about what they were reading. It looked bad. It looked terrible. I wouldn't have wanted us as part of this idyllic community either.

What trash.

We were. We were trash, and this flyer didn't even detail the half of it.

Easton made terrible choices. There was a list of them grasped in my hand. But *I* had dragged him across the country because of *my* issues, and he'd acted out because of it. I was selfish and thoughtless. He'd needed to stay home and *heal,* to remain with the people and things familiar to him and I hadn't let him. *I* was the one who'd caused the trail of wreckage in our wake. Me.

Travis reached out. "Haven, please," he said, "Let me make this right. I'm so sorry."

The loud whir of a plane flying low overhead could be heard above the murmurs. "It's trailing a banner," someone near the window could be heard saying.

Travis's eyes widened. "Oh, dear God, no," he gasped.

"It's an ad for parasailing lessons over in Calliope," another person answered, turning away from the window back to the more interesting drama unfolding in front of the crowded room. Travis's eyes closed briefly and his shoulders dropped and he exhaled a big gust of breath, evidently relieved about something.

Most unwanted.

Us.

Travis looked at Easton and then back at me. "Let me explain this," he said.

My gaze moved slowly over the room, the people a blur, hurt a gray pulsating fog before my eyes. Perhaps Travis hadn't meant this to happen, or perhaps not to this extent, or in this way, but he'd had a hand in it nonetheless, and now the damage was done.

Give us a chance, Haven.

His words, they'd been lies.

And I'd been lied to over and over and over and yet I'd kept on *hoping*.

I'm clean.

I'll never use again.

I won't spend the grocery money on drugs.

And the worst of them all: I'll be *there this time.*

All those old wounds ripped wide open and I bled, fresh pain in the light of this betrayal. He'd said he cared for me and he'd *let* this happen. Somehow.

"Congratulations," Easton said, his voice still dull, his lips tipping humorlessly. "You exacted the perfect revenge. You waited, and you struck, just like you said." He held his hand out. "Brilliant strategy. The win goes to you."

Travis's lips thinned, and his jaw ticked as though he was clenching it. He looked down at Easton's hand, but didn't take it. "This isn't how it seems—"

"It doesn't matter," I said, lifting my chin. I felt a sob moving up my throat and I could not cry in front of these people. I could not. "There was no need to make flyers to get rid of us," I said to the crowd at large. "I'm sorry you wasted the ink. And the research time. We were never staying anyway. Let's go." I batted Easton's hand down, still held out in the air, yanking at his sleeve.

Easton only hesitated a moment before he took my hand. We turned just as Travis reached toward me, but I avoided him, walking on legs that felt like rubber, my deep self-consciousness making my muscles twitch as I focused solely on moving. *Away. Away. Run.*

I waited until we'd gotten in the car and Easton was pulling out of the lot before I allowed the tears to flow, my heart and my pride in utter ruin.

CHAPTER THIRTY

Travis

Devastation rolled through me. What had I *done?*

I groaned in despair, gripping my head in my hands. She'd never forgive me, and why should she? It had been my stupid, misdirected need for revenge that had started the ball rolling and ended in Haven and Easton's very public humiliation.

I'd wanted to *kill* Spencer when I'd approached him after Haven and Easton had left. But his eyes had been wide with shock and shame and he'd said miserably, "We didn't know they'd *be* here." I'd tried to hang on to my rage about the fact that he hadn't sought my approval regarding the flyer, but I knew it had all started with me, and that I'd been negligent in letting it be printed at all. I was the chief. The fact that that had gotten past me was unacceptable. The buck, so to speak, stopped here.

As a result of me being asleep at the wheel, I'd destroyed Haven, and Easton too. *Dear Jesus.* I pictured the wounded looks in their eyes, the way they'd both tried so desperately to hold on to their pride and only barely managed to do it. Two people who'd been unwanted all their lives. It felt so . . . callous. *Heartless.*

All things I'd been called before. And rightly so.

I'd collected all the flyers, telling the crowd they were a mistake, but it was pointless by then. The whole place was buzzing, debate springing up about whether calling out individuals for misdeeds was right or wrong. I'd been too sick about it to engage, my head spinning uselessly with ways I could fix this.

Bree and Archer had approached me, the looks on their faces such stark examples of *disappointment* that I'd wanted to sink into the floor.

It would have been *easy* to place the blame on Spencer, and on Birdie Ellis too, but I'd always taken the easy way out, and I sensed, on some cosmic level, that this was my final lesson.

Lose it all, or lose it *all.*

I'd come to the crossroads, both paths seemingly leading in the same direction.

I looked out the front window of my truck, raindrops streaking over the glass and blurring the old red barn, misery tracking through my veins.

I hadn't slept a wink and as soon as the sun rose, I'd driven here, trying to grasp some peace, some clarity. Because all I kept seeing was her expression the moment she realized what she was holding.

The look on her face had ripped my heart to shreds, the way she'd stood there, the judgmental eyes of all of Pelion upon her. The place she'd considered such a dream. The place that had brought her peace.

Raindrops streaked, clouds rolled by, and I couldn't avoid another harsh truth.

Archer had felt that way once upon a time too.

I'd been part of it.

I deserved to feel like this.

Haven did not.

And neither did Easton for that matter.

The flyer had highlighted Easton's transgressions, but I knew the list had hurt Haven just as deeply, because she loved him. And they'd both been there to ask for acceptance from the town. I let out a staggered breath. The thing was . . . I knew what reading a list like that must feel like because I'd *been* him. I'd done things purposely to hurt people. I'd left destruction in *my* wake, and for longer than two years. But *unlike* him, I'd been embraced, not shunned. I'd been given a second chance. Hell, I'd been given more than a second chance. I'd been offered not only acceptance, but love.

But I'd *wanted* what had happened at that meeting, or some version of it anyway, not so long ago.

They'd been there to join the community, to be part of something. To *risk* asking for acceptance when risk was so very difficult for people who'd been through what they had. I'd known the reason they were there the second I'd seen her and it had sent happiness whirling dizzily inside me. I wanted to know how and why and when she'd arrived at the decision because even before she'd seen the things written about them, she looked like she'd been crying. I knew the choice had taken immense courage. Her eyes had been red and swollen but there had been such raw *hope* on her face.

"Idiot, idiot, idiot," I murmured, sitting up straight.

The rest of the photo albums my mother had given me still sat on my passenger seat and I picked one up, leafing through it idly, seeing photos of my father and me as a baby and then as a little boy, photos that stopped after the one of me in front of a cake with seven candles on it.

Why are you doing this? To torture yourself? For the reminder that you're not worthy of anyone's love?

To remember why he left?

I closed the album. The only other amendment to the original land deed had stuck to the top and I glanced at it. I'd already read it. It posed no threat to Archer so there was no need to burn it. If anything, it posed a threat to me, but I wasn't concerned. Archer was reasonable, and I knew he'd be willing to overlook or void it. I tossed it aside, picking up the heavy album to set that back on the seat as well when an envelope with my name on it fell out of the back, the handwriting both unfamiliar and immediately recognizable.

My heart lurched.

I reached for it with shaking hands. My stalled heart suddenly beating erratically.

Don't read it. Whatever it says might destroy the final piece of you.

But I had to. I *had* to.

My heart slammed against my ribs as I opened the flap. The seal had already been ripped. *This had been read before.* But not by me.

I unfolded the letter, my breath hitching. He'd printed the note.

Of course he had—I had only just learned to read that winter. He'd been writing to a seven-year-old.

May 15th

Dear Travis,

This is the hardest letter I've ever written but you are a good, smart boy, and so I know that you will try your best to understand what I have to say to you.

Sometimes mommies and daddies get married for the wrong reasons, and sometimes they stay together longer than they should even though neither one is happy. That's what happened with your mother and me and that's why we won't be living together anymore. What will never ever change no matter what, is our love for you. Someday, you'll know of all the mistakes that were made, but one thing you must never believe, is that you were one of them. You are my inquisitive, insightful little man, and I'm so very, <u>very</u> proud to be your father.

I'm leaving for a little while, Champ, but not for long. I will be back for you because I would never leave you behind. And when we are face to face, I will try to explain all the things that I know you are a big enough boy to understand.

You know the land that I took you to see right on the lake? The one with the red barn and all those rows of fruit trees? When the timing is right, I'm going to build a big house on that plot, and we are going to be happy there. I see it in my mind's eye, Champ—me and you sitting on the dock with fishing poles in our hands.

Can you see it too?

You hold that picture in your mind.

Between now and then, please trust me. And most importantly, please trust your own wise and tender heart. Listen to that part of yourself. It will never lead you astray.

We have so many years ahead of us, Champ. Years to live and laugh and learn all sorts of lessons, good and bad and everything in between. And when you have questions, or need guidance, I will be there.

I will <u>always</u> be there.

I love you with all of my heart, Dad

I let out a strangled gasp of air, hot tears burning my eyes as I sat, reeling.

He hadn't left without saying goodbye. He'd written to me, only I'd never known.

My dad had been leaving for a short time, most likely to get Alyssa and Archer to a safe location until both divorces were filed, and hot tempers flared and cooled.

He'd been leaving temporarily in an effort to protect them because he'd been in love.

I'd never understood the lengths a man would be moved to go to for a woman he loved. Because I'd never felt that depth of feeling. I did now though.

The world tilted, everything I'd ever thought to be true turning on its side.

Yes, my father had been in love. He'd loved me too though. *I would never leave you behind.*

I looked up, staring unseeing at the old red barn, a ray of sunlight streaming through the clouds.

Lose it all, or lose it all.

And suddenly, in an instant, I knew what I had to do.

Fear trembled through me. Fear, and a sense of rightness unlike I'd ever known.

Trust your own wise and tender heart.

I'm going to, Dad.

I turned the key in the ignition. First though, I had a few stops to make. The tires crunched on the wet gravel as I turned, heading toward the road that led out of town.

****

My mother adjusted the bags in her hand, digging in her purse for what must be her keys as I stepped toward her. It was barely ten a.m. and she'd already been out shopping.

She startled slightly, blowing out a breath when she saw it was me.

"Travis. You didn't tell me you were coming over."

I held up the envelope containing the letter from my dad. Her brows knitted as she again, adjusted the shopping bags in her hands. "What is—" I saw when understanding dawned. "Oh, I see." She gave her shoulders a small shake, stepping toward her door. But I'd also noticed that her face had suddenly lost some color beneath the heavy makeup.

She flicked open her lock, stepping inside and I followed her. "You kept it from me," I said. I'd driven the whole way without considering what I'd say to her, so many thoughts and emotions running rampant through me that I had no room left to plan for anything. I only wanted to know why.

She tossed the bags onto the couch, facing me. She'd regained her composure. It'd only taken a moment. "It wouldn't have done you any good, Travis. It would have only poured salt in the wound. You were seven years old. Later, I forgot it even existed."

I shook my head, in disbelief that anyone could be so incredibly, *blindly* self-absorbed. "It would have meant everything to me," I choked. "You didn't keep it from me because you thought I was too young to understand. And you didn't forget about it. You *wanted* me to carry the same bitterness toward him you did because it worked for you. He left you. He couldn't stand your lies and manipulation. But he didn't leave me. He never left me. And all my life . . . all my *life,* I've carried the grief that came from thinking he did."

She fiddled with her bracelets, two spots of color appearing on her cheeks as her eyes narrowed. She was gathering her anger. And her anger was a shield, I supposed, but it also shot daggers. It was meant to protect . . . and to wound. And I had never been exempt from it. *What happened to you?* I wanted to ask. But it didn't matter. She was never going to change. She'd had opportunities to become better— to reinvent herself—and she'd never taken them. "He didn't even *want* you!" Her words fired out. "You should have seen his face when I told him I was pregnant! It was like someone had punched him square in the gut."

"Because you tricked him into it!" I yelled, and drew satisfaction from her flinch. I *knew* what it was like to be strapped to this woman, so I didn't have to wonder how he'd felt. He'd made mistakes too, but he'd tried to do the honorable thing. And I wasn't going to let my selfish mother convince me that, though I was unplanned, he didn't love me. My heart told me differently. I'd *felt* his love. And believing he'd loved me and then left anyway had created a deep pit of devastation inside, one I'd carried since I was a child. I wasn't going to carry it any longer. I took a deep, cleansing breath, blowing out the anger, the resentment. I wasn't going to hold on to that either and risk turning into her. "I burned those amendments you gave me," I said. *Except one.* But I wasn't going to tell her that.

315

Her eyes widened, lips twisting. "You did *what?* My God! I thought I could trust you by giving you the originals! Do you know what you've lost? Do you even know?"

"No, you're the one who lost, Mom." I took her in, one final time. "If you'd loved me at all, you would have given me this letter," I said, holding it up again. "You were so unwilling to let go of trying to control everything and everyone, that you lost. You lost it all. Including me."

And then I turned and walked away.

As the road back to Pelion—back home—stretched before me, her words echoed.

I thought I could trust you, she'd said.

You can't, I thought.

But maybe I can finally start trusting myself.

****

I made a few other quick stops, notably one to the firehouse where I had some explaining to do, and a favor to ask, and then I headed home.

It was strange being in my house again, surrounded by all the things that felt both familiar and not. It didn't feel like home anymore. Not the way The Yellow Trellis Inn had, that house full of misfits and laughter. Affection, and even love.

And it went without saying, plenty of hooch.

I took a seat at my dining table, pushing a letter from my landlady aside. I'd deal with that later. My computer sat in front of me, and for a few minutes I simply stared out the window at the trees that blocked the lake beyond. There wasn't a clear lake view from here, but I could see tiny sparkles of blue through the feathery branches, and feel the peace that the water brought. How many countless times had that lake comforted me? Too many to count. How many times had the *people* in this community comforted me, in one way or another? Far too many to count.

I thought about what Burt had told me about Betty, and about her lost words. I thought about how they completed each other, each providing what the other was missing.

I thought about Haven, and about Easton too.

I thought about how they were nomads, searching for a home.

And how I was a man with a home I'd never fully appreciated until I saw it through their eyes.

I felt ashamed, and grateful, and devastated, and humbled.

I let it all fall over me, soaking into my skin, filling my heart, weaving into the fiber of my bones, who I was and who I might become. Who my father believed I would be.

Listen to your wise and tender heart.

I thought about all the ways I'd taken the multitude of gifts I'd been given for granted, abandoning all faith and embracing the very worst parts of myself.

And I no longer wanted to be that man.

I wanted to be someone better.

I slipped on my reading glasses, opened a document, and began to type.

CHAPTER THIRTY-ONE

Travis

"Thank you all for coming to, uh, the follow-up to the town meeting," I said, the microphone giving out an ear-piercing shriek that traveled along my already-frayed nerves as I winced, leaning back slightly. I cleared my throat. "I know this is irregular, and I appreciate you all making time to be here. Again."

I bent, lifting a box of stapled packets at my feet and handing it to Deb. She took it with a small huff, staggering slightly under its weight. I leaned away from the microphone. "There's a dolly over there," I whispered, inclining my head.

"Thank goodness," she murmured, taking the few steps to where I'd parked the dolly I'd used to cart the boxes in.

The crowd murmured, expressions rife with interest, and some concern, as Deb wheeled the first box toward the crowd, asking everyone to take a packet and pass them down. I waited a few minutes while they were distributed, Deb wheeling back and getting a second box to hand out to the middle and back rows. I avoided looking at the first of the citizens who'd already received the list I'd compiled throughout a long week and several sleepless nights. I couldn't bear to see their faces. I was bone weary, and yet fear and humiliation roiled in my gut.

"The flyer distributed at the annual meeting about the Torreses was wrong on every level," I began. "I didn't intend for any of that to be made public"—I shot Spencer a look and he bowed his head, ashamed—"*but*, I take full responsibility because I was the one who, because of my pride and my shortcomings, planted the seed that resulted in that list being compiled." I looked around, watching the packets being passed down one aisle and then the next. "We're better than that, as a community, and as individuals. Eight years ago, we learned what making outcasts of people does, and what gifts we all receive when we embrace a welcoming spirit."

I cleared my throat. The murmurs were rising in volume. Yeah, there was a lot to murmur about.

"Regarding the Torreses, I'd also like to make it clear that I'm biased. I'm biased because I'm in love with Haven Torres. Deeply, miserably, completely in love with her." I was pretty sure more mouths dropped open but my vision had gone slightly blurry. "Maybe it seems quick—"

"Maybe it seems like it's about damn time!" someone yelled from the crowd below. I thought it sounded like Mrs. Connick, but I couldn't be certain.

"In any case, I'm sure it will be some consolation to many of you that you'll enjoy witnessing my torment and suffering for a long time to come. Possibly for the rest of this life. Potentially into the next."

Murmurs. The sound of pages flipping. Someone in the back shouting, "What the *hell?* Who *does* that?" as they read over one bullet point or another.

"Haven Torres is the bravest, most big-hearted person I've ever had the pleasure of knowing, and any community would be lucky to have her in it. Communities should hold lotteries to win people like her. She cares for people, and even things, deeply and we don't deserve her because no one does." I glanced around quickly. "Easton Torres has made mistakes. But so have I." I squinted, clearing my throat again. "I, of all people, have no right to pass judgment on others. *I've* done things to ruin lives. *I've* acted in ways some might judge irredeemable." I paused, gathering what little courage it felt like I had left. "And the further truth—and a fact that wasn't included on that list—is that Easton acted as a hero when he saved his sister's life and for that, I will spend the rest of mine grateful to him. As an act of contrition, and of public apology for my part in what happened at the first town meeting, I've compiled a list, of every immoral, shameful, in a few regrettable instances, sacrilegious, and . . . well, in some cases downright illegal things I've ever done. Because I can't make excuses for Easton Torres, nor for myself, but I can join him. And that's what I'm here to do. I'm here to join him."

I dared a glance at Moira Cormier in the front row, who ran the pet grooming shop in downtown Pelion. Her eyes were wide and her mouth hung open as she scanned one page, flipping to the next. "There are some doozies in there. As you'll see, names and specific dates are redacted to protect the privacy of the individuals involved." I swallowed. The murmurs rose again, this time not only in volume, but in intensity. My face felt hot, muscles achy with tension. I didn't want these people to know these things.

"Er, I realize . . . well, I realize that some of these items might make you consider a chief of police recall. I wouldn't blame you. I'm prepared for that if you all deem it in the best interest of the town," I finished. I felt scared, miserable, and yet there was a strange weight that had been lifted off my shoulders. I didn't know if I was grateful for the release of pressure, or if that empty spot would come to be filled by a different, weightier burden.

But I'd accept whatever fallout this might cause. I'd earned it.

I'd never fought for anyone before. I'd been too busy fighting for myself. Thinking only of myself. While Haven had only done the opposite. And I loved her. God, I loved her.

Ellen Russo, the elderly high school chemistry teacher stood up, shaking the packet, a look of horror etched into her ancient features. "You did *what* in the chemistry lab at the high school, Travis Michael Hale? You're lucky you don't have chemical burns on your—"

"That was *me!*" Tracy Berry stood up with her toddler in one arm, her other arm raised high. "That's *my* name that's redacted!" She grinned around, her smile fading when she saw her husband's face in his palm. Her raised arm fell limply to her side. "He was the captain of the football team. *All* the girls wanted him," she said in explanation. "Oh, get over it, I hadn't even met you yet," she grumped, rolling her eyes and dropping back into her seat.

Citizens turned to other citizens, exclaiming about this or that, turning the pages quickly, as my face continued to burn, shame sitting like a rock on my chest.

You deserve this. Every bit of it.

"A strip club? A *strip* club?" Maggie shouted, rising, and pulling an obviously uncomfortable Norm with her to stand in solidarity to her outrage. She tapped her finger on the page. "You took that innocent boy to a *strip* club?" she yelled, shock and disappointment clear in her tone. I shivered. "How *could* you? I oughta take my wooden spoon to you! *Despicable,* Travis Hale!"

"I know, Maggie," I said into the microphone. "Believe me, I know." I stuck my hands in my pockets, both wanting to be swallowed into the floor, and knowing the point of this was to stand in front of these people and experience their disdain, waiting as they all read through each and every item.

We were all going to be here a while.

I glanced at Amber Dalton, the girl, and then woman I'd conspired with on more than one occasion to harass Archer, most notably in a strip club she'd worked at on the other side of the lake many years ago. Her mouth was hanging open. I

322

knew pieces of her story. She'd had a rough time at home too—we'd been messes together for a time and eventually outgrew each other. Despite her issues, and the part she'd played in several of my schemes, Amber had a sweetness to her. Unfortunately, we had never brought out the positive in one another. We'd never filled each other's hollow spots. She'd gotten her life together, was married to a mechanic, and had two little girls at home. The police department was never called there, not like they'd been to the home she'd grown up in. She caught my eye, and despite her shocked expression, her mouth hitched up slightly and she winked at me.

A small gust of breath released, something lightened minutely inside.

"That was *my* mailbox you sumabitch!" Linton Whalley shouted, raising his fist. "Three times I replaced that!"

Oh, right. I grabbed the folder on the table next to me, stepping down off the stage and walking toward the row where he stood at the end. I opened the folder, rifling through the stack of checks in a total that had drained every cent I had combined in all my accounts, including a cash withdrawal from one of my credit cards. "I've written out a check. I, er, looked up the average price of a mailbox, uh, times three, and added a five percent interest rate."

Linton grabbed the check from me, his eyes flashing with indignation. "You vandalized my property," he said.

My shoulders dropped, and I nodded. I'd been eighteen years old. I'd known better. Linton paused, his eyes narrowing as he considered me. "But," he finally said, "you also held my wife's hand when she collapsed last summer.

You were the first one there, and you kept her calm. Me too, truth be told." His lips thinned and he held my gaze as he lifted the check and ripped it up. "We're even, Chief."

Another exhale, the blessing of grace. "Thank you," I breathed.

I returned to the stage, leaning in to the microphone. "I apologize to all of you," I said. "The ones I hurt. The ones I used. All those things I did were about me, never about you. I wish I'd wised up sooner. I wish I'd been quicker on the uptake." I paused, trying desperately to contain my emotion enough to make it through this. "Most of all," I said, taking in a gulp of air and finally gathering the nerve to turn my body to where my brother stood off to the side of the room. His expression was one I'd never seen before and I didn't know how to read it. "Most of all," I repeated, "I want to apologize to you, Archer, because you're family. And I... I was supposed to be there for you. Instead, I made things worse." I turned the pages on the packet sitting on the lectern in front of me. "If you all turn to page seventy-three to one hundred four, you'll see every despicable thing I did to Archer. Addendum 1a outlines the times I was cruel. And addendum 2a–3c lists the times I was manipulative. I wanted to break them down so you knew I had considered the difference and how each might have affected you. And uh, well, addendum 4a outlines the times I *publicly* shunned you, which might have been the worst. You're my family and I shunned you. God, I'm so sorry. Haven said something to me recently about having apologized to you, but I never actually did. So you couldn't have fully forgiven me. I've never said the words, but I am. I'm so incredibly sorry for all the times I looked away from your pain, from your loneliness. If I could go back, I'd do things so differently. Because I hurt you, and I hurt Bree, and God"—I hitched in another breath, a lump filling my throat that I could barely speak around—"if anything I'd done had resulted in those two boys and that little girl not existing, I would have been responsible for ruining not only your lives, not only mine, but ruining the entire world."

Burt had described the way two people sometimes completed each other perfectly, helping to fill the empty gaps, and that's what Bree and Archer had been for each other. Her ability to sign had opened up his entire world. And he'd helped her overcome the loss of her father too. I didn't know the details, but I knew that much.

And I'd attempted to get in the way of that through trickery and manipulation.

The murmurs had stopped, heads swiveling between Archer and me, waiting. Bree came up beside Archer, standing quietly by her husband's side. As if her presence there had spoken to him in some silent way only he understood, he glanced at her, giving her a smile.

My heart picked up speed, thumping rapidly. I still had something else to say. "Our dad and his brother came to such an ugly end, on a highway, smeared with blood. You were there. You know." I closed my eyes momentarily. Winced. My hands were shaking. The whole room had grown silent, only the sound of my whooshing blood echoing in my head. I met Archer's eyes again. "I used to drive out there to the spot where it happened quite a bit . . . just sit on the side of the road . . . picturing a scenario where I could have intervened, stopped it somehow. I drove there today and it suddenly occurred to me that if you can find it in your heart to forgive me, really forgive me, then in some way, we *will* have stopped it. We will have broken the cycle. I want that for us, Archer. I want that for your sons, and for the ones, God willing, I might have someday."

My heart continued to pound, fingers trembling as I waited. He glanced at his wife, another unspoken something moving between them and then he turned, walking toward me. When he'd stepped onto the stage, he raised his hands. *None of us can go back,* he said. *But we're here now. And as far as new beginnings go, it's a pretty great place to start from. I'm all in if you are.* He walked up to me, placing his hand on my shoulder, and then removing it to speak. *Brothers till the end,* he signed.

I let out a small choked laugh that was filled with the enormous relief I felt. "Yeah. Yeah, I'm all in." I wrapped my arms around my brother, grasping him tightly, seeing Bree wipe a tear from her cheek, watching us from where she stood. I signaled her to join us and she walked toward the stage. The town might not forgive me, or ever trust me again. But I had my family back. They'd given me another chance, and I was going to grasp it with both hands. And now I knew, with absolute certainty, that my dad had loved me. He hadn't thrown me away. He had never thought of me as second best or someone he hadn't wanted. *I had been loved.*

But even if I hadn't been, I was *now* and God, I was grateful.

Bree made it to where we stood, wrapping her arms around us both.

"Is there a reason you're wearing"—her brow knitted as she stared at my hand on Archer's shoulder—"a donkey thimble?"

"Oh, er, it brings back a moment," I said, as we all stepped apart. "And I wanted that memory here tonight." *To give me strength. To remind me why I was doing this.*

"That's a nice show of family affection," I heard someone say. "But I don't know if he should still be chief. Have you read page forty-seven? What kind of role model is he?"

I had no argument for that.

Bree leaned toward the microphone, the murmurs beginning again, a few people still engrossed in my packet of shame, others asking questions about *repercussions.* Family was one thing, I heard someone say, but public service required higher standards. "We all have lists of things we're ashamed of," Bree said, glancing around. "Perhaps not with so many, er, *addendums.*" She gave an uncomfortable laugh. "But each of us could make one of our own. What would be on yours?" She pointed into the audience randomly. "Or yours?" She moved her finger to the left.

Apparently, assuming the question was non-rhetorical, Elmer Lunn stood up, put his hands in his pockets, hung his head, and confessed, "Sometimes when I'm bored, I go to the library and switch all the book jackets. Gives a little thrill."

A loud, sharp inhale of breath followed. "You evil *bastard!*" Marie Kenney, the town librarian said, standing up and glaring hatefully at him.

The whole crowd swiveled as Clyde Chappelle stood. "I pretended to be a spirit named Alucard."

His sister, June, came slowly to her feet, her eyes wide with disbelief. "The one we spoke to through the Ouija Board for years as kids? The one who demanded to know all of our secrets and threatened to pull us out of bed by our toes if we refused? *That* Alucard?"

"Yeah," he said sheepishly. "That's him. Er, me, I mean. I'm him."

"I've been in therapy my whole adult life over *Alucard,* you sick *devil!*" She lunged for him, but was restrained by her best friend, Honey Smythe.

"I ran over my in-law's dog and replaced it with a new one," Bill Donnelly confessed.

"Chewie?" Marie Flanders gasped. "Chewie's not . . . *Chewie?*"

Norm rose, head bowed, Maggie's eyes widening with what looked like panic. "I buy my secret-recipe potato salad by the tub at the Costco off the interstate." There was a collective gasp as Norm sank back down in his chair. "It's the best," he muttered defensively.

"Well now you'll *have* to retire. In *shame,*" I heard Maggie hiss accusingly.

Cricket stood up. "I killed Betty's husband and I'm not sorry about it." My head, along with Archer's and Bree's swiveled in unison. There was another collective gasp as the entire crowd turned her way. She reached down, took Betty's hand, and looked around. "He beat her. He knocked her in the head so many times, it's a wonder she held on to any words at all. And so I killed him. It was only an accident that I killed his cat, Bob Smitherman. He walked in front of the shovel I was swinging. But I do feel sorry about that. I bought him the biggest headstone I could afford, but it doesn't feel like enough."

Betty stood up, her hand still gripped in Burt's who sat beside her. "I should have been the one to go to prison for letting the abuse go on as long as I did. It's my fault you were . . ." Her brow dipped. Her fingers drummed on her skull as she struggled.

"Jailed," Cricket said.

"Imprisoned," Burt said.

"Incarcerated," I offered, leaning in to the microphone.

"Yes!" She breathed out a sigh of relief, smiling at me. "It was my fault you were incarcerated."

But Cricket shook her head. "No. It wasn't. I would have done it even if you had left and I still wouldn't have been sorry. Family is everything. I think Chief Hale has learned a lot about that recently if I'm not mistaken." She shot me a kind smile.

"Okay, okay," Bree said. "Point made. Um, thank you?" She looked around. "The thing is, we all have *other* lists too. Travis Hale answered the call that day in the diner that saved my husband's life, and most likely my own. He rushed in without a moment's hesitation." She looked at me, taking my hand in hers and giving it a gentle squeeze before letting go. "He's one of the *reasons* those two little boys and little girl are here." She focused back out to all the watching eyes. "He's answered countless calls over the years. I bet he's helped each of you, even in some small way."

The murmuring rose again, but this one sounded agreeable, several heads nodding. "He's a wonderful uncle who showers his nephews with love and too much ice cream," Bree said, sending a smile in my direction. "There are lots of other items on your list of good and heroic deeds, and *that's* the one we all hope you'll add to over the years, addendum after addendum. We're counting on it."

The community members nodded or shook heads, and chattered in unison, apparently too stirred to stop things now.

"There still might need to be a reckoning," someone to my left said. "Do we really need a public official who did what's on page fifty-three? And in a *church?*"

"To be specific, it was in the graveyard," another voice chimed in.

"That's worse!" came a shout.

In my peripheral vision, Lucinda Rogers made the sign of the cross.

My head buzzed. Someone stood near the back and shouted another confession of their own that someone on the other side of the room responded to. My vision blurred even while a laugh bubbled up my chest. Yes, there might still be a reckoning, and I had a stack of checks to distribute that represented my entire life savings, but for a minute, I just had to *sit,* overwhelmed, and *shaken* with too many competing emotions to name. I breathed out, taking a few steps to the plastic chair nearby and sinking down, turning as someone else rose, then another. Shouts ricocheted around the room and I sat there watching as the whole place broke out in utter mayhem.

CHAPTER THIRTY-TWO

Haven

I placed my blue sundress into my suitcase, my heart twisting as the memory of the day I'd worn it to the blueberry festival came rushing back, and I swore for a moment I heard the laughter and felt the warm sunshine on my shoulders. I balled it up—the dress *and* the memory—and shoved them under some shoes.

Blueberry sat propped against my pillow and I stared at him mournfully, remembering the flood of excitement when Travis had won him, the joy when he'd placed him in my hands. I should leave him here. It would always hurt to look at him. And he was nothing but a dumb stuffed animal. I brought him to my chest, closing my eyes and burying my face in his flat, patchy "fur." He smelled like dust. He'd sat on a shelf for a very long time. I placed him atop my clothes, gently pressing him down and creating a travel nest.

A sharp pounding on my door jerked me from my despondent reverie and useless attempt at balling up memories and shoving them beneath shoes. They just kept rolling in, vision after vision of my time in Maine. And I was so afraid they always would. "Haven! Open up, it's me."

I pulled open the door and he came rushing in. "Easton, what are you—"

He gripped my upper arms, shaking me lightly, his face lit in a grin. "You won't believe what happened."

I looked him over. His smile was bright, and yet the rest of him looked . . . rough. His hair was sticking up in every direction, dark circles were smudged beneath his eyes, and it looked like he'd slept in his clothes. "You look awful." The greeting was beginning to get repetitive. But so was my brother showing up in the morning looking like death warmed over.

"I know!" he answered, letting go of my arms. "The guys at the firehouse invited me to a get-together. Even after what happened, they rallied around me." Something that looked like surprised gratitude altered his features momentarily, and it made my throat feel suddenly clogged. The kid who'd regularly been shunned, the man who'd very recently been *publicly* shunned, had been embraced. "I've been up all night, drinking and smoking and gambling," he finished proudly.

I felt the blood drain from my face. "Gambling?"

Oh God. I hadn't thought things could get worse, but leave it to Easton to prove me wrong. "Please tell me you didn't gamble with our money. It's all we have." I'd known he'd been devastated after the town meeting . . . embarrassed . . . ashamed, but was he really so self-destructive that he'd leave us high and dry in the middle of Maine without jobs (we'd both quit) and a place to stay (I'd let Betty know we were checking out of The Yellow Trellis Inn today)?

But he shook his head. "No, no. I mean, yes, three thousand of it—"

"Three thousand!" I sputtered. We only had thirty-two hundred that we'd been saving over the past two years so if we settled somewhere and didn't immediately find jobs, or my car broke down, we'd have a safety net. My mouth dropped open. We had both promised not to touch it. I wouldn't even be able to pay Betty for our stay. "Oh my God, oh my God—"

"No, listen! I won! I won! I *doubled* that money." He spun away, raking his hand through his already disheveled waves. When he turned back, the grin had widened.

I was frozen to the spot, watching him, my heart in my throat, my stomach churning as I shot daggers with my eyes. I was going to *kill* him.

"Did you hear me? I said I doubled our money!"

"You could have lost every cent of it," I said between gritted teeth. "Don't you ever *think*, Easton?"

"I know. I thought I was going to puke, Haven. But I didn't lose. I won. And get this. At the end there, the pile got so big, Haven. Holy *shit!* It was, like, three a.m., right? We'd all been up drinking for hours. And Eric Philippe, you know the captain of the firehouse? He's all out of cash, right? So he throws this deed to some land in the pot. 'I have no real use for it,' he says. 'The wife and I have the perfect little place at the other end of town. Why should I pay taxes on a place I don't even need?' So in the pot it went. Every cent we have, plus the deed to that land in Calliope." He raked his hands through his hair again, his eyes widening as if re-living the memory. "I was shaking so hard, I swear to God. But I won. I fucking won!"

I shook my head, trying to catch up, my heart slamming in my chest, anger and the desire to *murder* him for risking our security warring with any gladness I might have had that he'd doubled our money.

What if he'd lost?

But he hadn't lost. He'd . . . won.

That meant we'd be able to get far, far away from here now, which brought both heartache and relief.

"Land?" I finally asked, his words organizing in my head as I gave it another shake. "In Calliope? What in the world are we going to do with that?" *Sell it? Give it back? The man who'd gambled it had been* drunk. *His wife was likely burying his body as we spoke.*

Easton let out a big breath, his smile softening. "Stay," he said. "Wait until you see the property, Haven. I went there this morning. The air smells like fruit. It's beautiful, right on the lake, with this old red barn. I told you about the position available at the firehouse and that it's just a test to apply . . .

the guys tell me they're sure I can ace it. They've even offered to help me study." He paused, breathless, as I stood, listening with my mouth hanging open again. "You said there's only one nursery in Pelion, that all the residents of Calliope have to drive there to shop."

My mouth snapped shut, chin tipping. "Yes," I muttered. "And the way the plants on their clearance rack are treated is disgraceful!" I said, a burst of indignation energizing me momentarily.

He eyed me. "Yeah? So . . . what if we did something about it? What if we started a business on that property? We own the land now. The barn would be the perfect spot to set things up. There's plenty of room for parking. We could use the money we have to start buying some inventory. You know, it would start small but I bet soon enough—"

"*Stay?*" I let out a humorless laugh. "*Stay?* Start a *business?* Join the firehouse? No, no we can't stay. I'm glad the guys at the firehouse accepted you back, at least as a gambling and drinking buddy." I couldn't help the bitterness that still seeped into my tone. "But we're *pariahs* here."

I clenched my eyes shut. How many years would go by before I stopped cringing at the memory of that flyer?

My every fear and insecurity summed up in two words. *Most unwanted.*

"We don't belong in this town, Easton." This perfect town where people drank lemonade on their porches, and set apple pies to cool on windowsills while their children played in sprinklers watering lush, green lawns. They didn't even know the half of it when it came to who we really were. The extent to which we *didn't belong.* What would they all say then?

No. *Run. Run away.* We had to.

But Easton was still smiling. He looked dead tired, hungover, wrinkled, and exorbitantly happy. He tilted his head, his smile growing. "I think you should watch something."

Movement in my peripheral vision made me turn my head toward the doorway where Betty, Burt, and Cricket had come to stand.

"Before the party, the guys from the firehouse asked if I'd go with them to the town meeting. I didn't want to but . . . they sort of insisted. I put on a ballcap and hid at the back." He paused. "It was . . . well, it was interesting to say the least." My brow dipped as he grinned. "Come with me."

He took my elbow and led me to the door, Betty, looking practically giddy, looping her arm through mine as we followed the group of them down the stairs to the office. Cricket all but pushed me into the chair behind the desk and pulled up a video. I recognized the same room I'd been in several nights before for the town meeting.

"It's . . . well . . ." Betty began, leaning forward to press play, but pausing, her brow wrinkling the way it did when she'd lost a word.

"Astonishing," Burt said.

"No . . . no, not quite."

"Remarkable."

Betty's frown deepened.

"Extraordinary."

She grinned. "Extraordinary! Yes. Yes, it is. Oh, wait until you see." And then she pressed play as Travis, appearing sleep-deprived and moving stiffly, took the stage. He looked miserable . . . and scared. I leaned closer, my heart thrumming, barely registering the soft sound of the door clicking shut as I was left alone.

I sat in that chair and watched it all, my emotions swinging wildly between one extreme to the next. At the end, I sat back in the chair, tears streaming down my face as I swallowed back laughter.

Then, fingers shaking, I started the video over, needing to hear him say it again. *I'm in love with Haven Torres. Deeply, miserably, completely in love with her.*

And what he'd *done* to back up those words. He'd put *everything* on the line . . . for us. No one had ever done that. No one.

I stood, flinging the door open. Betty, Burt, Cricket, and Easton were all waiting outside. "Oh my *God*." There didn't seem anything else to say.

"We thought you'd say that," Betty said, her smile as soft and gentle as her heart.

Oh my *God*.

"The town's still talking about it," Cricket remarked. "I imagine they'll be talking about it for a long time to come. Most people didn't go home until the wee hours of the morning. From what we hear, families were reunited, friendships reconciled, consciences cleared, forgiveness and repentance spread far and wide. Pelion is a more beautiful place this morning." Betty smiled. "Cricket and I were even invited to join the community relations group. It's been renamed The Bob Smitherman Citizen Outreach Council. Of course, its mission has been drastically . . . oh . . . oh . . ."

"Altered," Burt said.

"Yes. Yes, it has. *Drastically*," she emphasized.

Bob Smitherman . . . the dead *cat*. I recalled what I had just watched Cricket confess at the meeting. Poor Bob Smitherman. And poor Betty. Poor Cricket. I gave my head a small shake. But all that . . . that was going to have to wait until later. "I . . . I don't know what to say."

There was a *lot* to say.

"I don't reckon this is the time for talking. At least not to us," Burt said.

Right. No, probably not. My head whirled. "I have to go," I said.

"I'd say." Cricket smiled.

"I'll keep your rooms available, dear!" Betty called as I rushed past them, grabbing my keys on a hook by the front door, and throwing it open.

Gage stood outside, leaning against his red sportscar, his face breaking wide in a smile when he saw me. I halted and he pushed off his car, carrying a humungous bouquet of cut roses. I descended the steps slowly as he held the flowers toward me. I took them, needing two arms to do so, bringing them to my nose and inhaling their muted fragrance. "Gage? What are you doing here?"

He tilted his head, looking just a little self-conscious. It surprised me. And charmed me. Perfect Gage Buchanan was humbling himself in front of me. "I heard you might be staying."

"From who?" I frowned.

"From Travis. Listen"—he looked behind me momentarily and then met my gaze—"I think we could have something special, Haven. If I haven't pursued you wholeheartedly, it's only because I'm at a point in my life where I want something serious and you were only passing through town. But now . . . well, I'd love to see where things might go."

I stared at him, my mouth falling open.

I was going to *kill* him.

"Excuse me?"

"Not you," I said, realizing I'd made the threat out loud. I handed him back the flowers. "I'm honored by your offer, Gage. And you *deserve* someone serious, someone perfect, someone who *you're* perfect for." Because Gage Buchanan *was* perfect. "That's just not me." I leaned up and kissed him on his cheek. "I hope we can be friends. I have to go."

And with that, I jumped in my car and peeled out of the driveway of The Yellow Trellis Inn. When I glanced in my rearview mirror, the crew, including Easton, and now Gage, who had walked up the steps to join them with his massive bouquet, were all standing on the porch, watching as I drove away.

CHAPTER THIRTY-THREE

Haven

The door to his house was wide open, an old-fashioned bike with a white woven basket featuring a daisy leaned against the porch. My heart stalled. Was there a *woman* here? I got out of my car slowly, closing the door and hesitantly headed toward the house I knew from the Pelion directory was Travis's.

I knocked on the open door, leaning my head in. "Hello?" I called, walking inside, my heart rate increasing now, thumping in my ears. It smelled like fresh paint. "Travis?"

He appeared from around the corner, a box in his hands, his eyes wide with surprise. He set the box down slowly, his gaze held to mine as he straightened. "Haven?"

"Hi." I walked inside, noting the other boxes piled here and there. "You're moving?"

He looked around as though searching for the answer. "Uh. Yeah. Not for a couple of weeks but I'm getting a head start on packing."

"Where?"

"Where?" he parroted.

"Where are you moving?"

He gave his head a slight shake. "Just . . . down the street a ways. The landlord's cousin is moving in so I got kicked out." He was standing so still, watching me carefully. "What are you doing here?"

I ran my finger along the chair rail, walking closer. I spotted Clawdia stretched out near a window, basking in a pool of yellow sunshine. I looked back at Travis, raising my eyebrows in question.

"I, uh, took her off Betty's hands," he said in explanation. "She dropped her off this morning. Said I was doing her a favor." He glanced at the cat in question. "Clawdia gets skittish around so many moving feet. A B&B isn't the ideal place for her." His gaze flickered away, and Clawdia meowed from her patch of light, as if corroborating his obvious lie. Little accomplice.

My lip trembled. It turned out this big policeman was a *cat* lover.

But I'd already suspected as much.

I cleared my throat. "My brother came into some land."

His eyes moved over my face. "Oh yeah?"

"He won it from a guy down at the firehouse last night. The firehouse where they've all but offered him a job." I paused, giving Travis a sideways look. "The funny thing is, those guys asked Easton to go to a certain town meeting that I heard was . . . well, *memorable*."

He kept staring. "I . . . see," he finally said.

I nodded, sucking on my bottom lip. "It's as if they knew what was going to happen at that meeting. As if they'd been told in advance."

"I . . . see," he repeated.

"And then, shocker of all shockers, my brother won some money and a plot of land later that night from one of those same firemen."

"Lucky," he all but choked.

"You'd think, right?" I tapped my finger on my chin. "Only . . . we've never exactly been the lucky types. So I got to wondering . . ."

"Uh-oh."

My lip quirked, but despite his joke, he still looked mildly ill and as though everywhere except his mouth might have suddenly turned to stone.

"I remembered *you* mentioned owning a plot of land. And I got to wondering what I'd find if I looked up the deed to the one Easton now owns. When might it have been transferred to that fireman so he could *'lose'* it in that poker game? And by whom?"

He watched me silently, finally moving as he shoved his hands in his pockets but not before I noticed they were trembling. "Don't do that," he said.

"No? Why?"

"Because . . . I won't take it back. I'm moving to a smaller house near the lake, right down the street from Archer, Bree, and the kids. The owner said she might be interested in selling at some point. Which will be great if I still have a job and can save up some money. It's in Pelion. Close enough to the gym. But I've found I enjoy running on the shore more anyway." He let out a whoosh of air as though saying so many words had winded him.

"What in the world will *I* do with that land?" My God, he looked like a statue, as though if he moved at all, he would shatter.

He squinted past me. "Seems like the perfect place to help others plant ten thousand gardens," he said after a moment, meeting my eyes again. *Oh.*

It's what my brother had suggested too. But how could I accept it? How? "That land was yours," I said. "Why would you do that, Travis?"

He shrugged. "I can't do anything with it anyway. See, I came across this amendment that clearly states the Pelion chief of police has to live within Pelion town limits, which I am. The chief of police, that is. For now. Anyway, Archer agreed with the bylaw. He filed it this morning. There's no turning back now. I would have had to sell that land anyway."

"But you would have gotten the money!"

"I don't care about the money, Haven," he said softly. "And I don't think you do either. But if you'd prefer to sell it and settle somewhere else, that's your decision to make. I hope you do though. Settle."

I sighed. This man. He'd gifted us his land. His roots. The ones that went back hundreds of years. I was still reeling. About that. About so many things. "You sent Gage to me. Why?"

He paused. "I want you to be happy," he said. "I want you to have the perfect life, everything you want." He looked down. "Even if that's not me." The wince was slight. He almost hid it.

"Gage *is* pretty perfect. I concede."

He looked to the side. "You deserve perfect."

I moved closer. "He has the perfect family."

Travis nodded. "He's looking to settle down. If things . . . progressed, he'd be able to provide you security for life . . . a family . . ." God no one had ever looked more miserable than Travis Hale in that moment.

"I'm going to *kill* you."

"Excuse me?"

"Why would things progress with Gage when I'm in love with you?"

Blatant hope bloomed across his handsome face. "You're in love with me?"

"I am." I put my hands on my hips, attempting to look stern. "I have some decisions to make though," I said. "Considering the circumstances."

"Oh." He looked down, defeated.

I eyed him. It wasn't exactly right to draw out his pain. After all, I had hurt him too. But it wasn't exactly wrong either. He'd hurt me in a room full of strangers. "I'm either going to walk out that door because honestly, Travis Hale, I'm not sure you have much in the way of material possessions to offer me. It seems you've lost it all."

"It's true. I did. Every last bit."

"*Or*, I'm going to come over there and kiss you silly because as it turns out, your heart is made of gold, even if it's a bit tarnished. Which one do you think I'll choose?" The corner of my lip shook as I resisted a smile.

"The one that means I can take a full breath again?"

I laughed, rushing to him. He took me in his arms, murmuring sounds of love and relief, planting his face in my hair, his shaking hands running down my back. "I am so sorry," he said. "So, so sorry. You are wanted. You are so wanted by me."

I leaned back, bringing my hand to his cheek. "I *know*. I watched the video of the meeting."

He stilled again, but only momentarily. "So you know the extent of it. I might not have a job. There's a town meeting next week to decide whether to circulate a recall petition. It seems page fifty-three of my shame manifesto is the sticking point."

Shame manifesto.

I smiled softly. I wasn't worried for him. Like I'd just said, I'd watched the video.

And I had no desire to know what was on page fifty-three.

Ever.

"I also don't have a vehicle. My engine blew. Bree let me borrow her old bike. Clawdia enjoys riding in the basket."

"You're kidding?" I couldn't help the laugh that threatened as I pictured this strapping man riding around town on an old-fashioned bike with a cat in its basket.

He shook his head. *Well.* No house, likely no savings after that pile of checks I'd seen him distributing on the video, no truck, possibly no job, and no land because he'd gifted it to me. I leaned in and kissed him, luxuriating in his mouth, his taste, him, for many minutes. "I've been scared," I admitted. "Scared of the connection I felt to you right from the beginning." I paused, gathering my words. I wanted to say this right. "It scared me. No, it terrified me because I had this sense that if I let you in, I wouldn't be able to let you go. And I thought . . . if I could just put you in a box, things would be okay. But it didn't work. I just kept falling deeper. You just kept busting out of every box I tried to put you in. And I panicked. I ran in the only way I could. I threw Gage up between us. I convinced myself you were still in love with someone else. And at first that was a relief, but then, then it became a torment." I halted, forced to suck in a breath.

Travis was looking at me with something like awe. "I understand that fear, Haven. I do. And I want to talk about all of it. I want to reassure you, not just with words, but with actions. But right now, I think I need to hear you say it again," he said, his voice gritty with emotion. "Please say it again."

I knew what *it* was. He didn't have to clarify. "I love you, Travis Hale. I want you to know me. I want to tell you about my past, my life, the things that have hurt and all that I was running from. Not to wallow in it, but because it's part of who I am, and I'm proud that I survived it."

"You should be. You should be proud." His gaze washed over my face. "There's a lot I'm *not* proud of. But if you watched the video, you already know." His expression was searching. "That reinventing you spoke of that night on the porch . . . maybe we can both help each other figure out what that looks like. Together."

I nodded shakily. "Yes. I want that. But most of all, I want a future with you. I just couldn't let my mind go there, because it hurt, and I feared it, and when I did, when I *do,* it starts unraveling out of control to a wedding in a meadow, and children, and all sorts of things you don't want to know about." I bit my lip, vulnerability washing through me. If we were going to be blatantly *honest . . .*

His eyes danced as he picked up a curl and attempted to push it back, unsuccessfully. "You don't deal in half measures, do you?"

"No. That's the problem. It's why I've kept moving. Because when I stop—"

"Haven, I'm kidding." He smiled softly. "I love you too. I'm in love with you. For the first time in my life. I had to lose everything to figure out what's important . . . what I want." His lips tipped, eyes gentled. "What I've had all along, and what's still mine, even when it seems like I have nothing. What I hope to share with you if you'll let me."

My heart soared and I leaned in, kissing him on his beautiful mouth. I was ready. Ready to grasp happiness, moments at least, and whole seasons if I was able and life allowed. I wanted my life to *count,* not just be an endless cycle of struggle and survival. I was ready to risk, to trust, to stay in one place, to glory in the warmth of summer, to feel the subtle shift as fall arrived, to snuggle into winter, and watch with bated breath for the new green of spring breaking through the cold and the hard.

"You want children?" he asked, breaking from my lips, as if those words had just registered.

"A whole brood of them. I want roots. Noise. Chaos," I admitted, because in for a penny, in for a pound, and the way he was *looking* at me, made me believe he'd move heaven and earth to make all my dreams come true.

"Define brood," he said on a grin.

"Ten. Twelve."

Travis laughed, the sound filled with joy. "We better get started then. No time to waste."

I grinned back. "But before that, you have some dating to do." Because as much as I loved the idea of noise, and roots, and broods of whiskey-eyed Hale boys, I first wanted more blueberry festivals, and antique fairs, and moonlit lake rendezvous with the gorgeous man looking at me with love. I wanted morning upon morning where I woke first and marveled at his slumbering beauty in the still light of dawn. And I was determined to do it without that knot of fear in my belly.

"Oh, I'll date you, Haven from California. I'm going to date the hell out of you. No one will have been dated harder in the history—"

I planted my lips on his and he laughed against my mouth as he swooped me up in his arms.

And in my mind, the future appeared, and it was incredibly, brilliantly *bright.*

EPILOGUE

Three Years Later

The breeze rustled the trees, the scent of ripened fruit sweetened the air. I looked out to the horizon where the first wash of lavender spread across the sky, casting the water a deep purplish-blue. A smile tilted my lips as I raised an arm, wiping the sweat that had gathered on my brow. It'd been a long Saturday spent digging in the dirt.

"Hey, handsome," my wife said, coming up behind me and encircling my waist. "How's my hard-working man?"

I turned, wrapping an arm around her shoulder and kissing her temple, careful not to rub my sweaty, probably dirt-smeared face in her hair. "Filthy," I said.

"Don't I know it," she murmured, raising her eyes suggestively. "That's how we ended up in this predicament." She smirked, running a hand over her swollen stomach.

I grinned. Damn right. She was due any day now. It was a boy. Naturally. We'd named him Ryder. Pride swelled. I was going to have a son.

While I still had a regular job—the town had voted and generously decided to keep me as chief of police three years before, even after I'd made public my manifesto of shame—Haven and I wanted to accomplish the work of getting her nursery turned over for the changing of seasons before our little guy made his grand entrance. It was an all-hands-on-deck weekend at Haven's Gate, Plant and Garden Center.

"It looks amazing," Haven said, glancing around at the tiers of violets, dianthus, rosemary, ornamental peppers, and kale, and over to the neat rows of young trees. Easton, Archer, and I had unloaded them just that afternoon, arranging them by type and height. "Thank you." I knew the small frown that followed was only due to the fact that she wanted to be involved with more of the heavy lifting than her body was currently allowing for. But if I knew my wife, she'd be back at it soon enough, a baby boy strapped to her chest as she helped some client or another plan the perfect garden.

"You're welcome," I said, kissing her again, inhaling her intoxicating fragrance, sweeter than any flower that had ever graced this nursery.

In the two and a half years since the garden center had opened, it had grown exponentially. It wasn't only a wildly successful business, it was a place to gather. To plant the future. To encourage roots, deep and strong. Haven's Gate had hay rides in the fall and fruit-picking in the summer. In the winter we sold Christmas trees and wreaths, and Bree made trays of hot chocolate with homemade marshmallows. And in the springtime, we started all over again, lilac bushes and new dogwood trees filling the old red barn that protected them from the frost until they were ready to find permanent ground. And though I only helped out on weekends and when necessary, it was soul-nurturing work, joyful and fulfilling.

Somehow, I knew in my gut my dad would be happy and proud of what his land had become. And someday soon, I'd sit on the dock nearby and fish with my little boy, teaching him to bait a hook the same way my dad had taught me, with patience and with love.

"It looks like you have it all covered here. I'm going to stop at the market and then head home and get dinner started," she said, leaning in and kissing me once more.

I nodded, smiling. "I'll be home in an hour or so." *Home.* The small house on the lakeshore in Pelion with the creaky hardwood floors, and the original shiplap walls. The one where we whispered in bed in the quiet of night, words of love and tenderness, but also our fears, and insecurities, and the things we sometimes worried about. The one we'd need to add on to once our planned brood began materializing. I didn't know a lot about what was involved in "adding on" to a structure, but I knew my brother would help me when the time arrived. I watched as Haven walked away, stopping to fuss with the tiered arrangement momentarily, hesitating on a violet that had gone into a bit of shock at being moved. Her face wasn't visible, but I knew for a fact she was whispering words of care and encouragement. It's what she did. She *loved,* fully and wholeheartedly, until withered things that had the will to thrive, found the strength to do so.

Like me.

Three years of loving her. Three miraculous years. We'd taken our time dating—after all, falling in love had been somewhat of a whirlwind. I'd courted her through all four seasons, and fallen more deeply in love by the day, which was exhilarating but not surprising. As Bree had said, when you know, you know, and we'd *known.*

We'd married at sunrise in the orchard behind the barn, the air redolent with the scent of apple blossoms. Easton had walked Haven down an aisle of clover, delivering his sister to me, as he'd done in more ways than one. My eyes had burned when they'd reached the place where I'd waited, gripping his scarred hand in mine and promising to take care of her always.

As for Easton, he was moving up quickly in the firehouse that served three counties, but despite his busy schedule, he always made time to help at the nursery when asked. For the most part, he'd changed his wicked ways—the respect of the community was important to Easton and motivated him to act accordingly—but he was still very much a *single* man.

Only Bree, Archer, their children, and Easton had attended our marriage ceremony, but we'd thrown a big party that evening in the old red barn, decked out with twinkle lights and tables adorned with pots of sunflowers that we

354

later planted along the fence. The sight of those grand, happy flowers still reminded me of that beautiful day filled with love and, thanks to the crew, plenty of homemade hooch.

I had arranged for Mrs. Kim to be there as a surprise and when she'd arrived, she and Haven had sobbed and held on to each other until there wasn't a dry eye in the place. She'd already been back once since then, to visit and help Haven plan and conceptualize the garden behind our home.

Clawdia limped over, breaking me from my reverie, rubbing her body against my leg. I leaned down, picking her up as I walked toward the barn where more heavy lifting awaited. Clawdia often spent her days at the nursery, lounging in the sunshine of the loft, far out of reach of potentially trampling feet.

"Do you two need help?" I called as Connor and Charlie walked by, each hefting a bale of hay.

"No, we're good. Thanks, Uncle Travis," Charlie called. I ran my hand over Clawdia's fur, turning and watching as they added what they were carrying to the other bales that would be sold to customer's seeding grass, but also used as part of a display of vibrant red, yellow, orange, and white chrysanthemums. My eyes narrowed slightly as Connor gave a covert head nod to his brother, pointedly looking out to the dock where Juliette Moretti sat at the edge, legs dangling, as she leaned forward watching her feet swish in the water. Juliette's mother did the accounting for the nursery and often brought her daughter with her if she was only working for an hour or two on a Saturday. Juliette was a pretty girl with a sweet disposition who enjoyed helping plant flowers and arrange displays. But in her innocent smile, I also caught the glint of mischief and perhaps just a dash of devilry. I understood the qualities well. After all, it took one to know one.

Charlie gave his brother a head nod back, and they began slinking toward her in unison, stopping when she turned her head slightly, moving again when she looked away. Clawdia's purr vibrated, my hand moving idly on her back as I took in the scene.

Something was about to go down.

My nephews moved swiftly behind her, obviously up to no good, likely plotting on pushing Juliette into the water. For a moment I considered stopping the obvious crime in progress, but . . . well, I knew for a fact Juliette was an excellent swimmer and all lake kids needed to learn to expect being pushed in when standing on the very edge of a dock where a mere finger nudge could pitch you in.

The twins made it to her simultaneously when very suddenly, Juliette reached behind her, giving a hard yank to the towel she was sitting on, the one currently directly under the boys' feet. With dual yelps, both boys went flying off either side of the dock, belly flopping onto the surface of the lake. Juliette turned around slowly, bringing her hands to her cheeks in feigned surprise. "Are you *okay?*" she asked, her eyes round with faux innocence. And yes, a spark of that devilry. Again, it took one to know one.

"Try to be more careful," she said, looking down at them, her lips curling into a saucy smile.

Well, well. Juliette Moretti had just taken on both my nephews with apparent eyes in the back of her head and the singular flick of one slim wrist.

Connor and Charlie were very clearly outmatched.

I worked to hold back a laugh as they glared up at her, floundering with outrage, and what I thought might be a hint of . . . awe. And perhaps love. *Uh-oh.*

The boys dragged themselves out of the lake, their fists clenched as they walked onto the shore. "No time for a swim when there's so much work to do, boys," I said as they approached me. "Better go lay out back in the sun to dry off for a little while and then get back to it."

"Sure, Uncle Travis," they said, both attempting a nonchalant smile that Charlie pulled off better than Connor, who still looked, in equal parts, bitter and bamboozled. I waited until they rounded the corner of the barn before breaking out in laughter. Clawdia meowed in agreement.

My laughter dwindled, but the joy remained. I took time to revel in the moment, the beautiful season of life I was living, thinking of Clarice and her prophecy, and realizing the truth it'd contained.

I *had* lost it all.

Willingly. Joyfully. While following my heart.

And because I'd lost it all, I'd gained . . . *everything.*

ACKNOWLEDGMENTS

Seven years ago, I wrote a book called *Archer's Voice.* My only editors were two friends who read with a critical eye, a good grasp of grammar, and—most importantly, I think—a personal understanding of my heart. The latter meant that in many areas they knew what I was probably *trying* to say but had come up short, and showed me where they believed I had more to offer. Notably with the instruction, "make better." ☺ Angela Smith and Larissa Kahle helped me find my voice in those early days, and in turn, I helped Archer find his. All of *you*, the many hundreds of thousands of readers, bloggers, Instagrammers, and now TikTok'ers worldwide, helped amplify it, and continue to do so. The success of that book changed my life, and my gratitude is endless and forever.

My team is bigger now, but I have been blessed to have found others who similarly strive to help me tell the best story *I* can tell, in the unique way they believe I can tell it. What an incredible gift. Thank you, Marion Archer, and Karen Lawson.

Huge thanks to my beta readers who not only provided feedback, but did re-reads of Archer to make sure I wasn't forgetting any small details as I moved ahead in years. JoAnna Koller and Ashley Brinkman, I am so appreciative for your time and your support.

And to Elena Eckmeyer for not only beta reading and providing suggestions, but for laughing with me, loving my anti-hero first, and understanding the wild, curly-hair struggle like no other.

To Sharon for your final glance, and during a time when you would have had every right to step away from this job. I don't deserve you, but I'm never giving you back.

Thank you to Kimberly Brower for being all-around amazing, always.

Everlasting gratitude to Mia's Mafia—who stepped into Pelion, Maine first, and have journeyed with me to each successive location (some stranger than others).

To my husband, who fills my soul, and my coffee cup when I'm on a deadline. I couldn't do any of it without you.

ABOUT THE AUTHOR

Mia Sheridan is a *New York Times, USA Today,* and *Wall Street Journal* Bestselling author. Her passion is weaving true love stories about people destined to be together. Mia lives in Cincinnati, Ohio with her husband. They have four children here on earth and one in heaven. Her works include the Sign of Love collection (*Leo, Leo's Chance, Stinger, Archer's Voice, Becoming Calder, Finding Eden, Kyland, Grayson's Vow, Midnight Lily, Ramsay, Preston's Honor, Dane's Storm,* and *Brant's Return*), the standalone romance novels, *The Wish Collector, Savaged,* and *Once We Were Starlight,* the romantic suspense duet, *Where the Blame Lies,* and *Where the Truth Lives,* and the romantic thriller, *Fallen.*

The standalone romance novels, *Most of All You,* and *More Than Words,* published via Grand Central Publishing, are available online and in bookstores.

Mia can be found online at:
MiaSheridan.com
Twitter, @MSheridanAuthor
Instagram, @MiaSheridanAuthor
Facebook.com/MiaSheridanAuthor